AUTUMN

in

WOLF VALLEY

~~~~~

ED A. MURRAY

~~~~~

Also by Ed A. Murray

In a Northern Town

Somewhere More Than Free

Between Two Slopes

Published independently in the United States.
www.edamurray.com

ISBN-13: 978-0-9986889-3-0

Printed in the United States of America.

For my girls
Cara, Maeve and Mara

Autumn in Wolf Valley

Prologue

You have probably never heard of Wolf Valley. Most people haven't. Before last fall, I was one of those people.

Its flood was a forgotten tragedy in American history, overshadowed by 9/11 and the war and eventually Katrina, I presume. But retelling that story was now my job. I have spent the last few years trying to break into the freelance writing world. The gig came from one of my most reluctant clients, a small literary magazine based in the northeast that you have surely never heard of. Why they cared to run an anniversary article on the flood more than 20 years later I am not entirely sure, but I wanted to nail it.

The assignment was to document the progress that has been made since the flood. "Talk to some locals," my editor said. "Get a feel for how things have changed, what's rebounded, what new struggles persist. Find a story to tell. Make it human." So that's exactly what I did, packing up the car and kissing my wife and baby girl goodbye. It took me about seven or eight hours to reach the valley. As the Wolf River winds, the state highway traces the bends and small towns appear along the way—Livingston, Huell, Elmswood, Jefferson City. For the better part of two days, I stopped into coffee shops and gas stations and libraries—anywhere I thought there would be people who could help me tell this valley's story.

I met some interesting characters along the way, that was for sure. One man owned a barbershop that flooded and so he spent nearly 48 hours sitting on the roof in the rain. I met two sisters who were asleep in the same room when a tree came crashing through their ceiling, pinning them to their mattresses until help arrived hours later to cut them free. But the most interesting story came, as they often do, sitting in a bar.

This was a weekday afternoon and I was occupying a stool going over notes and listening to interview recordings I had made. It was one of those local haunts: low ceilings, dark even in the middle of the day, walls lined with beer signs and pictures of local high school teams. Despite some decent leads, I was feeling discouraged about my prospects of spinning a good story to the tune of eight thousand words, as my editor requested. The bartender was a young woman who looked to be flirting with the legal drinking age herself, with tanned skin and long, black hair that was braided and draped over her shoulder. She must have noticed my angst and brought me another Yuengling.

"What's eating at ya?" she asked.

I sighed and set my pen down on the bar. "I'm supposed to be writing a story about this valley," I told her.

"What about the valley?"

"About the flood, basically, and how the area rebounded. I can't imagine you have any stories yourself," I said, a nod to her age.

She smirked, still holding an empty pint glass with a thin layer of amber at the bottom swishing back and forth. "If you're writing a story about the flood, there's a guy you should talk to."

The next day, I walked into the same bar to meet a man named Howard Lynch. I found him sitting at a table near the back, reading a worn copy of *The Empty Hills of History,* a novel I hadn't read since high school.

"Mr. Lynch?" I asked as I stepped toward him. The first things I noticed were his hands. One was wrapped around a coffee mug, making it look more like a shot glass. He donned a white undershirt and had close-cropped gray hair that was receding. For a brief moment he ignored me, then he glanced my way and then back at his book, all without changing the expression on his face.

"You want to know about the flood, or you want to know my story?" he said more as a statement than a question.

Unsure how to respond, I asked if I could sit down. He nodded toward the vacant chair across from him. "Well, sir, I'd like to know it all."

"Everyone wants to know it all these days," he said and then finished his coffee. "Let me ask you, do you like stories? Because if you have some time, I have one you won't believe."

The assignment, as I said, was to write eight thousand words for the literary magazine. I didn't do that. Instead, I passed on the assignment altogether and wrote this book.

This is Howard's story.

1

Wolf Valley, 2001

In which Howard is 47 years old

He buys the pistol the day he puts his wife in the ground. That was of course never his plan. None of this is. In years past, he would pull one of his wife's books from the shelf and read it with fondness, stealing the occasional peek over the top at the woman in the next room pecking away at her old typewriter or scribbling something with the pen she refused to abandon—shaking the ink after what seemed like each sentence. That's not what he does anymore. Now, the books are a desperate escape. The gun is his backup plan.

When he walks into his house after the funeral he is numb. Empty. It takes him a few moments, but once he allows his senses to return, the first thing he notices is the smell. For days he had forgotten about the dog. Now there is garbage spilled across the kitchen floor. At the side door a rug sits soaked in urine, a pile of feces on the linoleum nearby. The dog—a shaggy brown mutt with white paws, some kind of shepherd, he thinks—looks thin and is lying on the floor, paws beside his face, whimpering. Anytime in his previous life, Howard would have been overwhelmed with guilt at the sight, of what he had allowed to happen. But that was then. Now, he instead walks right past the animal toward the liquor cabinet and pours himself a drink. He blames that dog, whether fairly or unfairly—a distinction he is far from able to make at this time.

Rain, since that night, stirs something in Howard. He sits upright in his recliner staring out the window. Droplets batter the glass and then smear downward in uneven tracks, blurring his sight out to the yard. On a clear day, he could sit there and look beyond the grass and down to the river, watch it flow by lazily in the hot afternoons. When it rained, he used to love grabbing a cup of coffee and sitting under the covered part of the patio, listening to nature's song on the metal awning overhead, watching the millions of dimples punctuate the normally idle river.

The rain stopped for the funeral, an overcast autumn morning. Those gathered stood huddled around the hole in the ground, the rich wood casket sitting before it. Thirteen people could have been there, or thirty thousand. Howard never glanced around to notice. On the drive home, his tunnel vision gave way to a sign he had perhaps driven past hundreds of times but never paid the time of day: Hanson Arms. That's where he bought the pistol—a 22-caliber revolver with a beige handle. The man at the counter tried to talk him into something a little more powerful, something semi-automatic, but that was a conversation for defending his life, not taking it. Howard knows if this gun ever discharges, it will be both the first and last time.

In those initial moments of your world crumbling, you feel every twist of the knife. Howard did. He didn't sleep for nearly a week. But then the funeral happens and there is supposed to be some kind of closure, that it is okay and expected to move forward with your life—an impossible task when your life was just laid six feet beneath the earth. *Anyone who thinks that has obviously never buried his wife*, he thinks. But his particular brand of torment is only half-driven by grief; the rest is coming from guilt.

When he isn't torturing himself, his mind stirring into regretful knots, he is instead vacant. The whiskey helps him find that state. Not so much cloudy or anxious or even sad—simply vacant.

One afternoon, when he comes to, he is standing in Amber's study. It is a small space just off the living room with French doors. From his recliner, he could look through those glass doors and see his wife sitting at the desk positioned in the center of the room, hunched over her typewriter. Expansive bookshelves lined the wall behind her, filled from top to bottom with inspiration and classics and reference guides and books her publisher had begged her to blurb. When they moved into the house, Amber set strict boundaries: during writing hours, which were from dawn until she stood from the desk—usually sometime in the evening—Howard would not enter the study. Afterward, if he wanted to browse the bookshelves for something to read, he could do so. She needed confidence in her isolation, and Howard respected that.

That is why he is startled to find himself standing beside her desk. As he looks around, a photo hanging on the wall catches his attention. It is from their wedding day, taken by Howard's boss, Wendell. It's just the two of them. They are kissing, a bright blue sky the backdrop, the rolling forested hills of Wolf Valley below and, somewhere out of frame, there is the river. It's tragic how reality today can shatter the reality of yesterday.

On her desk, papers are stacked neatly in piles and the typewriter has a blank page already curled in its platen, awaiting the words that will never come. The sight turns his stomach. A large manilla envelope with the words *Near and Far by the River* scribbled in Sharpie is sitting on the edge of the desk. Howard peeks inside but it is empty. Instead, he turns toward the bookshelf, which she also kept meticulously organized. Books are arranged by purpose, by author, by genre—except the top shelf, which she never had the opportunity to fill. Off to the left, on the bottom shelf, Amber kept copies of her own novels. So he crouches and lets his finger slide gently across the spines before tilting her first novel, her most famous novel, *The Empty Hills of History*. He then picks up her other book, *A Stranger on Charles Street*, opens the inside cover and sees Amber has scribbled: *To my biggest fan*. These are books he has read countless times. But as he knows is the case, literature has the power to change with your life, and he knows he needs to understand how his wife's words have changed. *Not how they have changed*, he corrects himself, *how you've changed*.

Still crouched, book in hand, he hears a whimper and the dog is inches behind him, head hanging low. Howard never heard him approach. He thinks the dog has lost weight and it gently paws at Howard's pant leg. Howard shakes his head and stands to return to his chair. "We're all suffering," he says.

Outside, the rain begins falling once more. This time Howard is oblivious to it, not knowing that the God who brought on the storm and took his wife would next come for his life.

2

Pennsylvania, 1962

In which Howard was 8 years old

There is a place, somewhere in the world, or somewhere in Howard's mind, where a small piece of land juts out into the ocean. At the right time of night, if it's clear and calm, you can stand on the shoreline and look out into a kaleidoscope where the water and sky and stars and reflections are all blended into one black canvas spotted with twinkling lights. There is no separation. Ultimate mindfulness. It was a place, whether real or imagined, that lived in Howard's mind frequently during childhood. He first discovered it in his bedroom closet.

As a child, Howard hated the fall. Autumn was the time of year that reminded him the holidays were right around the corner, which were typically accompanied by disappointment. That cool air meant even colder nights. Baseboard heating was expensive, and so

Howard was regularly relegated to chopping wood for the fireplace or hiding beneath mounds of blankets to suffer through the night. The old man certainly wasn't going to do it. Fall, also, for whatever reason—call it playoff baseball, football season—meant more of his father's late nights drinking, coming home to a pissed wife and a lonely son, which meant, often, just not coming home. The nights his father didn't return were actually better for Howard than when the old man stumbled through the door drunk. That's when the fights happened.

They were pretty innocent the first few times. "Where have you been?" being the accusatory question, followed by hushed disagreement. But later, that's when things started breaking. First a lamp. Then a window. Then his mother's orbital bone. Of course, the old man claimed it was an accident. And for the first few days, his mother played along. But it ate at her. Howard knew it ate at her. She was left with a few different options. She could remain silent and go on like nothing terrible had happened to her. She could go to the police, file a report, press charges. But neither of those options must have really felt, to her, like she was solving the problem.

Instead, on a crisp afternoon in the fall, eight-year-old Howard walked home from school, opened the front door and found a note lying on the kitchen table. Of course, he didn't see it at first. No, first, he stepped into the house and felt the chill. The heater was off again and he knew better than to ask his folks to turn it on. Rather than wait for the wrath of the old man, Howard dropped his book bag by the door and went outside to find the axe. He spent a good half hour out there splitting wood before stacking it neatly under a tarp beside the shed, and then he tied a small bundle and carried it inside.

On his way to the fireplace, the note caught his eye. Setting down the wood, he picked it up and unfolded it. All it said was, "I've gone. Won't be back," and then his mom's signature at the bottom. That was it. Simple words. Concise. No, "I love you, Howie."

At the time, Howard didn't entirely know what to make of it. His mother had left before, for days at a time. She always came back.

Those were the worst days. His father would drink until he teetered on death, but remained just coherent enough to berate his son for the simplest of mistakes. Howard learned to stockpile books and hide in his closet with a flashlight. He'd stay there until he heard his father stumble through the door, and then he'd click off the light and pray the old man didn't find him. With any luck, his father would think he'd gone with his mother. But she never took him. His father would tear through the house looking for him, shouting his name, then hers, and thrashing things around until finally the chaos stopped. Presumably, when his father passed out.

For some reason, this time felt different. Howard stood there holding the note, reading it over and over. Before he even set it down, his father walked in the door. The boy didn't look up at the old man, who walked over and snatched the note from his hand.

"Gone again, eh?" he said. He crumpled the note and tossed it in the direction of the garbage can without looking. It fell to the floor and rolled against the wall. He jingled his keys while staring off aimlessly, then said, "You good? I'll be back," which Howard loosely translated to, "I'm going to get piss drunk again. Feed yourself."

Howard waited for the old man to drive off before retrieving the crumpled note, taking it back to his room and smoothing it out, over and over, and then sticking it between the pages of his thickest book.

Restless nights are followed by restful mornings. Howard's father never came home, which wasn't entirely unusual. The boy sat at the kitchen table eating cereal when his old man finally walked in the door. Without saying a word, he looked at his son and then went to the fridge for a beer. Then he took a seat across the table. He slurped the foam from the top of the can and let out a big exhale.

"What your mother never understood is that I'm a salesman first," his father finally said. "Everything else comes second. She never could get that through her brain."

The boy sat there in silence.

"You want a beer, son?"

"I'm eight."

"You're eight. 'I'm eight,'" he repeated in a mocking tone. "What's that got to do with it? I asked if you wanted a beer."

Howard didn't say anything and his old man laughed and then stood and walked out of the room. He didn't come back for two days and the boy thought, just maybe, he had been orphaned. It wasn't exactly as terrifying as it should have been.

But then, as always, his father came home, and he brought the waft of whiskey with him.

Once it became clear that his mother was not returning home, Howard fell into a depression. It only took his father a matter of days to collect all the photos around the house and burn them in the backyard. Not just the ones of Howard's mother, but all the rest —the family photos, the shots of Howard as a baby.

When his father wasn't home, Howard snuck into his bedroom and snooped around. He was convinced that some photographs survived. The room was almost vacant. Before his mother left, she would make the bed every morning, stacking a mound of pillows against the headboard. Now, it looked like the house had been robbed. Very few belongings remained, to the point where Howard felt that perhaps his father had moved out, too.

Just as the boy's search for a surviving photo began, it ended. He heard the crash of the front door thrown open. *Oh boy*. He was going to be in big trouble for being in there. Not *you're grounded* big trouble, but *thrown into the wall and starved* big trouble. His only hope was to try dashing across the hall before his father caught him. Just as he entered the hallway, he saw his father standing there. *Here it comes. The belt this time.*

The man had a wry smile on his face, a look Howard had surely never seen before. He was breathing heavily and his hair was breaking from its slicked-back shell.

"There you are," the old man said.

Howard braced for a lashing.

His father looked too out of breath to say much. "With me," he said with the flick of a finger and then turned toward the front door. Howard followed. Outside, the old man never broke his pace. Howard followed. They made it to the end of the driveway, then turned onto the dusty road and kept walking. Howard trotted occasionally to keep up with his father. Out in the country where they lived, houses were few and far between—plus, they were heading in the opposite direction of town. The boy had only been down this way a handful of times his entire life. This is the way his mother left. Go left for town, turn right to leave. That's what he always told himself. Where they were heading now, he had no idea.

A quarter mile or so later, his father turned up another driveway and ascended over a small hill and then back down on a slow descent all the way to a modest homestead set behind a farmyard and in front of a thick line of trees. From the road, the house was barely visible, and as they approached Howard didn't think he ever remembered seeing it before.

"What are we doing here?"

His father completely ignored the question and continued onward. When they reached the front porch—a rickety structure with warped boards—his father simply walked right inside. Howard followed. The first thing Howard heard was the anxious shouting. It was coming from a room in the back of the house. His father headed straight for it, but Howard hesitated for a few moments in the front room. It had old planks that were scratched and faded, and the space was littered with junk and plates and cups with leftover residue. The curtains were pulled tight and there was a stench that he couldn't quite decipher. On the wall near the entryway, a framed photo hung crooked. Howard glanced at the photo, then a double-take. It showed a mother standing with her little boy, her arms wrapped around him. Howard knew that boy. He rode the same bus, was in his class. *Willy. Willy McNabb*, he thought. He never knew where the kid lived.

"Back here, boy!" his father hollered from the other room, and Howard hurried in, completely unprepared for the scene that was unfolding. They were in a utility room with only slits for windows. Exposed lightbulbs hung from the ceiling with dangling pull chains attached. Howard's father, Willy's mother and Willy gathered around a kiddie pool that was sitting on the cement floor. Inside the pool, a black dog lay panting and whining in pain. Its stomach was bulging and Howard could see rows of protruding nipples underneath.

"She's having a litter," his dad told him.

Howard's head started spinning. "What did you need me for?"

"It's all hands on deck, son."

Willy looked at Howard and calmly said, "Hey," as if they had just sat down beside one another on the school bus.

Howard nodded but then started looking around the room. He had an unsettling feeling about all of this. Whatever was happening, and why Howard and his father needed to be there, was a complete mystery. Howard lost trust in his father for normal things like bringing dinner home—he certainly didn't trust him with mysteries.

"Thank goodness you're here," said Ms. McNabb to Howard's father. "We didn't even know Lulu was pregnant until last week!"

Howard's old man took charge, his authoritative voice cutting through the tension of the situation. "We've got a job to do, boys. Willy, you hold Lulu steady, and Howard, grab that clean towel from the kitchen."

Doing as he was instructed, Howard dashed into the kitchen and grabbed a towel that was folded neatly on the counter, the whole time wondering who the hell this man was thinking clearly and ordering people around. All four of them positioned themselves around Lulu to help however they could.

Willy leaned over to Howard, who was beginning to tremble. "You ever done this before?" Howard shook his head and Willy smirked. "Me neither."

"Willy—pay attention!" his mother snapped.

"Yes, ma'am."

The atmosphere grew increasingly tense as Lulu struggled with each contraction, her whimpers filling the room, each one sending a rush of adrenaline through Howard. His heart ached for the poor dog, but he knew he had to try to stay focused if he was going to survive this.

"You're doing great, boy!" Howard's dad shouted. "Keep supporting her, just like that." He looked ultra-focused, waiting to help each pup slide out. Ms. McNabb was holding the towel and looked ready to clean them up. "Yeah, she knows what to do," the old man seemed to say to Lulu as he gently rubbed her side.

After what felt like an eternity, the first puppy arrived. The boys shared a glance of relief. But that quickly faded and Howard stared at the pup, which looked more like a rat to him. Its brown fur was matted and slimy, and its eyes looked almost sealed shut. Little pink paws flailed and tried to latch onto anything. Whatever kind of dog this was supposed to be, the only thing it didn't look like to Howard was a puppy.

As the afternoon turned to evening, Howard and Willy assisted in the delivery of six more puppies, each a different combination of black and white and brown. The boys' hands were stained with blood and sweat, and a mix of exhaustion and relief hung in the air.

Ms. McNabb turned to Howard's father and took him into a firm embrace. "Thank you. Oh, thank you and your boy for coming down here. I'm not sure what I would have done..." In the anxiety of the labor, Howard didn't notice how pretty Willy's mom was. She looked younger than his own mother, by at least a few years, and she had soft brown hair pulled back that helped emphasize her blue eyes.

The gruff exterior of Howard's father momentarily softened. "It was our pleasure. Isn't that right, boy?"

Howard nodded and then turned to Willy. "Didn't expect to be doing this, that's for sure."

The puppies were in the kiddie pool beside Lulu fighting over the available nipples.

On their way out, Howard's father gave Ms. McNabb another hug and Howard saw the woman flinch and then blush.

"So, I'll come by in the morning to check on the pups," his father offered.

Through a crimson smile, she nodded and said "Thank you" again, before recognizing that the boys were staring and shouted at Willy, "Go get Lulu some water, will ya?"

Howard and his father didn't say anything as they walked down the driveway and turned onto the road. The evening was already fading into night and a gentle moonlight lit the tops of the surrounding trees but didn't make it down to the road.

Finally, Howard's father said, "You know how you ain't got a mama no more? Well, Willy ain't got a daddy."

Those words hung in the air while Howard's emotions ran circles around his head. He had a mama until his father drove her from him —but she still existed. Somewhere.

His father added, "So, I'm gonna have to lend a hand to Ms. McNabb with all these puppies. Gonna need your help a bit, too."

Howard didn't say a word and fell back a few strides, and that's how they walked, slowly in single file until they reached their front door.

In the quiet of his room, Howard tried to distract himself from the puppies, the McNabbs, his father—who, shortly after their return, was gone once again without a word. The boy crawled into his closet and slid between the hanging clothes and blankets. A normal boy would not have intentionally draped blankets over the bar in his closet, but this gave Howard an extra veil of privacy. His closet was slightly deeper than most, and he discovered young that with the right coverage, he could build a hidden sanctuary. With some old wire and a leftover nail in the wall, he was able to fasten a flashlight into an overhead light. Stuffed with blankets and pillows and books, that was the only place in the world he felt safe.

The house was quiet that night, as it had been so many nights since his mother left. When it wasn't dead quiet, it was maddeningly loud—there was no in-between. He picked up *The Adventures of Tom Sawyer*, one of his favorites, but before getting through the first page had to set it down. Then he picked up *Charlotte's Web*, but the same thing happened. The books weren't doing their jobs—they weren't forcing his thoughts from the real world into the make-believe. Instead, his mind continued to linger at the McNabbs' house. He saw what looked like blood and other fluids. He saw the slimy, rat-like puppies. He saw the look on his father's face and the fear in Willy's.

But mostly what his mind kept returning to was Ms. McNabb and that redness that washed over her as they left her house. It was a look Howard had seen his father put on his mother's face once upon a time. That was always during the good times. They all ate supper at the table in the kitchen as a family. His parents would tuck him into bed together. In the morning, they would be making breakfast hand-in-hand.

As Howard thought back to those memories, it felt like peering into someone else's life. The strangeness of the unfamiliar. Most of all, because he knew what came next.

Over the next several days, Howard and his father frequented the McNabb house. Howard, who was nearly always tucked away in his reading nook, would hear his father's faint whistle from the front entryway, and then they were off down the dusty road.

The boy didn't know a thing about puppies, and he quickly surmised that his father probably didn't either. The man was a bullshitter, first and foremost. Ms. McNabb would greet them at the front door, Willy off to her side or playing marbles on the living room floor. The first day she was wearing a full-length dress with a winding, floral pattern. The second day her dress lost several inches and swished with each step she took. By the end of the week, she answered the door in a fuzzy white robe, her hair draped over one shoulder and dripping with water. The boys rolled their eyes and jumped off the porch and tore around the house.

Not quite friends but no longer acquaintances, they kicked the dirt, snapped sticks, climbed trees and tossed rocks into a small brook that snaked through the woods out back. Willy was a small kid for his age, with freckles dotting his pale skin and shaggy hair. Howard, for his part, could have been his older brother. Other than the height difference and the freckles, he and Willy were nearly identical—right down to the dusty old blue jeans.

"You think yer pops likes mama?" Willy finally asked.

Howard shrugged. "Dunno. But I'm betting he fancies her enough."

Willy was poking at a dead bird with a stick. "Haven't had a daddy around my whole life, is all."

"He ain't much of a daddy. Better to not have one around."

"Easy for you to say."

"He's about the worst daddy."

Willy dropped the subject, along with his stick, and shoved his hands in his pocket. "Let's go see how the pups are comin' along."

The boys slipped off their shoes at the backdoor and went inside. Howard's dad and Willy's mom were sitting in the kitchen drinking coffee, hands desperately close to one another as they rested on the table.

"Check on the pups, will ya?" his father said without more than a glance in Howard's direction.

The boy rolled his eyes and then looked over to Willy, who shrugged and went inside the other room with the dogs. Still in the plastic pool, the pups squirmed and fought for their mother's teats. They were finally starting to look more like puppies now, the boys thought, before Willy uttered quietly aloud, "What are we checkin' on, exactly?"

"He just wanted more time with your mama is all."

The cool breeze of oncoming autumn seeped in through the window and refreshed the room of the stale, wafting odor that a litter of dogs creates. They sat there, hands in their pockets, leaning against the concrete wall for what felt like ages.

"Do you remember Mrs. Haskins' class?" Willy finally asked.

"What about it?"

"Just how rotten it was."

"Yeah, what about it?"

"I just think even cleaning poop off puppies is better than that class."

Howard smirked, not realizing until that moment how good it felt to smile again. It had been weeks. He and Willy had spent two years in the same class in school and barely said two words to one another. Now, there they were, tending to a litter of puppies as if they had grown up brothers. "So, which one is your favorite?" Howard asked.

"Hmm." Willy crouched and looked at the pups closely. "I think I like this little one." He pointed to a runt with brown fur and a crescent strip of white around the back of its collar.

"Yeah, I like that one too. It's always fighting for milk and barely gets any. I feel sorry for the little guy."

"Let's name him."

"Didn't your mom name them yet?"

"Nope," said Willy. "She was just going to sell them, I think. Didn't want any names attached."

"What should we call him then?"

Willy studied the pup again. "How's Bingo?"

Howard thought. "Doesn't seem quite right." Then, "How about Pluto? Because that white mark looks like it's from outer space."

"Pluto, like from Mickey Mouse?"

"Oh, right."

"Let's just call him Moon."

"Moon it is."

As the afternoon wore on, Howard's father finally grabbed the boy from the back room and told him it was time to go. Howard had already put his shoes on and was waiting for the signal. Lingering heat from the summer months seemed to find its way inside and burn up a perfectly good autumn coolness.

On the walk home, his father said, "In a few days, we're gonna sell those pups for Trish." He paused. "Ms. McNabb. We're gonna take those pups down to town and sell them for her."

Howard nodded but it didn't matter. "Do you think they're old enough to sell?"

"They're old enough. Any pup is old enough."

"Don't they need to be with their mama longer?"

"A little, yes. But then we'll sell them. I'll tell you when."

"In a few days?"

"Yes, maybe. Maybe a week. We'll see."

After a moment of listening to the breeze on the trees and the crunch of the dirt beneath their feet, Howard asked, "Did Ms. McNabb ask you to sell them for her?"

"That's a mighty dumb question, son. Of course she did."

"Is she going to keep any of them?"

"No, she doesn't need any more mouths to feed. And before you go askin', we ain't keeping one either."

A few days turned into nearly two weeks. The boys hung out in the backyard while the adults hung out in the house. Their guise was taking care of the pups, but Lulu was doing that just fine on her own, and Lord knows Lulu doesn't need any caring for. The dogs were growing quickly and had more than doubled in size. It was quite amazing to Howard. He had never seen anything so incredible and cute and disturbing in his whole life. They were balls of furry mystery.

"How's Moon doing?" Howard asked as he and Willy walked in the woods. Twigs snapped beneath their feet and the boys peeled bark from the trees as they passed by. The rich scent of evergreen lingered around them.

"He's okay." Willy looked down.

"Something the matter?"

Willy stopped walking and stood there. "I don't think Moon is doing too good, to be honest."

"Is he gonna make it?"

"Yeah, mama says so. But I don't know. He looks awful rotten compared to the others."

"I'm sure it's just the way some dogs are."

"You're probably right," said Willy, continuing his pace.

When they stepped back into the house, Howard's father was in the kitchen making a pot of coffee. His shirt was unbuttoned and his socks were missing. A cigarette hung from the corner of his mouth.

"Boys," he said as a way of greeting. His voice had a new energy to it.

"Everything okay?" Howard asked.

His father took a sip from the mug and then smiled a smile Howard had never seen before. "Today's a good day, boys. Howard, you and me are goin' to town to sell those pups."

"Today?"

"Today. It's time."

The boys spun and went into the backroom. The puppies had outgrown the plastic pool and were corralled inside a makeshift pen made from chicken wire. They knelt beside it and stuck their hands through the wire and tried to pet every puppy like they wished they'd done for the last few weeks. Last chances always sneak up on you. Once again, the little Moon was being boxed out by his siblings, wiggling and clawing to gain ground.

Howard's father had built a wooden box for transporting the puppies, with more chicken wire for the sides so that you could see them inside. Howard and Willy helped load them into the box, scooping one up at a time and gently lowering it inside. With each one, they gave it a little rub, looked it in the eyes and told it, "You're gonna be a good pup for some family."

Howard's father stood in the doorway, his gut still hanging out of his unbuttoned shirt, the cigarette on his lip still unlit. Ms. McNabb appeared beside him and pressed her hip into his.

"Good luck today," she whispered.

As each pup was taken from the pen, Lulu looked on helplessly. It wasn't concern on her face so much as confusion. But Howard's father assured the boys that she understood what was happening and that it was natural for all dog mamas to eventually say goodbye to their young. "Dogs are bred for that kind of thing," he told the boys. But Howard wasn't so sure. When all the pups were in the box, Lulu finally climbed to her feet and let out a gentle whimper.

"Ah, hush," Howard's father said. Then, "Son, let's get these pups to town."

The town was more of a stoplight, comprised of three blocks of two-story brick buildings. There used to be an old opera house but it caught fire back in the 1910s and they never renovated it. Its charred remains sat in the center of town as a reminder of what this place was. Still, the steel industry had been generous to the neighboring hills and cities, all leading to Pittsburgh, and this little place reaped the benefit when passersby would stop into the saloon or the Italian restaurant. Every town's gotta be famous for something.

The street corner where Howard and his father set up shop was a prime location. They had parked the truck on a nearby side street and, once his father had finished two beers and taken a pull from a little flask, carried the box and a handmade sign that read PUPS FOR SALE to place in front. The foot traffic was decent. The weather was nice and it was Saturday. People were out and about, but they didn't come into town to leave with a new puppy. But still, they came. Howard's dad had positioned his son in front of the box and, after an hour without luck, told him to hold the sign. Not five minutes later, a woman stopped by with two children in tow.

"Look at those little things!" she said. Her kids were tight by her side, peering around her leg at the squirming pups in the box.

"You folks have any dogs at home?" his father asked, trying to seize the opportunity.

"Not at the moment."

"Well, these here pups come from a long line of championship dogs. The mom, God rest her soul, didn't make it through the labor, so these are all that are left of that award-winning lineage." The lies spilled out of his mouth. They sounded second nature to him.

"Is that right?" She was intrigued.

"Is there a mister at home?"

"Mhmm."

"And what, may I ask, does he do?"

"Oh, he works up in Clement at the Steel Works."

Howard could see the wheels turning inside his father's mind. He had seen this show before, many times, play out in their own living room.

"Just you and the boys at home all day then?" his father said, gesturing to the little guys hidden behind her dress. "Two boys like that," and then he crouched down to their level. He was still talking to the woman, but he was at eye level with the boys. "These little guys need to grow up with a dog to chase around. Shoot, I remember the family mutt when I was their age. That thing kept me out of trouble, I'll tell ya." He gave the boys a wink and then stood. "What do you think, ma'am?"

"How much are you wanting for one?"

"Hmm," he brought his hand to his cheek and looked her up and down. "Heck, normal price is $50 per pup, but I'd sell one to you for $30."

"Oh? And why is that?"

"Pretty gal like you? With two lads who probably run her crazy back at home? You need a pup more than any of these other folks walkin' these streets."

The woman blushed and looked into the distance. She thought about it. "Say. Can you do $25 apiece if we take two?"

His father's face lit up. "I'd even carry 'em to the car for ya."

And just like that, the first two pups were sold.

"Okay, boys, which ones do you want?" the woman said to her sons, who suddenly shed their shyness and pressed themselves up against the box. Their eyes lit with excitement as the dogs fought to squeeze their snouts through the wire. Howard stood nearby and watched, praying silently that they overlooked Moon.

Just then, as the boys looked on: "How about that little one?" their mother suggested. "He's cute."

Howard felt a twist in his stomach.

"I want one of the big ones!" one of the boys shouted, pointing through the chicken wire, the puppies rushing to lick his finger.

"Okay, okay. We'll take those two big ones, there." She slipped a few bills from her purse and handed them over.

Howard's father said, "Mighty fine choices, mighty fine," and then scooped up the pups and handed one each to the little boys. "Keep 'em close, boys. If they start nibblin' just bop 'em on the nose," he said tongue-in-cheek.

As the afternoon pressed on, more people stopped by to see the remaining puppies. Men, more women with kids, a few old-timers, a group of older girls from Howard's school that caused his cheeks to redden. But as the heart of the evening set in, the box was left with just one pup: Moon. Howard was thrilled.

"Alright, son, let's get this cash back to Ms. McNabb."

His father carried the box back to the truck and Howard trailed behind. On the drive, Howard tried to devise a plan to keep the puppy, raise it all by himself in his room if he had to. Heck, he knew Willy would walk down the road and help out any chance he could.

"Surprised, got to be honest, that no one took the little one," his father said along the drive, though the tone in his voice—an unfamiliar one—said it didn't bother him much. To the old man, it would have been gravy had someone bought Moon. "Just figured once the others were gone folks wouldn't see how little he is."

Howard shrugged but didn't say anything. He didn't want to say anything until he knew exactly how to say it. They continued driving and his father passed the turnoff that led to their dirt road. For five minutes, the road winded through hills and down into a nearby pass, overgrown with trees that were showing the first hints of autumn orange on their branches.

"Where are we going?" Howard asked.

"Gotta take care of something."

Howard fell quiet and hoped whatever the errand was kept them out of trouble.

Finally, they pulled off the road onto a two-track with thick grass growing in the middle. The grooves in the path were so warn that Howard heard the grass tickling the bottom of the truck. In the distance, Howard saw a creek appear and as they got closer and his father idled the engine, he could hear the water trickling off the rocks and picking up speed downstream.

"What are we doing?"

"Gotta take care of something," his father said again, a little less patience in his voice. He stepped out of the truck and walked around to the back. In the side mirror, Howard tried to steal a glance but couldn't see his father. He heard the truck bed click and the groan of the metal hinges. Then it slammed shut and Howard heard, "Come out here, boy."

He didn't want to move. He wanted to stay right there in the truck, close his eyes and wait until he was back in the safety of his closet at home. But he peeked through his eyelids and saw his father in his direct line of sight through the side mirror. The man was staring at Howard with a look even he had never seen, so the boy climbed out of the truck.

"Good boy," his father said condescendingly. "Now take this here pup over to the river."

Howard looked at Moon, who was sitting on the tailgate looking at him, ready to play. "What am I going to do with him over there?" He was afraid to ask the question but did anyway.

"Toss him in."

Howard's heart was racing. He felt a flutter in his chest, then again. A pounding now. He could barely breathe. "But, dad..." The words fell out involuntarily. There were tears in his eyes that spilled down his cheeks. He wanted to plead to keep the dog, but he couldn't talk.

"Ain't no time for cryin', son. Toss the pup." His father watched him stand frozen. He bent over to Howard's level. "Listen, boy. This here runt ain't gonna grow up to be a good dog no more than you are. He ain't got no future. Toss him in the river and get on with it."

"But—I can't. Dad. That's Moon." His voice squeaked with fear.

"You went and named him? Fool's mistake." The old man picked Moon up by the skin on the back of his neck and shoved him into Howard's chest. The pup yelped and then let out a soft whimper. Howard wrapped him in his arms. His father spoke again, slowly. "You take that pup over to the river. Now."

"Wh-wh-why do I gotta? Why are you making me do it?" There was desperation in Howard's voice now.

"There's some things a man's gotta do in this world. Time for you to get to findin' out what those things are. Now git."

His father leaned against the side of the truck. Howard looked down at Moon, tears streaming onto his fur. He tried to wipe them away but they smeared into it. One last glance at his father, who made a simple gesture toward the water. Howard kept his head down and shuffled his feet, but he couldn't feel himself moving. He could hear the creek before it entered his peripheral vision. Then he planted his feet. He kissed Moon on the top of the head. He closed his eyes. He tossed as far as he could. Time stopped. Off in the distance, he heard a splash and that was it. The river was still rushing by as if nothing happened.

"Good boy," said his father.

The silence in the car was deafening for the rest of the drive back to the McNabb house. Howard had his head pressed against the window, the vibrations of the old truck rattling his brain. Good, though, because he wanted his brain rattled. Removed altogether would be better.

Just as they pulled off the dirt road, his father said, "Oh, and best not say anything about that runt. If Ms. McNabb asks, we sold all seven." He reached around his seat and grabbed his silver flask and took a long sip.

Howard wanted to hit him, but he had been fighting back nausea since the river. When the car stopped, he opened the door and vomited. He did so quietly and off in the grass so that when his father came around the side of the truck to see what was happening Howard was able to conceal it. The last thing he wanted was for his father to see how shaken up he was.

"All good over here?"

"Mhmm." He wiped his mouth with his sleeve and started off toward the backyard. He knew the old man was going to head inside to offer Ms. McNabb her cut of the money—undoubtedly less than she deserved—and so if he headed around back he wouldn't be followed.

Ms. McNabb opened the front door and stepped out onto the porch, leaning back against the frame. "Well, how'd it go, boys?" she asked, her voice full of anticipation.

Howard's father grinned confidently. "Went just fine, ma'am." He stepped onto the porch in front of her and stood close enough to smell the perfume coming off of her body. "Sold all seven pups, just like I promised."

"I knew you would," she said, setting her hand on his chest. "You are a lifesaver."

"Just thank that dog of yours for givin' you a litter to sell."

"I'm thanking *you*."

Reaching for his back pocket, the old man withdrew a folded stack of bills and held it in front of her. "Here's your share, Ms. McNabb."

She rolled her eyes and smacked him playfully. "Call me Trish."

He ignored her. "That's a good deal more than I expected, given the pedigree of those pups."

She took the money and then pulled him inside by his shirt. Willy, who was reading a magazine on the living room floor, jumped up and ran out the backdoor. The sun had barely set behind the backdrop of the trees, casting a bright glow off in the distance. Howard was sitting out in the yard by a pile of chopped wood, kicking at rocks and staring into the emptiness of the world.

"How's it going?" Willy asked as he approached. "Did you sell all the puppies?"

Howard ignored him. He couldn't bring himself to answer. He stared at the ground instead.

Willy could sense something was wrong and pressed further. "What about Moon? Did someone buy him?"

The mention of the pup was like a knife to Howard's heart. Unable to restrain tears any further, he broke down. Uncontrollable sobs overwhelmed him and he collapsed into himself. Willy stood a few feet away, unsure how to respond. Howard didn't know if he should lie or tell the truth. The truth might kill him. But lying wasn't in his nature. He was afraid to lie, even as a boy, mostly because he was afraid of becoming his father. Still, it was in his blood and could be retrieved, he decided, in moments of desperation.

"Yeah, some nice lady," Howard finally said through labored breaths.

Willy waited a second and then said, "Are you okay?"

"Fine." He picked up a stick, snapped it and then discarded it into the nearby trees.

From where they stood, they were still within earshot of the house. In their silence, they began to hear sounds from inside. At first, it was a startling pounding on the wall. Then a few bursts of screams. They weren't exactly painful—no, something different. The boys looked at each other.

"This has happened before," Willy said.

Howard looked confused.

"Best give 'em space." Willy waved Howard over toward the woods and the boys headed into the trees without looking back.

The woods were dark, but a dimming light made just enough of the way through so they could watch their step. Willy led them through thick pines and across a small, trickling stream. Howard looked into the water and envisioned Moon's panicking body trying to wrestle free of the current. The boy quickly closed his eyes and leaped to follow his friend. They came to the base of a large tree. When Howard looked up, he could see a series of planks nailed into the trunk that led to a sizable structure overhead.

"What is this?" Howard asked.

"Dunno, exactly. Found it one day a while back. Not sure who built the thing."

"It looks pretty neat."

"Wanna check it out?"

With Willy leading the way, they scaled up the tree and settled in the makeshift fort. Twigs and brown, crunchy leaves littered the floor. Hanging on a nail was a small lantern that Willy retrieved and lit. It provided enough light to see the warped wood, the stack of magazines that had accumulated in the corner, the tops of the surrounding trees. This, Howard realized, was Willy's sanctuary. His hidden reading closet. The place where he escaped his resentment for his lousy childhood, his absent father, his train wreck of a mother. Adults were selfish beings who had no business raising children.

3

Wolf Valley, 2001

In which Howard is 47 years old

Without much thought, Howard begins to establish a ritual—setting the gun on the coffee table in front of him, beside a glass of whiskey, and drinking until he dares to use it. He sits in his chair; the dog lies across the room near the fireplace. The pup's fur, despite any kind of grooming, remains shiny and soft. With his white paws tucked beneath him, the dog is a ball of brown hair, with two eyes that glare at Howard. The two maintain steady eye contact, neither flinching, neither offering so much as a single emotion. As the sun sets in the evening, it becomes all the more important to remain in the deadlock. There is something in it for each of them. The dog is hungry, needs food, needs water, needs some instance of affection. Howard needs the dog's spirit to break so that he can re-focus his energy on the breaking of his own spirit.

That is when it dawns on Howard: he hasn't given the dog a name. For the last several days, he simply called him 'dog' or nothing at all. After the funeral, Howard noticed a stench in the house. The mutt was lying on the kitchen floor, whimpering, as it often did. He walked past him to grab a bottle from the liquor cabinet. Pouring a few fingers into a small glass, he took a long drink and held the liquid in his mouth for a moment. When he swallowed, it burned the whole way down. Howard knew there was a technique to drinking whiskey so that you minimized the bite, but this was intentional. He wanted the burn. Needed it. But the stench lingered in the air and even the alcohol could not dissipate it.

The dog doesn't stand but keeps his paws beneath himself and army crawls across the wooden floor past Howard and around the corner to the side door. It's strange. Howard sets the glass down and follows. That is where he finds a urine-soaked rug and a pile of feces. It dawns on him that he hasn't let the dog outside in days. Careful not to step in any of the wet spots, he opens the door and shouts, "Out." The dog finally lifts itself off the floor and walks, head down, outside—more like a prison sentence than a reward. The ground is still soft from the rain and once he reaches the grass he lies down. Howard loses it. "You piss and shit all over my rug and then I let you out and you just lay there!" He slams the door and hopes that, eventually, when he opens it back up, the dog will be gone.

Hours later, Howard is back at the cabinet pouring the last of the whiskey into his glass when the motion-sensor light on the side of the house clicks on. It catches his eye and he walks around to open the door, this time too drunk to avoid stepping in the dog's prior mess, which he hasn't yet cleaned up. There, sitting in the cold autumn night, is the dog. He is sitting nicely, patiently, with a slight tail wag. Howard shakes his head. "Alright then," he says, waving the dog to come inside. He does promptly, heading right into the kitchen where he stops and stares at the sink. "You want some water?" Howard asks aloud, though he is already reaching for a bowl. He turns on the faucet and flicks his finger through it a few times until he can feel it cool down, and then he fills the bowl and sets it on the floor. The dog drinks until he is licking the metal. "I suppose you're hungry too, huh?" The cupboards are pretty bare. Howard untwists a loaf of bread and drops a slice on the floor. Then he heads over to the refrigerator and retrieves a block of cheese and slices a couple of pieces. By the time he drops them on the floor, the bread is already gone. "Greedy little bastard," Howard mumbles to himself, before grabbing his whiskey and heading back to the living room. The dog follows and calmly curls up at his feet.

Howard stares at the dog now. The dog blinks and Howard feels some sort of satisfaction. Then he thinks that, if the dog were to stay—and he isn't telling himself he is keeping him—that he should at least get a name. Even a temporary name. Amber used to assign names all the time. To all those characters. *How did she do it?* There are no names that come directly to Howard's mind. Namelessness, he decides, is a cruelty he will not inflict. A few moments pass and he stands and walks into Amber's study. He brings his glass with him and sets it down on the lip of the bookshelf, smearing a ring onto the wood. There is a book of baby names he hasn't picked up in years. The dog, he notices, is at his feet, as if intrigued by what's unfolding. Howard flips open the book and points. Jasper. He looks at the dog—*not a Jasper*. He does it again. Olive. He gives the dog a look, then crouches down and lifts its leg, just to be sure. *Boy dogs can't be named Olive.* This exercise is dumb, he decides, because it doesn't matter what he calls the dog; it is likely going back to that shelter anyway. But he flips the book open one more time. Coby. Unisex? *Good enough.* "Congratulations," he says matter-of-factly to the dog trailing behind him as he returns to his chair. "Your god-damn name is Coby."

Coby makes a habit of following Howard around the house, from room to room, often leading to doors being shut in his face. Then he sits patiently, or sometimes lays, until Howard emerges from the room, and then the shadow resumes.

The house is a one-story brick ranch on a dusty road. A steep mountain—or, at least what Howard considers a mountain—overlooks the road opposite his house. A wide lawn has a subtle slope to it, which runs down to the river out back. In this valley, most people know their neighbors out of both necessity and boredom—although that was more of Amber's area of interest than Howard's. Where he lives just outside of Elmswood, no two houses are closer than a quarter mile. His road isn't quite an isolated path carved into the valley, but it is the next closest thing, with fields of wildflowers and forests littered with thick underbrush beckoning throughout.

This is one of Howard's bad days, where the guilt overwhelms. The kind where he sits in his chair, staring at the pistol, staring at the bottle, and contemplating which will ultimately cause him more harm. Before the accident, he had already neglected himself for too long. Now he sits, unbathed for days, hair growing long and greasy, the semblance of a beard—speckled in streaks of gray. It's the opposite of Coby, who is asleep at Howard's feet, fur shedding a bit and shaggy but otherwise miraculously still somewhat soft despite who-knows-how-long without a proper bath. But Howard doesn't pay that much attention. He is living a single-minded life.

A knock on the front door startles him. It has now been more than a week since the funeral, almost two without Amber. There have been no knocks, so this one seems to echo throughout the emptiness of the house. Coby picks his head up and stares at the door as if waiting for it to open itself. Howard does the same, and then they share a look of confusion. Through the peephole, he sees an older woman with dark, leathery skin, her black hair swirled up on top of her head. He has never seen her before, but she is holding something, a box. At this point, Howard has no awareness of his appearance. He thinks he probably looks a bit disheveled, perhaps even presentable, but the truth could lie on either extreme and he would not know. The woman is unfazed by it and introduces herself.

"Hi, I'm Edna Druthers. You must be Mr. Lynch?"

Normally Howard would correct someone for saying such a thing. "Call me Howard," he'd say. But he does not say anything. His blank, confused state lands quickly with Edna and she continues.

"I live just down the road a piece. I can't imagine what you're going through." She pauses to let the words hang in the air, allowing an opportunity for Howard to respond, but still, he remains silent. She gestures toward the box in her hands. "I baked you a chicken dish. Mama's old recipe."

Howard offers the semblance of appreciation, a false smirk. "Very thoughtful," he says.

Coby is now nosing his way to the front door. He looks up at Edna but just stares and takes a few sniffs in the air at the lingering scent of baked chicken.

"Look at you," Edna says, crouching down to pet the dog. "I didn't know y'all had a dog. He's a cutie."

As she scratches his head, Coby's mouth falls open, tongue hanging to the side—his first affection since stepping foot in the house.

"We didn't," Howard says after a moment. His voice is serious, telling the visiting neighbor that he'd rather not breach the subject.

Edna stands and reverts back to Howard. She gives a friendly smile. "Well, please enjoy the chicken, and if there's anything you need, just holler."

Howard nods.

"Sorry again for your loss," she says as she backs off the porch and returns to her car. She is walking gingerly, not from injury but from age. For a moment Howard watches her drive away, trying to picture which house is hers, but he can't muster up a guess. Finally, he retreats inside. Coby follows him to the kitchen counter and waits patiently for a meal that isn't coming. Inside the box, Howard sees the chicken dish that Edna had mentioned. When he lifts it, there is a note beneath, written on a small prayer card. The prayer comes from John 6:22. "So also you have sorrow now, but I will see you again, and your hearts will rejoice, and no one will take your joy from you." The note that accompanies it, which is handwritten, simply says, "Please enjoy the chicken. Jesus comforts when we need

Him most." In one motion, Howard folds it in half and slips it into the trash.

Outside, it is another gloomy fall day in Wolf Valley. The river is full from all the rain, but it does not seem to be moving at any pace greater than an ordinary day. That is the only constant in Howard's life at this point, the river, which reminds him of past sins. The colors have begun to change over the last couple of weeks but he has not noticed until now. Lush shades of green have transformed into a yellow forest, save for the pines that now speckle the landscape like the gray in Howard's beard.

Several ducks are floating in the water and Howard stands in his kitchen watching them through the window. The current is too slow to see on the surface but their kicks create subtle ripples that bring life to the river. From his periphery, Howard can see the red light blinking on his answering machine. He doesn't check it because he knows what it is. Perhaps some condolences, from Amber's agent, Kim, he presumes, or a random person he doesn't know. Maybe a telemarketer. But likely it's Wendell from work asking when Howard's coming back. The market is in limbo and Wendell needs him back on-site to scoop up as much cash as he can muster. That is the last thing on Howard's mind. Instead, he unplugs the machine and sets it on top of a kitchen cabinet.

Behind him, he hears a growl. Coby is sitting in the center of the room. When Howard looks at him, he darts his eyes to a food bowl that was recently set out empty and then back to the man. Then a whimper. He darts his eyes again. Howard doesn't flinch. Coby barks.

"Cut that shit out," Howard says, but it is enough for him to parse through the cupboard for something. A can of beans has been tucked away in the back for months, maybe years, and Howard opens it and slops it into the bowl. "Eat up." But he knows he needs to get some real dog food. Just enough to last until he takes the mutt back to the shelter.

Back in the living room, there are a couple of stacks of novels on the small table beside Howard's chair. They are the classics—some

Hemingway, Steinbeck, Faulkner, Fitzgerald, Wolfe and Woolf—with Amber's mixed in. He has read them all multiple times. They sit here on the table because he is limiting his trips into the study, a room where he thought he'd find comfort but instead finds grief. From his chair, he can feel the warmth of the fireplace, which reminds him that he needs to split more wood before winter. Through the bay window, he also has a clear view out to the road and, more importantly, the driveway and the front walkway—both of which are as lonely and empty as he is. Most of the time, anyway. That is why he is surprised to see a man leave the road and begin walking up to the house. "Jesus, two in one week," he mumbles to himself. The man is tall but built, with a flannel shirt tucked into gray jeans. Coby doesn't see him.

A few moments later, there is a knock at the door. Now the dog, with some renewed energy, springs to his feet and barks his way over to the door. *Seems he's settled into the house,* Howard thinks to himself as he tucks his pistol into the rear of his waistband and heads to the door. He pulls it open without saying anything. Coby tries to bull past him onto the porch, still barking, but Howard gives the dog a firm kick back into the house before stepping outside and closing the door behind him.

"What can I do for you?" Howard asks.

"Mornin', sir," the man says in a powerfully deep voice, respectfully ignoring the heel Howard has just put to the mutt. "My name is Stu Steiner. The wife an' I live just down the road a piece."

"Another one," Howard thinks aloud to himself.

Stu hears. "Pardon, sir?"

Now Howard is embarrassed. He regroups. "Sorry, I'm just not used to visitors, and a woman stopped by the other day saying the same thing."

"Who's that, if y'don't mind me askin'?"

"Edna, I think she said her name was."

"Ah, yes, Edna. Sweet old God-fearin' lady."

"Mhmm."

"Well, I come by—somewhat embarrassed to say empty-hand-ed—but the wife an' I wanted to offer our condolences. We heard about yer wife. Awful tragedy, sir."

Howard nods in a short, quick rhythm, trying to say, "Thank you, but I don't want to talk about it with you."

"Well, listen, mister. Pardon my mindin' yer business but I don't see much comin' and goin' from this here house, and I reckon it'll do ya good to git out. Y'like fishin'?"

"Haven't fished in years," Howard says.

"Livin' on this here river and ain't been fishin'? That's just a crime, if y'askin' me. I got myself a little fishin' boat. How's about you an' me take 'er out later this week? Not sure what's bitin' this time a year, but the fresh air'll save yer life."

The cold metal from the handgun presses against the small of Howard's back and sends him into a rush of embarrassment. Stu waits patiently for a response, his bushy eyebrows raised in anticipa-tion. What Howard wants to say is that he'd rather sit in his chair reading and drinking bourbon, that the thought of sitting on a cold boat in the wee hours of a fall morning sounds like the last place he'd want to find himself.

Instead, he says, "What the hell."

"Fantastic," says Stu. "I'll bring my boat over Saturday mornin'." As he turns to leave, he adds, "Y'all take care of yerself, now."

Once again, Howard finds himself watching a neighbor, a stranger, a new acquaintance walking away, all the while wondering how his life came to this. And then he feels it start to rain.

By the time Saturday rolls around, Howard has all but forgotten about his fishing outing. He awakes in his chair, now in a reclined position. The first peeks of sunshine, which on cloudy days do not crest over the mountains and into the valley, have still yet to appear. Instead, he sees the lights from a pickup idling in his driveway, the heavy exhaust hitting the cool air and looking like a fire lit out front.

Shit. His head is pounding and he has to take a piss. Suddenly something on the table catches his eye. The bottle of bourbon has been knocked onto its side. He falls to a knee and pats the floor, then smells his hand. No moisture, no whiskey scent. He figures he must have finished the bottle and then kicked it over accidentally in his sleep.

On the walk from the living room to the bathroom to the bedroom to change and finally back to the front door, he has a familiar shadow. Coby has learned to keep his distance, but he refuses to allow Howard to forget about him. Survival instinct, more than anything. When he opens the front door, the dog dashes past him into the yard and lifts a leg to relieve himself on the first bush he sees.

"Dog sure did hafta piss," Stu shouts. He's patiently leaning against his truck.

"Dog shouldn't be out of the house," Howard says, snapping a finger at Coby and using his boot to usher him back inside.

"Dog's welcome to join, if he can handle the boat."

Howard shakes his head. "This dog's fine right where he is."

Stu clearly doesn't want to push the subject and pivots. "Didn't wanna drive over yer grass here without the okay from you first," he says as both a statement and question. The trailer is hooked up to the truck and an old beige fishing boat with blue and white stripes is loaded on top. On the side, the faded name SWEET SUN DAYZ is printed.

"Fine by me," Howard says, motioning for him to pull the boat down to the river. He has his canteen in hand and follows slowly behind on foot. This is a moment he should relish: a crisp fall morning, dew on the grass, trees forming a kaleidoscope of green and yellow that is dimmed in the dark of the morning. In front of him is the river, which comes into view from the west and runs eastward, appearing around one bend and disappearing around another, so that this one sliver of tributary feels like it was carved out by God just for him. He should suck that pure morning air into his lungs and let it free him.

That's not how he feels.

Stu approaches the river and swings his truck wide so that he can back the boat trailer right up to the bank. He has evidently done this many times before. Howard watches with dull amusement. A few minutes later, the two men have the boat in the water. It's a calm morning on the river. The recent rain has left it fuller than it would normally be this time of year. The truth is that they have been getting much more rain as of late. While the river moves fairly swiftly in the spring, the autumn always seems to, ironically, bring it some new life after the hot summer months.

Pushing off from shore, they glide peacefully for a moment while Stu starts up the engine. Once moving, the lures in the tackle box and the metal rods rattle with the rumbling of the old craft. Upstream, there are a few spots where the river widens into what some might call a lake, and Stu says he knows a few places where they can drop anchor or just drift and fish. All this time, Howard is regretting accepting the invitation. He sips from his canteen, which is perhaps more whiskey than coffee, and hopes that Stu can't smell his breath from across the boat. *There is enough of a breeze*, he thinks. *Should be okay*.

If Howard didn't regret coming before, he certainly does once the conversation starts. "Can you believe those goddamn terrorists?" Stu says with clenched teeth, referencing the attacks on the World Trade Center only weeks before. Howard shakes his head in agreement but doesn't say anything. Nothing needs to be said, especially not about that. "So, Howard, what d'you do fer work?"

This question makes Howard pause. It is obviously simple enough, but he has spent so little time thinking about his career— and what will come of it now—that he does not answer immediately. Finally, he says, "I'm a contractor," and leaves it at that.

"Like, buildin' houses?"

He nods.

"Well shit, good line'a work to be in."

"Except," Howard begins, then second-guesses himself.

"'Cept what?"

After a deep breath, Howard finishes. "I just have a hard time picturing myself going back to work, is all."

"I totally understand. Y'have some money saved up so y'can take it easy a while?"

He says, "Enough." Could have said, "Plenty." He doesn't know what Stu knows about Amber's work, but he also has no interest in elaborating.

"Hate to say it this way, but did yer wife have any insurance?"

That was something, believe it or not, Howard had not even considered. He ponders it for a few seconds and thinks maybe she did. After another sip from his canteen, he makes a mental note to look into that. When he looks up at Stu, he realizes he is still waiting for an answer. "Not sure," he offers.

The two sit in silence for a short while. They have baited hooks and the repetition of casting, reeling and casting again is calming. The sun is up now, spreading a blanket of wrinkled orange over the water. Though they aren't speaking to one another, the air is far from silent. Birds are flying overhead. Ducks swim in groups. Herons stand near the shore like statues. The smell of the algae in the water reaches their nostrils. Occasionally, another boat putters by and gives a friendly wave. That is how most of the rest of the morning goes before heading back to his property.

As they drag the boat from the water, Coby is in the window watching them. They can hear his barks and Howard sighs.

"Don't wanna overstep my mindin' here, mister, but you should treat that dog a little more like the rest'a folks 'round here."

Howard gives him a look.

"All's I'm sayin', ain't no reason that dog shouldn't be on that boat with us. Or waitin' in the yard fer when we pullin' up."

"I appreciate your concern, but that dog is right where he belongs."

Stu leaves the subject alone and they load up the boat. "Shoulda thought'a this b'fore, I s'pose, but what d'ya think'a me keepin' this here boat tied up right here next time? Sure beats me havin' t'drive down the road to the launch ev'rtime I wanna use it. I got a big stake I can put in the ground right here that it'll tie to."

"Yeah, that's fine," Howard says. "I appreciate you taking me out." The words of gratitude almost catch him off-guard.

"Well, I appreciate y'comin'." Before he drives off, Stu rolls down the window and says, "Hope y'don't mind my askin', but y'wanna come to church tomorrow? Sure is good fer the soul to pray to the Good Lord."

"Not sure I'm quite ready to start talking to God again yet."

Stu nods in understanding. "Well, sure hope ya pick up the phone soon."

Howard remembers about the answering machine he unplugged. *Not likely*, he thinks.

That night, Howard sits in his chair. A new bottle of whiskey is already empty. The pistol is sitting on the table in front of him. A single bullet sits on its end beside it. Howard leans forward and picks them up. Briefly inspecting the bullet, he slides it into the chamber, draws back the hammer, sticks the barrel into the roof of his mouth and squeezes the trigger.

The click of the hammer startles him. He sits for a moment shaking. He can't help but feel like he's still alive.

4

Pennsylvania, 1972

In which Howard was 18 years old

With only his father around, the life Howard knew, the one he'd imagined coming true, was completely upended. Not long after selling Ms. McNabb's puppies and bedding her, his father sat him down and explained his philosophy on life. "I'm a salesman first," he told the young boy. "Just look at those pups. Everything else comes second. Sooner you understand that, sooner things start goin' smoother around here." Howard stared into his father's eyes with a vacant expression, wondering if he had the same whiskey on his breath when he told his wife that she came second to his career—if he'd even had the balls to say such an honest thing to her.

Not long after that day, the frequent visits to see Ms. McNabb became less often until one day he stopped going there at all. Howard knew exactly what happened: she got tired of his shit. The old man moved on to the next woman, and then the next, and then the next. Over the years, it became impossible to keep track of.

Still, Willy and Howard remained friends all through elementary school, junior high and into high school. Now they were approaching the end of their academic lives, something neither could see as a negative.

Howard outgrew his closet hideaway, but no longer feared his father's wrath. He had matured into a sturdy young man with visible abs and veins down his forearms, and the last time his father laid a hand on him was the last time. The old man knew better now. No, Howard didn't strike back. But there was a look in his father's eye—instant recognition that their situation had changed.

The books that were once piled in the corner of the closet, out of sight, now took up space on a small desk or scattered about his bedroom floor. He was lying on his stomach reading *East of Eden* when he heard a knock on his door. Without looking up or answering, it gently swung open and his father stood in the hallway, hair disheveled and shirt untucked. Without even stepping foot in the room, Howard could smell the Wild Turkey. Howard didn't say anything, just waited for the old man to speak. He hoped he was going to address the eviction notice that the county had posted on their front door the day prior.

"Old Bill Pratt fired me. That cranky old bastard."

He was looking for some sort of reaction, but Howard wasn't going to give it.

"You hear me, boy?"

"Mhmm." He was still trying to read.

"You got anything to say? This here is your home too."

"Bank gonna take the house?"

"Hell no, I ain't lettin' that happen."

So then Howard asked, "Did you have it comin'?"

"The hell is that supposed to mean?"

"Did you have have it comin'? Seems like a simple enough question."

His father stepped into the room but hesitated. "You might wanna check that attitude, boy."

Without flinching, Howard shrugged and kept reading.

The old man didn't quite have the same fight in him that he'd used to drive Howard's mother away. The drinking got worse and his health had deteriorated over the last decade. Even if his father found new employment, it wouldn't last long. Then they'd be right back here having this same exchange all over again. At times, it had pushed Howard to his limits. On more than one occasion, he had contemplated heading down to the army recruiting station and volunteering his name. He figured that was better than getting his number pulled from the draft—though both routes achieved the same goal: getting him out of his father's house.

Not long after Howard's father and Willy's mother ended their affair, the two boys discovered a path through the woods connecting their two houses. It was a saving grace, as was that tree fort. The two of them fixed it up over the years. It now had a real ladder, a sturdy floor and a roof that didn't leak. Pair all that with their cordless radio and the occasional six-pack, and the boys had a regular retreat. As the years went by and his father stopped caring whether the boy was around the house or not, Howard would sneak off and spend days on end up in that tree. Willy would bring him water and snacks and they'd read books and magazines and talk and listen to music and whittle and do all the other things teenage boys tend to do in the woods.

It certainly started off more innocent than it eventually became. When they were kids, it was just them. Then in junior high, the first girl glimpsed the fort. Then two more girls. And before they knew it, it was the safest place in those hills to hide out with your crush. The girls came before the drugs and alcohol, but it all came. As they stared down graduation, that fort nearly killed them but also may have been the only thing that kept them alive.

Howard loved those nights. But he loved the peace that the fort gave him much more than Willy seemed to. For Willy, it was a temporary escape. For Howard, it was the only place in the world where he could think. He'd sneak up there by flashlight, sometimes with a bottle tucked under his arm and sometimes without. It wasn't difficult to get his hands on booze. Though he was legally underage in Pennsylvania, all it took was a road trip over the state lines to stockpile for a while. It was during those late nights drinking alone in the treehouse by lantern, the still of the night or the swishing of treetops in the breeze his only companion, that Howard felt he could think. His brain seemed to run on reserve power most of his life, but in that stillness, he could access its completeness. He hated the thought that he could wind up like his father—drunk, alone, failing. And yet, that was the only path he saw before him.

His mother, he decided after years of spinning in circles on the topic, was smart. And selfish. But smart. She had no life living under his father's domain. Walking out of the house that day wasn't her abandoning Howard, he now believed, but an act of self-preservation. It was live elsewhere or cease to live at all. It was a decision that may have saved her life. And one that may have condemned her son.

As Howard returned through the back door, his father stepped through the front. It was late—the middle of the night, as most people would call it—and the old man stopped dead when he saw his boy. A grin crept upon his face. It was a look Howard hadn't quite seen since his father connived to swindle Ms. McNabb.

"What is it?" Howard asked. But he knew the answer: He found a new job, the one that will take off and make them rich one day. For as many books as Howard had read, this was the one he'd read most often.

"Landed me a gig," his father said as he walked into the house. He crossed the room and Howard noticed something missing: the reek of alcohol.

"Where at?"

"Whistle Stop."

"You're working at a bar? Is that really a good idea?"

"Think what you will about me, son," his father said as he reached into the fridge for a beer, "but I ain't got a problem. I can turn this shit off whenever I please if it means makin' some dough. Just look at me tonight. First night bartendin' and didn't have a drop."

Howard gave him a look.

"This here? This is a victory beer. Says the world tried to keep me down but couldn't."

The victory, of course, lasted until the sharp rays of the morning sun pierced through the front windows. When Howard emerged from his room to head to his own job—bagging at a local grocery store—the old man was disoriented and trying to roll off the couch. Howard walked right past him as if he didn't exist.

It took the old man one day in his new job to spiral.

With only a side lamp lit, it was calm inside the house. Howard knew the home as still or chaotic—not much in between. He was back to reading Steinbeck with his feet kicked up on the couch when his father stumbled through the front door. They shared a look, but Howard instantly knew this was the father that he left on the couch earlier that morning, not the sober one who boastfully returned the previous night. His father stepped inside and began pacing. A tense energy began to fill the space. Desperation clung to the man.

"What?" Howard asked flatly. He set his book down.

The old man waved him off with a finger.

Howard stood. "Dad. Tell me what's going on."

Attempting to gather himself, his father paused and faced his son. "I'm not working at the Whistle Stop anymore."

"You got fired your second day? What the hell did you do?"

"It was a misunderstanding, is all. I borrowed some money—was totally going to pay it back—and the boss fired me. Threatened to call the cops."

Howard shook his head, sat back down, picked up his book and went back to reading.

"You gotta help me think outta this one, kid."

He shut the book. "What am I supposed to do? You're the one who keeps fucking everything up."

"You're 18 now, kid, you gotta do your part."

Now Howard was standing, looking eye to eye with the old man. "You keep calling me kid. I worked all day, just like I've been doing every weekend and most weeknights for the last three years. How the hell do you think these lights are still on?"

His father went quiet. He paced some more and then sat down at the kitchen table. "Well, it's not just the lights I'm worried about."

"We're losing the house, aren't we?"

His father didn't answer, but then Howard's question also wasn't really a question. They were losing the house.

As the days passed, the atmosphere inside the house grew tense and suffocating. Howard spent nearly all his time with his back propped against a tree thirty feet in the air. The notice had been posted to their front door, and Howard knew that one day he would return from the woods and the doors would be locked, the windows boarded up.

One afternoon, he approached the house and saw his father loading bags into his truck.

"Is this it?" Howard called.

His father dismissed him with a wave of his arm and continued filling the vehicle.

Howard jogged up beside him. "We officially outta here?"

"Pack your shit, kid, we got a place to stay."

"What? Where?"

"Harvey place. That old prick has a trailer out back he said we can crash in for a bit."

Living in a trailer with his father sounded like pretty much the worst thing imaginable, though he knew the old man would likely not be around much. Out drinking, chasing women, perhaps sprinkling in some job hunting.

The move was quick: Old man Harvey lived just down the road, on the other side of the McNabbs' place. Howard and his father loaded as much of their stuff into the truck as they could, drove down there, unloaded it, and then returned for another trip. The trailer, surprisingly to Howard, was in decent shape. It had a functioning bathroom, two small bedrooms and a kitchenette. Harvey took good care of it, which only gave Howard more anxiety about what his father would do to the place. The last thing he wanted was to get comfortable there. He knew their days were likely numbered before they found themselves homeless once again.

When they were nearly moved in, his father opened a beer and sat down on the old couch that Harvey had left in the trailer for them. "We're gonna make this work," he said.

Before Howard could even respond, there was a knock on the door, and then Harvey stepped inside. He was a wide-set man with hunched shoulders and a wispy gray combover. Ducking to fit through the doorway, he stood before them with his hands on his hips, looking around. "Everything okay?" he asked.

"Everything's great," Howard's father said, standing from the couch and setting the beer on the nearby side table. "I appreciate you helping us out."

Harvey nodded slowly and continued scanning the space. "Just know," he said in a low, gravelly voice, "you've got a short leash, Lynch."

"Yes, sir, we'll be the best tenants you've ever had."

This newfound neutering of his father was unbecoming, Howard thought, and yet he enjoyed every second of it. Nearly worth being evicted.

"And you," Harvey said, nodding toward Howard. "What's your story? You in school?"

"Yes, sir. Bound to graduate here pretty soon."

"And then what? Live with your dad here forever?"

"No, sir," Howard said, though he hadn't given much thought to what would come next.

"What then?"

"Still working that out, sir."

"Hmm. You do that. Maybe get far away from this place when you do." With that piece of advice, Harvey turned and ducked back out of the trailer.

"You give any thought to your plans after graduation?" Howard's father asked him when they were alone.

"Nope."

Howard knew he had some thinking to do. The last thing he could permit was graduating—a task his father had never accomplished, nor had many other kids from his town—and then bagging groceries for the next several years. He needed to figure out a plan.

That's what he was thinking about as he set off on foot behind the trailer and into the trees. He had walked these woods for the last decade and knew just about every square inch. He knew where he was entering, he knew where the hidden streams ran, which way to turn to head toward any number of places—but especially the route along the backs of the neighboring properties that would bring him to the foot of the tree that held his refuge. This time of year, the ground was soft, the blanket of fallen leaves from autumn soaked by the spring rains and matted into a soggy layer that molded around every step.

When he eventually made it, he was surprised to hear music humming overhead. He looked up. The evening sun barely cut into these woods so it became darker earlier, but there was still enough light to see. Coming from the treehouse was an orange glow to accompany the music. Shadows danced on the wall and along the trunk of the tree. He contemplated walking away. Instead, without saying a word, he quietly climbed the ladder. As he rose, the sounds grew, and a picture of what was happening sharpened in his mind. At the top, as his head became level with the floorboards, he was careful to peek inside first.

Two beer cans lay crunched in the corner. Several more stood upright, looking unopened. At the far side of the fort, on the makeshift sofa that Howard and Willy hoisted into the tree a couple of years prior, he saw his friend necking with a young blonde. The glow from the two lanterns sitting on the floor beside the sofa didn't shed enough light, and from his vantage point, Howard couldn't quite make out her identity. He climbed back down the ladder as quietly as he could and walked off a little ways so that he was outside of earshot but could still see the treehouse. He wasn't going back to the trailer; he'd wait it out.

Keeping a close eye on the structure in the sky, Howard looked for any sign that the moment he witnessed had passed. Fortunately, within 10 minutes he could see Willy stand up and change the music to something more upbeat. Howard took that as a signal and approached the tree, hearing the cracking open of another can as he did. Quickly, he rushed to climb the ladder before he could be boxed out by another round of intimacy.

Willy must have heard him coming because the second Howard reached the top his pal said, "What are you doing here?" It wasn't so much accusatory as it was friendly curiosity.

Before answering, Howard looked over at the girl, who was buttoning up her shirt, her hair a bit disheveled. He didn't recognize her. Back to Willy, he could tell that he had consumed more than a couple of the empty cans on the floor. "Oh, sorry. I just needed to get away from my pops. I didn't mean to interrupt anything."

"No, it's cool," Willy said. "Have a beer." He tossed a can in Howard's direction. The girl finished straightening out her clothes and sat politely on the sofa. Howard glanced at her and then back at Willy.

"Shit, sorry," Willy said. "Sophie, this is my buddy, Howard. Howard, Sophie. She's from over in Winston."

She smiled politely, but Howard could tell she was uncomfortable with the entire situation. Willy was messing with the radio and so Howard took the opportunity to walk over to Sophie and introduce himself, extending a hand.

"You know, Willy and his dad built this place a long time ago. He tell you that?" Howard was keeping his voice down, but there was no concealing the conversation from Willy entirely. Sophie shook her head. "Yeah, then me and him fixed it up a bit over the last few years."

She looked around as if this new information offered a fresh perspective.

"You're the first girl I've ever seen him bring up here." She brought her gaze to him but still didn't speak. "Honest," he continued. "And I've spent a lot of time up here. An embarrassing amount of time, actually."

Sophie glanced over at Willy, who was still messing with the radio, though slowly, methodically, in a way that made it obvious he was eavesdropping. She blushed and then nodded. "Thanks," she said.

Howard gave her a gentle pat on the arm and then walked back over to Willy and gave him a wink.

The three of them hung in the treehouse for a while, until complete darkness arrived in the forest and they ran out of beer. Then Willy escorted Sophie back to his house and gave her a ride home. As they walked away, Howard watched them from above, the single lantern lighting their way until it disappeared through the thickness of the woods.

While he was by himself, Howard quieted the radio and then dimmed his own lantern. He closed his eyes, wishing he had brought a book with him. Surprised, actually, because he always brought a book with him. Instead, he slept.

He awoke a little while later to the sound of Willy climbing back up the ladder.

"You're a lifesaver," Willy said, setting a pint of whiskey on the floor before hoisting himself up.

"What did I do?"

"That thing about never having a girl up here before? That might have saved my chances to see her again."

"Kinda true though," Howard said. "I mean, I know you've told me that you've had girls up here before, but I've never seen it."

"Fuck you," Willy said jokingly. He took a swig from the bottle and then passed it to Howard.

"Where'd you meet a girl from Winston, anyway?"

"My ma knows her pops. I didn't ask questions. Cute though, right?"

"Yeah, cute." Howard didn't want to boost Willy's self-esteem too much, but Sophie seemed out of his league. She had blonde hair and dimples and looked well put-together—not like most of the girls Howard had seen his friend pursue. "How old was she?"

"Sixteen. She's young for her grade, though. Goin' into her senior year in the fall."

"You gonna keep seeing her?"

"Shit. Maybe?" He took another swig. "If I'm still around here, that is."

"Where might you be going?"

"Got an opportunity to move up to Detroit this summer. I have a cousin who works at a construction company that's hiring."

"No shit?" Howard felt his heart sink with the realization that he may end up alone in this town, friendless, living with his deadbeat father in someone else's trailer.

They sat there, the radio playing quietly, watching the shadows on the walls cast by the low lights of the lanterns, until Willy finally said, "You wanna come?"

5

Wolf Valley, 2002

In which Howard is 48 years old

Perhaps the longest year imaginable has come and gone. Howard wasn't sure he would survive it, with endless nights spent gripping the handle of a loaded pistol. He even pulled the trigger that one time. That's the thing. Once is usually enough. He tells himself he's too chickenshit to move on with his life and even more chickenshit to end it.

At this point, seemingly endless advice has flowed his way, both solicited and unsolicited—mostly unsolicited. All the clichés, all the tips that feel like they were drummed up by someone who has never actually experienced grief. Time heals everything. Turn to prayer. Take it one day at a time. All that bullshit. But, as the anniversary of the worst night of his life draws near, he does think to himself that he's made progress. The pistol, for example, has not left the bedside drawer in a couple of months. He can't even remember if it's still loaded. He's also fished with Stu several more times. And in the warmer summer months, on days he didn't go out on the boat with him, Stu was often still cutting across Howard's lawn to where the boat was tied up, and those quick exchanges were enough to keep him sane.

July and August were hot and sticky, but not wet. Wolf Valley had experienced a fairly dry summer—something the fall was destined to make up for. Since September rolled around, the clouds moved in and each day seems grayer than the last. Perhaps that is just Howard's perception, but that makes it reality. With the clouds comes the rain. The grass, which went dormant in July with a brittle beige, is now suddenly lush and the ground beneath it soft, so that Howard can nearly see his bootprint walking to the river. Makes letting the dog outside a hell of a thing, too, since he has to wipe those damn paws pretty much every time or risk muddy prints spotting the floor.

After all those long, trying nights, Coby is still there—something Howard never thought would be the case. *It's not a bond*, he tells himself. He was too grief-struck to call an animal shelter. Then when the grief subsided—or, rather, more accurately, he learned to live with it—a degree of guilt set in and he began thinking that returning a dog after adopting it wasn't helpful for anyone. What he doesn't tell himself about keeping Coby is that it's what Amber would have wanted. That would mean connecting this dog emotionally to his late wife, which Howard will not do.

For as much as Howard complains about that dog, mostly to himself, Coby remains steadfast. On this late afternoon, the light rain beginning to pick up, along with the wind, Howard is back in his chair and Coby is curled at his feet—just as he was that first week. This is the routine they have established. In the last year, Howard has read numerous books—likely, he thinks, if he counts reading all of Amber's multiple times, that he has well surpassed 100 —and it's been his routine to steal a peek over the top of the page at Coby, who always nestles tightly at Howard's feet or occasionally against the cool brick of the fireplace. At one point, Howard sets his book lightly on the table and walks over to the window. Assessing the weather, as men do, with his wrist in hand behind his back, he gazes at his yard. Puddles are beginning to form on the dirt road. Out the back window, the normally still river is almost choppy. By evening, between the dark and the rain intensifying, he won't even be able to see the river.

Retreating into his chair, Howard turns on the news. A weather warning is scrolling across the bottom of the screen. Severe rainstorm. *No shit*. But what is worse is what Joe Weatherman adds: that the system producing this storm has stalled over the region. This is just the beginning.

In moments like these, Howard is thankful that he doesn't have a basement. By this time, he can see the puddles in the grass swelling. When he looks into the distance, he sees the boat rocking back and forth on the river. This is the first clue that the wind has picked up. The second clue is the branch that crashes into the yard with a crack. It is small enough that he reserves his concern, but big enough for him to realize that perhaps this storm should be taken seriously.

A scratch on the wooden door followed by a low whimper catches his attention. Coby is pawing, ready to go outside.

"Can't you see the storm?" Howard asks rhetorically.

The dog paws at the door once more. Then another whimper. He is not a barker, which Howard appreciates, but there are times when the whimpering is worse. Both pathetic and annoying—a dual threat. This is one of those times. Howard has a decision to make: let the dog out now and deal with the consequences, or wait and, well, deal with the consequences. With two losing options, he recognizes the situation will likely only get worse if he delays.

The door creaks as he opens it, but only for a moment before the sound is instantly drowned by the battering of the rain and the fierceness of the wind. Coby, fearless, takes off into the storm. Howard thinks about calling for him to come back but knows the attempt would be futile. Within minutes, he watches the puddles on the patio grow. It's dark, but a patio light and another across the yard on the back of the shed seem to illuminate far past their expectations, reflecting off the wet surfaces. Howard strains to spot Coby but he knows it's pointless. He finds himself hoping that the dog is smart enough to keep away from the riverbank. As the water crests, that area is going to become extremely dangerous—and he has decided that he cannot take another loss in his life. Not right now, not like this.

Suddenly, Coby emerges from the storm in a full sprint. His fearless demeanor that he left with is now gone—he looks spooked. With the door propped open to see the yard but so as not to allow too much rain inside, Howard wedges himself in the doorway to keep Coby from running directly inside. But that was a task the man was not quite ready to handle. Instead, the dog puts a shoulder into Howard's knee and frantically squeezes through the thin space and into the house. Howard nearly slips and topples over, but regains his footing only to pivot and see the disaster that is occurring behind him. Coby's white paws are gone. Thick mud runs up each leg, fading into the brown fur almost naturally. Before Howard can even get the words out, Coby has already dashed through the kitchen, rolled on the living room rug, and returned to the doorway to shake off. The look on the dog's face now is joyful. He is panting a bit from the excitement, and his mouth is hanging open just slightly with a canine smile. His antics have amused him; Howard's blood is boiling. Muddy paw prints scatter across the wood floor and spot the rug. What's not muddy is at the very least wet.

"What the shit are you doing!" Howard yells. He marches over to Coby, who doesn't even flinch until he is yanked forward by the collar and dragged back to the doorway. A gray towel with patches of dried mud hangs on a hook and Howard uses it to quickly and forcefully wipe the dog's paws. When he's finished, instead of running away, Coby presses his shoulder into Howard's knee gently.

He's sorry. He may not entirely know what he did wrong, but he knows his master is angry with him. The affection is easily recognizable. Still fuming, though beginning to slow his heart rate, Howard gives the dog a firm pat and then shoos him away.

The scene before him is unsettling. Across the mud-spotted living room is a large window, through which Howard sees a sizable branch come crashing down into the front yard. He watches it stoically, and then he walks to the kitchen and pours himself another glass of whiskey. There is a disaster to clean up. But it's not going anywhere. Years ago, had a dog run uncontrollably through the house causing this much of a mess, Amber would have been a wreck and Howard would have been quick to usher her to a chair and then get down on his knees to scrub everything clean. That was back when messes couldn't wait; now they could.

It's an attitude, an outlook, that is practical because moments after Howard flips on the news he hears the dreaded report: The Wolf River Dam will be breached. That is the way this storm is headed. Nothing can be done to stop it. It's time to prepare for what comes next.

Suddenly, muddy paw prints are an afterthought. The miscellaneous details of life are no longer important, either. A quick rush of panic and Howard finds himself in Amber's study piling copies of her novels into a box. His shadow is watching him, confused but intrigued.

What starts as fear and adrenaline wanes as the box fills and he realizes that acting out of senselessness is childish. *You are a man*, he tells himself, *and whatever is coming will come. You'll get through it*. It's a reassuring thought but perhaps not a sensible one. After all, he has no control. Once again, he finds himself living a reactionary life.

He sits back in his chair and looks down at the box of books. To him, it could be an urn. Amber—what he remembers about her, what he yearns for, what destroys him to even think about but that he cannot cast from his mind—lives on through those words. It is not without guilt that his mind wanders to the sound of her voice. Pictures of Amber are scattered all around the house. Books and notebooks and jotted-down notes fill the study. But her voice—he realizes he is beginning to forget. That is an unforgivable sin. How can his mind betray him like that? The cruelest truth.

He knows he must remember, if for nothing else, for his sanity. So he heads into the kitchen and finds the answering machine in the cupboard that he had unplugged almost a year earlier. It is the first thing he can think of. They never recorded many home videos—that is the kind of habit that starts when couples welcome kids into the world. The answering machine would be the only thing in the house that would replay that beautiful voice. Plugging in the machine, he waits for the little red light to illuminate. He gives it a few seconds, but nothing happens. Clicking the buttons, but nothing happens. Unplugging it and plugging it back in, but nothing happens. His face warms. It's fear. There are some things in this world that, once gone, can truly never be replaced. Losing his wife was devastating. Now God is twisting the knife, slowly carving what Howard has left of her from his memory.

Anger begins swelling inside him. It's a false feeling, a coping mechanism to dull the pain. He knows that. It doesn't stop it. He's leaning against the counter on his elbows, head collapsed, and for a long while he stays that way until he feels the light scratching on his pant leg. Coby is looking up with concerned eyes. Howard lets out a sigh and shakes his head. "Not now," he says in a stern but defeated tone. "I'm going through a goddam crisis."

The dog stays at his feet for a few moments and then wanders back into the living room, finally coming to a rest on the floor with his head lying upon a book that has fallen off the coffee table. Eventually, Howard calms himself and returns to his chair. He looks down at Coby. He sees the book under his snout and bends over to pick it up. It was the first copy of Amber's first book that she ever gave to him. Inside, Howard flips to the inscription that she left. He reads it aloud.

To my love,

In uncertain times, I find comfort at my typewriter. I hope that you will always find comfort in reading the words that come from it.
Yours always,
Amber

As the words leave his mouth, a rare tear falls down his cheek. The realization that these words, silently written, will be all that his wife speaks to him for the rest of his life is a suffocating feeling. His chest tightens and there is a burning behind his eyes. Coby nuzzles his nose against Howard's thigh and without looking the man gives the dog a soft pat. "It's just you and me now, bud."

The rain and the wind battering the roof and windows almost drown out the phone ringing in the next room. Howard snaps from his spell and tries to compose himself before walking over to answer. His eyes are puffy and he knows likely lined in red, and for a moment he's comforted by his isolation.

"Hello?"

"H'ard," Stu says with his drawl, a one-syllable version of Howard's name. "Can y'believe this here storm?"

"Pretty wild out there."

"How's the river lookin'?"

Howard isn't by the back window so he says, "Gimme a sec," and then sets the receiver down and walks into the kitchen. The glare from the window keeps him from seeing all the way to the river, so he flicks the lights off and squints. He can still see the boat thrashing back and forth, but he can't tell if the water is cresting above the riverbank yet. He strains to look through the dark and rain but it's futile.

"Still looks okay, I think," he says to Stu when he gets back to the phone. "Boat's sure rocking, though."

"I bet. I cain't see the river from m'house so I figured I check with you. Y'hear uh the dam?"

"Yeah, I just heard."

"Doesn't look good. The community center up there on the hill is gonna be a shelter if y'need to head that way. Me an' the wife might be goin'. You bein' on the river an' all, might wanna consider it."

"I appreciate your concern. I think we'll wait it out, at least a while longer. Hope for the best."

"We?" Stu asks.

"This damn dog and me."

"Ah, right. Well, y'all take care an' I check on y'all in the mornin'."

Howard isn't sure if his neighbor's unease is comforting or concerning. The pistol, which he now keeps in his bedside drawer, hasn't been touched in weeks, if not months, but that call makes him go and check on it. There is a box of ammo in a separate drawer and Howard grabs both and carries them into the living room. Staring at the gun and the box of ammo and the empty glass, he realizes he is acting out of fear. "Is this crazy?" he says to Coby, who, once again, has been following his owner around the house. The dog tilts his head in confusion. Howard pats him on the head as he stands up with his glass to walk into the kitchen for a refill. Before he can turn the lights back on, something catches his eye. It's Stu's boat, floating in the yard.

6

Detroit, 1978

In which Howard was 24 years old

If Howard charted the full spectrum of men, with his father at the far end of worthless, Lester Pitford would be his counterbalance. Lester was Howard and Willy's boss at Brent & Sons, the contracting company that served as a sort of jack-of-all-trades home remodeler in the Metro Detroit area. When the two boys stepped onto their first job site six years earlier as fresh-faced high school grads, Lester was one of them—a hired hand, although with considerably more experience. The rest of the crew took to Lester and he quickly worked his way up to be a project manager.

A tall, soft-spoken man with combed-back blonde hair, Lester didn't fit the mold for the type of person typically found with a hard hat and a hammer. But once his jeans got dirty, he fit right in with the rest of them. Willy and Howard, despite their admiration for

Lester, had their own conflicts. They trekked up to Detroit shortly after their high school graduation to work with Willy's cousin, Perry. But, as it goes, Perry was just about the only person at the company who didn't get along with Lester. After Lester's promotion, Perry started mouthing off more—and it didn't take long before he found himself out of a job. This left Howard and Willy in a tough position—where did their loyalty lie?

Given that their entire reputations in the industry—and this town—existed within Brent & Sons, they delicately protected their jobs while doing their best to bridge the relationship with Perry. But the stubborn cousin—a stocky Vietnam veteran who always had a pack of cigarettes in his breast pocket—drew a hard line in the sand. He wanted Willy to make a choice—a silly notion to the kid who was now a grown man at 24 years old. Alas, he deferred to Howard, who made the easy decision to stick with Lester.

"You sure?" Willy asked him one day after work, bellied up to the bar.

"Lester is the only leader I've ever wanted to follow. He's a damn good man."

"You gonna tell Perry that?"

"I don't give a damn about Perry. Sorry to say it. He helped get us these jobs years ago, but that's about all he's done for us since we got here. He tried to drag us into his bullshit one too many times."

Willy could feel the nerves firing up just from the thought of that conversation he had to have with his cousin.

But the decision paid off. Lester gave the men a vote of confidence, teaming them up on the same jobs as often as he could and naming them site supervisors when the opportunities arose. Howard quickly fell into the new routine, and the home renovation life became his only life.

He and Willy shared a two-bedroom apartment in a blue-collar neighborhood in the Detroit suburbs. It had thin walls, flat carpeting and depressing paint. But every morning before sunrise, Howard was up brewing a pot of coffee, taking a shit, trying to wake himself. With the one bathroom, they had to get on a schedule. He always made it a point to wake up 30 minutes before Willy, that way he could read a book on the couch until they had to head out the door.

Work days varied by the project. Some days they were remodeling bathrooms. Sometimes it was gutting an old house. Sometimes it was putting a second story on a ranch. Hell, they'd even tried their hand at landscaping and roofing—whatever was asked of them. They all required steel-toe boots, good jeans and a lot of sweat. At the end of the day, they usually picked up some food and ate it on the couch in front of the TV, or just grabbed burgers and beers at the local sports bar if there was a game on, or after a particularly grinding day.

For the first few years, this life suited Howard. He was out of his dad's house, living on his own, making his own money. He could drink as much or as little as he wanted. He could buy his own books. He controlled his own schedule and didn't answer to anyone outside the work site. For the first time, he felt like an adult. He felt the freedom that came with that.

But the years kept passing. By his twenty-fourth birthday, that freedom began to lose its excitement. He found himself sitting on barstools watching the crowds, the cute young girls on some guy's arm, the rowdy bikers always seemingly ready for a fight, even the suits who would occasionally wander in with a couple buddies for happy hour. His first thought was that everyone else had their lives figured out, leaving him alone to continue the search. That, or he was the only one with it figured out, which was equally as depressing but far less likely.

One morning Howard took a good look in the mirror. His teenage arms had finally developed. He leaned closer and barely recognized the person he saw. Real scruff. Tough skin. Dark circles under his eyes from the previous night's bender. A few gray hairs that he tried plucking with tweezers. It was no longer himself that stood before him—no, much more terrifying. He was beginning to see his father.

"What's got ya down?" Willy asked one morning on the drive to a kitchen remodel.

"I'm fine," Howard said, gripping the wheel tighter.

Willy shook his head. "You always pull this shit. Just tell me, okay? Save us both the time."

Howard glanced at Willy and then back at the road. "I'm fine, honest. Just tired."

"You're getting bored aren't you?"

Howard shrugged.

"You know Lester's gonna be onsite today? I hear he has a job on the West Side that needs quoting. Could be our big shot."

"Where's the West Side?"

"I mean, like, West Michigan. Across the state. He has some guy he used to work with who moved out there."

"And?"

"And? And I think I can get us on the project. Get us a free trip across the state for a few months!"

"Hmm." Howard was interested but made it a point in life not to get his hopes up. He would let the situation play out and whatever happened he would go with it.

At the current site, which they had been working on for a few days already, there was a full crew. Howard expected a couple of guys to be there to help, perhaps, but there were six of them. The house was a decent size, but eight guys gathering in an unfinished kitchen remodel site was crowded. Instead, they went outside into the driveway. It was a cool day in early fall, the leaves still firmly holding onto their green.

One of the men at the site was Lester, who was wearing a tucked-in golf shirt instead of his regular work attire. The shirt was red—normally not a detail worth noting, but he rarely added color to his wardrobe. He was a neutral guy, and Howard took notice. Maybe red meant this was a bad day. Maybe good. It meant that it was a different day, regardless. Or maybe, just maybe, Howard was over-thinking things again.

"Fellas, gather around," Lester said. He had an odd smirk on his face. The men stood in a semicircle around their boss, hands in pockets or arms crossed, a couple holding canteens of coffee. "We have a big opportunity ahead of us, gentlemen. You remember the Connelly home we built, a couple years ago in Plymouth? I think most of you were on board for that one. Well, Vern has another project that needs bidding. This one is over in the Holland area. Anyone know where that is? A couple hours from here, at least."

Willy gave Howard a look.

Lester continued: "If we win this bid, it could mean a lot of work for us, though some of you would have to live out there for a while. So, what I'm asking, is I need a guy or two—"

Willy's hand shot up before Lester could get the rest of the sentence out.

"Son, you better be careful volunteering before you know what it is you're volunteering for."

"You need someone to head over to Holland and meet with Vern about the project? Howard and I will do it." He patted Howard on the chest.

"I like the initiative," Lester admitted, grinning. "I've already done the bidding myself. I think Vern just wants to meet with some of the men who will actually be doing the heavy lifting, show you around. Maybe see if he can trust people from the Detroit area to actually show up. Can you boys handle that?"

They nodded. "Of course."

Lester took a step forward and placed his hands on his hips. "We're paying a day's wages to send you over there. Don't fuck this up." It was a seriousness, a tone that they had never heard from him.

After work that day, Howard, Willy and Lester circled up for a quick meeting about how the trip would play out. They had a couple of days to put their game plan in place, and then the guys would wake up early one morning, drive across the state before the sun came up and meet Connelly. Sounded easy enough.

Working as builders, early mornings were nothing new for Howard and Willy. They had worked on sites all over the Metro Detroit area, which could mean over an hour's drive each way until they finished and moved on to a new project. But getting up to head to Holland—hell, it was debatable if this was even considered early morning or late at night.

With a construction detour, they expected the drive to take about three hours, and they wanted to meet with Connelly first thing in the morning. The drive was long, longer than Howard had expected. The sun was just beginning to cast its first rays across the horizon as they passed Lansing, about halfway across the state. He rubbed his eyes, trying to shake off the last remnants of sleep. The coffee helped, but even it had its limitations. In the passenger seat, Willy was fidgeting. In contrast to Howard, the early morning didn't seem to bother Willy as much—he was eager to get there.

"I can't believe we're going all the way to Holland," Willy said, glancing at Howard with a grin.

Howard yawned. "I know. It feels like a cross-country trip."

As they drove, Howard's thoughts wandered. He couldn't shake off a mild sense of unease. Meeting with Vern Connelly was a big deal, even if Lester had already handled all the negotiating beforehand. They were going to represent Brent & Sons and that wasn't something Howard took lightly.

Finally, after hours on the road, they arrived. The morning sun was now fully overhead, casting a warm golden hue upon the town. The city sat on a small lake that led out to the far larger Lake Michigan, but they didn't see any water from where they were. The address that Lester had provided took them into a nice neighborhood just outside of town. When they arrived at the address, which was an extravagant house, they parked the truck out front and waited a few minutes until their meeting time. Then, they headed to the front door and knocked. A middle-aged man in a blazer and sunglasses answered the door and stepped past them without saying a word.

"Mr. Connelly?" Howard said after him.

The man paused and looked back. "Yes?"

"My name's Howard Lynch. This here is Willy McNabb. Lester Pitford sent us from Brent & Sons."

"Ah, shit," said Vern. "I had a meeting with you two, didn't I?"

They nodded.

"Sorry, boys. Can we do four o'clock instead?"

They looked at each other, not that there was an alternative answer. "We'll be back here at four sharp," Howard said.

They walked down to their truck parked in the street and watched from the road as Vern drove off in a Cadillac. Howard sighed. "Well, that's a bummer."

"After how long it took us to get here?" Willy said, disappointed. "Shit, man. I hate when rich folks think they can just do whatever they want."

With newfound free time, they drove to Lake Michigan, eyed a parking lot with a view, rolled down the windows to feel the crisp fall air coming off the lake, and then took a nap.

When they awoke, it was lunchtime. They drove into town and found a pub on a corner called McSweeney's. It had slits for windows, a few pool tables in the back and the floor looked like it hadn't been swept in years. It was Howard's type of bar. The place was nearly empty when they walked in. Thursday afternoons were slow for pubs like McSweeney's, Howard knew that. Taking a seat at a table in the back, he scanned the place. Most of the tables were empty, but down at the far end of the bar sitting alone was a young woman. She had dark hair pulled back and she was writing in a notebook. There was something about her that drew Howard's attention. Her petite frame in that blue floral dress looked out of place on that barstool.

"You good?" Willy asked.

"Yeah, good," Howard said, moving his eyes around the room and then back to Willy as casually as he could.

"I'm not blind. I see the smokin' hot chick at the end of the bar, too."

Howard felt embarrassed. "Yeah, pretty cute."

"Just about the only cute thing about this place. And I absolutely love it."

They ordered beers and burgers, and the entire time Howard stole glances toward the girl at the bar, who kept her head down writing.

"I think this project could be the turning point for me," Willy said.

"Hmm?"

"I've been looking for an excuse to get out of Detroit for a while. Don't you feel like you need a change?"

"Is that 'cause of your cousin?"

"No, not even that. We've been there six years. And don't get me wrong, I like the job, but I think I need a change of scenery."

"So how is this gig going to do that? Depending on the scope, if you're lucky it'll bring you out here for only a few months, most likely."

"A few months, sure, at first. Then, say, I don't go back?"

"Just quit?"

"I'm just saying getting away from Detroit could be a good mental reset. From there, who knows? See how it all plays out, I guess." Howard was only peripherally paying attention to the conversation with Willy because he couldn't stop thinking about the girl on the barstool. After a few moments, Willy said, "Man, just go talk to her."

Normally, Howard would ignore advice like that, finish his burger and say it was time to go. But he had barely even touched the food in front of him. His stomach churned with a sense of urgency. Without acknowledging Willy, he pushed back from the table and walked across the room. He stopped close enough that it was obvious he was there to talk to her, but kept a respectful distance between them.

"Hi."

She took a moment to finish writing her sentence and then turned her eyes to him without moving her head. The blue caught him off guard in sharp contrast to her short, dark hair, but was an almost perfect match to her dress. She smiled without her teeth and then put her pen back to the paper. She had an innocence about her. This girl didn't belong at the end of a bar on a weekday.

"My name is Howard," he said, extending a hand, feeling like his chance might rapidly be slipping away.

"Nice to meet you, Howard," she said without looking up.

So that's how this is going to go. "And do you have a name?"

"I do."

He smirked. "You're making this pretty difficult."

Setting her pen down, she finally spun on her stool to face him. She tucked a leg up underneath her. "My name is Amber. It's nice to meet you—Howard, was it?"

"Yep, Howard." He waited a moment. "What are you writing?"

"I don't mean to be rude, Howard, but I get this a lot. I'm flattered, but I'm really just here to write."

"To be honest, I just wasn't sure you looked old enough to be sitting at a barstool on a weekday afternoon. I simply came over here out of concern."

"Well, rest assured, I'm old enough—at least for a few more months."

"Why's that?"

"Because they're about to raise the drinking age back to 21. Have you not heard?"

He shook his head. "I suppose that means I should buy you a drink before it's too late."

"Smooth," she said, but Howard caught a glimpse of the smile coming to her face before she turned her head to hide it. "I'll tell you what. You know where the Copper River Inn is?"

"I'll bet I can find it."

"If you can, I'll be there later tonight."

"It's a date."

"No, Howard, it's not."

~∽~∽~∽~

The meeting that afternoon was back at Connelly's house. When they pulled up the second time, they saw the home through an entirely new lens. And the place was impressive. It was a tall brick home, two stories but the height of three, with a driveway that wrapped around the back to a three-car garage. Why, Howard thought, he would be contracting with Brent & Sons to build a new one was beyond him.

Inside was just as impressive. Connelly's wife, a tall woman dressed far too well for a casual afternoon, answered the door and escorted the two men down a long hallway with high ceilings to a study that was lined with dark wooden bookshelves. Behind a sturdy desk on the opposite side of the room, Connelly sat with glasses on the tip of his nose reading from a stack of papers. When he saw them enter, he looked over the top of his spectacles and waved them to the chairs sitting on the other side of the desk.

"Gentlemen," he said in a drawn-out expression, as both a greeting and a delay tactic while he wrapped up his work.

"Mr. Connelly," Willy said, reaching across the desk with an open hand. "Thanks so much for inviting us out here."

Connelly shook his hand, then turned and shook Howard's. He leaned back in his chair and inhaled deeply.

"If I can just say, sir, this house is magnificent," said Willy. "Truly. I'm not sure why you would even want to build another one."

"Well, son, it's a long story. But I have to be honest, I feel like I'm wasting your time."

"Oh? Why's that?"

"I have another builder for the project."

Howard's heart sank, and he knew Willy's did as well. Lester made it seem like it was a done deal, that this was a formality. "Sir?" said Willy, confused. "Mr. Pitford said—"

"It's nothing personal, boys, and it certainly doesn't have anything to do with you two or even Lester. I just found a deal that your company couldn't match. Couldn't even come close, if I'm being honest."

"Name your price and we'll get it approved," Willy shouted out of desperation.

Connelly remained calm. "Like I said, I already have a builder. I'm sorry for making you boys come out all this way and for pushing this chat to the end of the day."

Howard stood. "No apology needed, sir. You call us if anything changes and have yourself a great rest of your day." He shot Willy a look and his friend reluctantly rose and followed him back down the hallway and out the front door.

Outside, Willy said, "What the hell was that about? We should be in there trying to negotiate with him!"

"No, we shouldn't. You gotta learn when to cut your losses. Looking desperate in there would have just hurt our chances at any future work."

"Bullshit."

"Bullshit? Connelly has his hand in half the developments in this state, seems like. You really want to put him off?"

"I just think you folded a little too quickly, is all."

"I didn't do anything. You heard what Lester told us, we weren't here to negotiate. He took care of all that. This is on him, not us."

The boys climbed back into the truck. Howard turned the ignition but they just sat there, the low rumbling of the engine the only sound. The windows were down and a soft, cool breeze that traveled east from Lake Michigan felt good on Howard's skin.

"So now what?" Willy asked.

"I say we check in to a hotel and hit the town. Lester owes us a night out."

The previous afternoon, Lester had handed each of them a small wad of cash—a per diem, he called it. Spending money. "Get yourselves something to eat and have a good time," he said. They didn't intend on returning to Detroit with a single cent.

Contrary to what Howard imagined, the Copper River Inn wasn't actually an inn, although it looked like once upon a time it may have been. Now it was a two-story late-nineteenth-century building with peeling paint and a few missing shutters. They had dropped their bags at a motel off the main highway and then headed straight to the bar. As the days shortened into the fall, the sun began setting much earlier. If the circumstances were different, Howard would have loved taking a pint of whiskey to the lakefront parking lot with a book, watching the sun rest on the day. But this was not that day—no, far from it. This was a night for drinking—and looking for that girl.

The inside of the Copper River Inn looked much like the outside, like it was decades past its prime. Willy made his way to the bar while Howard trailed behind keeping an eye out for Amber. The place had low ceilings and country western music was playing over the speakers. He had to concentrate to see, the lights dimmed for effect. It wasn't exactly packed, but there were enough people to make his search difficult.

As he peered about the room, Willy nudged him on the shoulder and handed him a beer. "Let's sit down, shall we?"

They found a table in the corner and filled a paper bowl with peanuts—the floor littered with their shells. They began cracking them and adding to the crunchy mess beneath their feet. Howard had a vacant look on his face, barely sipping his beer.

Finally, Willy said, "You find her?"

"Huh?"

"I'm not an idiot, I know you wanted to come here because of her."

Howard didn't know what to say.

"It's cool," Willy continued, "just make sure you find her. This place is rotten."

They sat and chatted about baseball, mostly the Tigers.

"They have a good, young core. You got Trammell and Whitaker up the middle, Stanley in the outfield, Parrish behind the dish."

"And then look at the mound: Morris, Rozema, Wilcox, The Bird."

"I know, man. All the pieces are there. I'm tellin' ya, this team is going to win the World Series sometime soon if they can keep this group together."

The conversation continued that way, talking about sports and work and politics. The bar filled up a little more, they drained a few beers and Howard finally stood to look for the bathroom. Being pointed around the corner by the bartender, Howard made the turn into a narrow hallway where he saw the restroom.

After doing his business, instead of heading back out the way he came, he continued down that hallway. He could hear music coming from another room and decided to explore his curiosity. The hallway opened up to a space nearly as large as the front room where he left Willy. A man was playing a soft guitar on a makeshift stage and patrons scattered around the room, mostly pulled up to small round tables made for two apiece, though some people leaned against the walls or stood near high tops. Howard stepped inside and walked along the back, keeping his eyes open. That's when he saw her, just like he had seen her before—hunched over a journal, pen in hand, a small glass of brown liquor on the table. And still in that same blue floral dress—a choice that made more sense during the day, but as the crisp evening air rolled in and reminded that autumn had arrived, it increasingly seemed like an almost eccentric decision. What he didn't notice earlier that day was that her skin was vacant of any jewelry to speak of—no earrings, bracelets or necklaces. All natural.

Howard thought for a moment about the best way to approach, but the alcohol in his system said to abandon his sensibilities and step right up to her table. That's what he did. At first, he said nothing, his shadow cast from the few dim overhead lights blanketing her page. Yet she continued to write as if he didn't exist. The smell of liquor and cigarettes and cheap cologne wafted through the room.

He cleared his throat and then said, "Miss, I'm here for our date."

Without looking up she said, "I told you, sir, it's not a date."

For a moment he watched her write. Maybe he was too nervous earlier that afternoon, trying to think of the right thing to say, but now he looked at her deeply. Her skin was caramel colored, smooth. She could be part Native American, he thought, or maybe just Italian. Howard took the opportunity to sit in the empty chair beside her. Finally, her eyes rose with a look that questioned his action.

"Oh, was this seat taken?"

She paused. "Is there something I can help you with?"

"Actually, yes. I have been thinking all day about what a young, pretty girl like you is doing hanging out in bars alone without so much as looking up from her diary."

"Well..."

"Howard."

"Yes, Howard. Well, Howard, for starters, this isn't a diary."

"Sure looks like a diary."

"Not all things are what they appear."

"So, if it's not a diary, what is it? You writing your life story?"

"Actually," she said, lifting her glass and finishing the last of the tinted liquid, "I'm writing a novel."

"No shit," Howard spat out, clearly impressed. "Not much of a writer myself, but I sure read a lot."

She looked him up and down. His dusty jeans, his scuffed work boots. The look she returned was skeptical. "Why do I find that hard to believe?"

"If you want, I would be happy to get us a couple drinks and then tell you all about my favorite books."

She squinted and looked around.

"Fin Gamble would say to accept my offer."

That caught her by surprise. She looked back at him, trying to figure him out. "Is that so? Why would you say that?"

"Because I've read that book seven times, and I think he and I would be best friends," he said, nodding toward a worn copy of T.

Wilson Murphy's *Broken Souls and the Lovesick Pirates* that sat beside her journal.

Howard felt confident in her response, but she made him wait on it. She set down her pen, crossed her arms and finally said, "Whiskey. Neat."

"Whiskey neat," he repeated. When he returned a few minutes later with two lowballs, the pen was back in her hand and she didn't flinch when he slid one of the glasses across the table. Instead of saying something, he just sat there. He looked at her like he'd known her for years, despite knowing absolutely nothing about this girl. The music played in the background, and there was bar noise filling the rest of the audible space. Howard couldn't even hear the stroke of her pen across the paper, but she wrote so fluidly that he suspected it was nearly silent anyway. Through the smell of stale beer, whiskey and men, there was a subtle fragrance that tickled his nostrils. He leaned subtly across the table and it intensified. She smelled as pretty as she looked.

"So," she said, setting down her pen and picking up the glass. "You were going to tell me about all those books you've read."

And so he did. He talked about the regulars—Steinbeck, Hemingway, Woolf, Fitzgerald, Wolfe, Salinger, Faulkner. He quoted from books most people had never heard of. He described obscure scenes that buried themselves into his core memory while hiding in the confines of his closet. He told her about how his reading evolved— from a scared child to a confused adolescent to an angry teenager. And now, as a young adult just trying to figure out his place in this world, he knew there was probably a book that explained his feelings but it wouldn't come to him in this moment. The more he spoke, the more his mind began to trail off thinking about the girl in front of him.

Finally, he stopped. Her glass was empty and her journal was closed. She was leaning on an elbow and had committed to the conversation. He took a final sip from his glass and finished it. "Another?"

She nodded.

"And then I want to know more about you," he said as he walked away. He approached the bar with an urgency. It was all going too smoothly, he thought, that if he didn't get back as quickly as possible the entire conversation would deteriorate. But as the bartender placed the two drinks in front of him, he heard a familiar voice.

"Thought you might be taking the longest shit of your life." It was Willy. *Shit, Willy*. He had forgotten completely that he'd left him in the other room. There was liquor on his breath now and he had an energy about him. He glanced at the glasses and rolled his eyes, "Where is she?"

"Huh?"

"The girl." Then he spotted her. "Oh, nevermind. She's looking fine as hell, Howard. But sadly your night is over. C'mon," he said grabbing his friend's arm, "let's throw back these whiskeys like shots and find a new bar. This place is lame. It's all dark and depressing."

Howard hadn't noticed. But when Willy reached for one of the glasses, he grabbed his wrist to stop him. "I'm not going anywhere."

Willy gave him a look of betrayal. "Surely, you can't be serious."

"I'm into this girl, man. I'm not leaving now."

"We came here together. You can't leave me out to dry like this."

"I'm not leaving you like anything," Howard said and then retrieved the keys from his pocket and handed them to his friend. "Here, go to another bar. I'll find a cab or something."

"Find a cab," Willy mumbled, along with some other choice words, as he snatched the keys and stormed out.

The exchange left Howard feeling uneasy. He and Willy had been friends since they were kids. They were roommates, coworkers. They had been through a lot of shit together. Now he was ditching him for a girl he just met. Some friend he was being. But then he lifted the glasses, turned and looked back to Amber, who was sitting patiently alone, eyes locked on Howard.

By the time he returned, she had slipped the journal and the book into a small knapsack she had slung over the back of her chair.

"Who was that?"

"That was my friend."

"What was that about?"

"He's just mad that I'm talking to a cute girl without him."

Amber might have blushed but Howard couldn't see it through her tanned cheeks.

"Tell me about yourself," he said.

"What do you want to know?"

"Well, everything," Howard said. "But to start, tell me about that novel you're writing."

"That's the one thing I won't tell you."

"C'mon."

"I don't like to talk about my writing."

"You can't tell me anything? Where does it take place? How far along are you? Who is the main character? What's the title?"

She bit her lower lip and then said, "The Empty Hills of History."

"I'm sorry?"

She repeated it.

"And that's... is that the title?"

She nodded nervously. "And I haven't told anyone that, so you better keep your mouth shut."

"My lips are sealed," he said, making a gesture locking them and tossing an imaginary key over his shoulder.

Then they continued to drink whiskey. The glasses in front of them went down quickly and Howard returned to the bar for two more and then two more. Finally, they finished with Stroh's. In all that time, the band wrapped up its set, the place began emptying out and the bartender made last call. Howard opened up about his mother walking out, his father getting them evicted, the treehouse that he and Willy basically lived in and their decision to move to Michigan after high school. Amber told Howard about her overly religious parents, how she moved out of their house a few months earlier when she turned 18 and graduated high school, got her own apartment, worked a minimum wage job and wrote with every free second she could.

"You must have had good grades in school?" Howard asked.

"Good grades aren't everything."

"Still. You could be at Harvard or Yale or something." Howard was talking slower, smiling more and inching closer to her. She reciprocated.

"But if I were at Harvard, or Yale, or something," she said softly, "then I wouldn't be here, with you... or something." And then they kissed. It was a short kiss—gentle, kind, too loving for strangers. The kind of kiss that said more kisses were coming, but that they needed to find a better place to do it. When Amber pulled away, she looked embarrassed for a moment, but then said, "I saw you hand keys to your friend earlier."

"Mhmm."

"So how are you getting back to your hotel?"

"I guess I'm walking unless you have a better suggestion."

"I do, actually." She grabbed his hand and they slipped out the back door.

Their lips were back together before they even reached her bedroom. Without looking, she grabbed for the knob and then their momentum thrust them inside. Howard was singularly focused. He didn't know how big the room was, how tidy it was, the size of the bed. Darkness surrounded them, the only light piercing from the hallway that disappeared with his kick of the door behind him. All he felt was the softness of her kiss, her body pressing against his. She was so petite he could wrap his arms all the way around her. It caused him to keep it slow, to remain delicate.

In one motion, her blue floral dress fell off her shoulders and to the floor. She was exposed. He quickly pulled his shirt over his head and pressed his chest to hers, feeling the warmth of skin on skin. They continued kissing and she bent backward to the bed and he followed her, completely in sync. Her sheets were thin and cold, and Howard tried to pull a blanket over them but it snagged on something and he let it go. He ran his hands down her body, feeling its subtlety, slipping his fingers beneath her underwear. She grabbed his belt and yanked on it with a few hard tugs and then said through heavy breaths, "Take your pants off." It was clear she wasn't used to doing this. He could hear the nerves in her throat.

But Howard did as she told. He sat upright and slipped off his jeans and tossed them aside, while she lay there and did the same with her underwear. Howard looked into her eyes. They were innocent. "Are you sure?" he said.

Without hesitation, she reached up and pulled him back on top of her. His heart raced and they brought their lips back together. When it was time, he was gentle. He kept his hands on her body and he stayed on top throughout. It was a little clunky, a little awkward, but he suspected this was her first time and was sensitive to all the emotions that came with that. He listened for verbal cues but she gave very few, and so he moved slowly and softly.

Afterward, he slipped out and rolled onto his back beside her. Their bated breaths lasted for a short while before they turned their heads to face one another. Howard wasn't sure how she would react, but she smiled and then brought her hand to her forehead. He laughed and kissed her on the cheek. In the aftermath, it suddenly became evident how cold it was in the room and Howard tried to cover himself. She glanced down, laughed, and then crawled out of bed to find the blanket. He watched her the entire time. Without question, Amber was the most beautiful girl he had ever been with. The blanket was caught on the corner of the bed frame, but she freed it, pulled it over her shoulders like a shawl and hopped back onto the mattress.

She said, "You can move your hands, I've already seen it," and then smirked, rolled over and went to sleep.

Howard didn't dream that night—a rarity for him, especially when he'd been drinking. Sure, most of his dreams were nightmares, but he was surprised upon waking to notice how inactive his brain had been while he slept. That didn't last long.

The initial confusion he felt suddenly cleared when he saw the dark hair on the pillow beside him. Her eyes were closed and the blanket fell off her shoulder. He gazed at her delicate skin—soft, warm, young. After a few moments, he let his eyes drift around the room. It was a small bedroom, sparsely decorated. A desk sat against the far wall and upon it stood a stack of books. Howard recognized several of them as those Amber had mentioned the previous evening at the bar. Two notebooks, closed neatly and set one upon the other, were on the opposite side of the desk, a pen resting on top.

Finally, her eyes blinked open, the strain of a hangover apparent. She stretched and her arm bumped into Howard. That jolted her awake. She reached for the blanket and pulled it tight to her neck and then slinked out of the bed, ensuring full coverage.

"Uh, good morning," Howard said. He wasn't sure if he was offended, confused, or amused by her exit.

She hesitated and glanced around, then timidly said, "Hi." They let a few moments pass and she softened her mood. "Okay, I'm sorry," she finally said, embarrassed. But before she could say anything else, the bedroom door was nosed open by a Labrador. The golden dog peeked inside at first to see who was in the room, and then when he saw them he trotted over to Amber, tail wagging. The dog tried Howard next, who remained on the bed, uninterested in showing any affection.

"Who is this?" Howard finally said.

"Not my dog." She seemed to notice Howard's unease. "He's not big on personal space."

"Not yours?" A wave of relief washed over him.

"One of my roommates'. His name is Ralph."

"You don't sound too pleased."

"I'm just not much of a dog person, is all."

"Well, we have that in common."

Amber blushed and then said, "Okay, out, Ralph. Out, boy!" Then she looked up at Howard. "You too," she said with a smirk. "Out. Let me get dressed."

"Right," he said as if just remembering that they were both still naked. He rolled out of bed and attempted to cover himself as he scrambled for his clothes. "I'll just, uh..." He was muttering as she nodded and pushed him into the hallway. He slipped into the bathroom across the hall, got dressed, and then waited for her to come out. When she finally did, she looked as adorable as the night before. It was effortless, a natural beauty. "So, breakfast?"

"I wish," she said. "But I have work to do. That agent's not going to find itself."

"Agent, huh? Trying to make a career out of your writing?"

"Like I said last night, that's the only reason I'm not going to college right now. I have to at least give it a real shot."

Howard thought skipping college was an odd path to becoming a novelist, but he just nodded and looked around, then back to her. "I hope you make it work. And when you do, I'll be the first person to buy your book."

"If I somehow make this work, I'll send you the first copy."

"Deal."

The ride to the motel was quiet. The radio played softly—Fleetwood Mac, Bowie, Queen—but Howard could barely hear it over the rumble of the engine. In the parking lot, Howard stepped out of the car without so much as a hug or a handshake, but leaned back into the window and said, "I was serious about that book," to which Amber said, "Me too."

Before she pulled away, he asked, "Can I come back and see you again? Next week, maybe?"

She appeared to be thinking about it, but she said, "You know where to find me," and then pressed the gas pedal and left Howard watching her taillights. It wasn't until she was out of earshot that he instantly realized he never got her phone number. But she was right —he knew where to find her.

Howard was still watching the empty street long after the car had turned the corner and zoomed out of sight when he heard, "Just in time before I left your ass in Holland." Willy was walking outside, a duffel bag slung over his shoulder. Howard didn't say anything and Willy added, "Not so much as a 'sorry'?"

"For...?"

"For? What, how drunk were you last night?"

"You mean for going home with that girl?"

Willy looked through Howard. "Look, I'm not going to fault you for wanting to go home with her. She was cute as hell. But, shit—tell me, man. You just disappeared on me. Pulled an Irish exit."

"I should have, you're right."

"You're damn right I'm right." After slamming the truck door, Willy said, "Now get in or you're hitching your way back to Detroit."

The next week dragged by. Howard spent the days in a daze, going through the motions. His heart felt heavy and he was riddled with anxiety. Amber was the only thing he could think about. As each second passed, he worried that he was one second further from her, that some other guy was one second closer. It tore at him. Sometimes he found himself staring off, a rapid beating in his chest. He lost his appetite. During their lunch breaks, he'd nibble on a sandwich before slipping it back into his bag, hoping the other guys didn't notice. He drank coffee—that was about it. A little water. By midweek, Willy said, "Seriously?" The question snapped Howard from another hazy episode.

"What?"

"Is it that girl? You got it bad, my man."

Howard shrugged him off.

"Tell me you're not planning on going back to Holland to see her."

Another shrug.

Willy shook his head. "You're pathetic."

Fortunately, Howard didn't hear those words. They passed right by him without ever making contact, because he was still thinking about Amber. There wasn't anything that could shake him.

Until he got back to his apartment that night. His phone rang. It was a sergeant with the Pennsylvania State Police.

"I'm calling for Mr. Howard Lynch."

"This is he."

"Mr. Lynch, I'm saddened to tell you that your father was found deceased earlier this morning."

Howard stared at the wall.

"Sir? Mr. Lynch?"

"Yes, I'm here. Thanks for telling me. Is there something I need to do?"

"Well," the officer mumbled, caught off-guard by Howard's composure, "if you want to arrange for a burial..." His voice trailed off. "At the least, we'll need you to come claim the body."

After a moment, Howard said, "Yes. Yes, of course. I will make arrangements," and then hung up.

Even in death, his father was ruining his life. That weekend, instead of driving west back to Holland to try seeing Amber, he was heading south and then east, back to his hometown, to claim his father's remains. He swore to himself that he would make it quick—check in with the morgue, arrange the burial and leave town. Willy had offered to come with him, but Howard waived off his friend. "This isn't going to be worth anyone's time," he told him.

So it was just Howard. Walking into the morgue alone. Standing beside a hole in the ground, just a minister with a small bible, a grave digger smoking a cigarette and a few members of the church that his father apparently had begun attending over the last few years. The ceremony wasn't sad. Sad men don't get sad funerals.

When the final spade of dirt was dropped atop the grave, Howard nodded toward the gravedigger and then headed back to his truck. He checked his watch. It was Monday evening. He had missed the weekend, missed Amber. His boss, Lester, had given him a couple of days to get his father's affairs in order. Of course, there weren't many affairs to tend to. His father had been a frivolous man —spending the money as quickly as he earned it, never owning any property outright in his life. It made Howard's job much easier.

Back at his motel room, he rang Lester and asked if he could head back in the morning, meet the team on the job site in the afternoon.

"One P.M. sharp."

"Yes, sir."

Across the street from the motel was a liquor store, where Howard popped inside and bought a bottle of cheap bourbon and a six-pack of light beer—dinner and dessert. He spent the entire night in the motel room lying on a hard bed, watching a fuzzy television, drinking every ounce of booze he bought.

Come sunrise, he felt like shit. He could barely rise from the bed, staggering with one eye closed into the bathroom to relieve himself, his head pounding. He dry-heaved a few times but nothing came out. Then he put on his work boots and jeans, pulled on his jacket and went for a coffee. The drive was going to be a bitch.

Howard's grand plan of visiting Holland again was unraveling. Shortly after returning to Detroit, Lester put him on a new project that required working back-to-back weekends. He once thought he would be back a week later to see Amber, and now more than three weeks had passed—thanks to his father and his boss, the two men who have controlled his life the most.

Finally, though, on a foggy fall morning, Howard climbed into his truck before the sun was awake and drove west. The drive to Holland felt like a journey through uncertainty and anguish. He didn't know if Amber went back to her room after dropping him off at his motel and forgot about him completely. But he never forgot about her. Quite the opposite—his infatuation only grew. Along the drive, each passing mile was a reminder of missed opportunities.

As Howard arrived in Holland, he tried to reacquaint himself with the streets. The town was charming, and being back almost felt bittersweet. He couldn't help but feel the echoes of a moment that had already passed. By midmorning, he found the Copper River Inn. He idled his truck in the parking lot and tried to remember that night—*where was Amber's house?* The details were fuzzy. *They went out the back entrance? Was she parked back there, or around the block on the street?* He dropped his head into the steering wheel and closed his eyes. Then, in an instant, it came to him. Like an epiphany. They hadn't driven; they'd walked.

In a rush, he left the parking lot and drove, making a few turns and then idling once more in front of a familiar house. This was it. He took a deep breath, climbed from the truck and walked toward the front door. The memories started to rush back to him—this was the place. It was definitely the place.

He knocked. Then waited. Then waited. Then knocked. Then waited.

Inside he heard someone approaching the door, then a brief silence. The door opened. There stood a woman, several years older than Amber, probably older than Howard even. She had scraggly hair and dark circles under her eyes. "Can I help you?"

Howard cleared his throat. "I'm looking for Amber. Is she home?"

"Are you the guy?"

"I'm sorry?"

"The guy from a few weeks ago?"

"Uh, I might be." *I hope so*, is what he thought. *I better be.*

"Well, no matter," the woman said. "Amber isn't here anymore."

"Do you know when she'll be back?"

"No," the woman clarified. "She isn't here anymore. She doesn't live here anymore. She moved out a few days ago. You just missed her."

It hit Howard like a dagger to the heart. He tried to think but his mind wouldn't steady. "Do you know where I can find her?" he finally asked.

She shook her head. "Sorry. Didn't say where she was going. Just kind of packed up her stuff and left."

Dread settled over Howard. "Did she leave a phone number? Anything?"

"Sorry."

He drummed his fingers nervously on his leg. His breath was quickening. "She was writing a book, right?" He asked this as if saying it out loud would summon her back.

"Yep. Pretty much always writing that thing."

Nodding his head, the realization was falling upon him: the woman that left him sleepless without an appetite was now little more than a drifting shadow, a memory that he couldn't hold. He thanked the woman for her time and then returned to his truck. Suddenly, the streets of Holland felt strange, foreign—when only minutes earlier they'd felt full of hope, like a place he could call home.

Howard sat in his truck for a long while, just staring and thinking. Thinking that this dream he had been envisioning for the last few weeks had just evaporated before him. Thinking that Amber had slipped from his life as mysteriously as she entered it.

7

Wolf Valley, 2002

In which Howard is 48 years old

By the time morning rolls around, Howard hasn't slept a wink. The sight of the boat floating in the yard has startled him. The shot of adrenaline that followed never subsided. His eyes are blood-shot, he knows that, having spent the entire night nervously watching the water level rise. The rain and the wind are as powerful as they were the previous night, which is unsettling. Though it is still dark outside, the morning brings enough light for him to see his front yard scattered with twigs and branches and, perhaps most terrifying of all, the river has spilled up the back lawn and is rapidly approaching his patio.

Coby is whining by the back door. He hasn't gone outside since the evening before. The thought of letting him out hasn't even crossed Howard's mind. After all, the rug and kitchen floor are still spotted with dried muddy paw prints. But he knows nature calls—more mud is better than the alternative.

This time around, Howard decides to keep the dog under control. He will put him on a leash and venture out in the front yard with him. Aside from the mess Coby could cause when returning inside, there are too many dangers out there: wind, flooding, branches cracking and tumbling to the ground. Fortunately, Howard has rain boots in the closet. He pulls them on, then slips into a hooded jacket. In the basket by the door, Coby is burying his head looking for his leash. "I got it, boy," Howard says.

These autumn storms in Wolf Valley are entirely unpredictable. Howard has been here long enough to know that. Sometimes it's warm and tornados start swirling. Other times, the air bites and the rain stings. A year earlier, the rain that fell barely seemed like a storm—more like just a rainy night. No, the storm didn't arrive until afterward when his life instantly imploded.

Right now, this is unlike any storm he has ever experienced, in Wolf Valley or elsewhere. That was clear early. Each minute that passes, it only worsens. Standing on the porch, Coby is pulling on the leash to get out to the yard. Howard is hesitant. Then he steps out from under the awning and feels the rain pummel his coat. Coby continues tugging and lifts his leg at the first shrub he finds. That's where they stand for a long while. Howard is looking around the side of the house and sees the water advancing. It's another unsettling sight. There is nothing he can do. He's helpless. Rain is dripping off his hood and he has to wipe it from his eyes, but what he sees out here is a far clearer threat than what he could see from his kitchen window: this storm will eventually turn deadly—he's now sure of it.

When Coby finishes, he immediately tries to drag Howard off the walkway and onto the lawn. The grass is so soft that the dog's paws sink past the white. Howard is nervous about his first step and he can feel his boot splash and then sink as well. It's stuck and difficult to take the next step. Coby only takes a few more strides before assuming the position. The wind is whipping so hard that Howard thinks his anchored feet will cost him his balance. The moment Coby finishes, Howard shouts, "C'mon, boy!" through the storm and turns toward the house. It's so loud that he can't hear the truck approaching, but the headlights reflect off the front windows as it turns into the driveway and Howard spins to look. It's Stu.

He rolls down his window and motions for Howard to come over. The rain is coming down sideways now. Howard wants to let Coby in the front door first but doesn't trust him inside alone, so they turn and briskly walk over to the truck.

"Pretty damn crazy out here," Stu says.

"What's going on?" Howard asks. He wants to get to the point of the visit. The quicker he can get back inside the better.

"We're headin' to the shelter. You should come." They are talking with raised voices, not quite yells, to project over the sound of the rain.

"What now?"

"Gotta grab the wife, then we're leavin'. You comin'?"

Howard thinks about it for a moment. It's probably the safest option. It will only be a matter of time until the power goes out. Just about a miracle that it's still on. That river is also still on the rise. Before tomorrow's daybreak, it'll hit the foundation. "Let me gather some things and grab a bag for the dog. You mind waiting a short bit?"

Stu shakes his head, not at the thought of waiting, but at the part about the dog. "No pets at this place," he says with regret in his tone. "Apparently they're real strict about that. They ain't sure there's gonna be 'nough room fer the humans, I reckon."

"You want me to leave Coby behind?"

"Fill some bowls with food and water, he'll be alright."

Howard repeated himself, this time slower and firmer. "You want me to leave Coby behind?"

"H'ard, a year ago you was bitchin' about even takin' care'a that thang, now you suddenly have a problem lettin' him be?"

"I'm not leaving the dog, Stu."

"Y'gotta, H'ard. Leave the dog and save y'self. This storm is gettin' worse 'fore it gets any better."

"You're sure this place won't take dogs?"

"Positive. Leave the dog, we'll come back fer him first thang we're able."

The decision is clear: he can't leave Coby behind. For as much as he didn't want the dog, in trying times his mind always goes back to his wife. *This isn't my dog*, Howard thinks to himself, *it's Amber's dog*. Still, he knows that choosing to stay behind could mean risking both of their lives.

"Gotta have a decision," Stu says. There's urgency in his voice.

"I'm staying."

Stu shakes his head. "Yer makin' a mistake, H'ard."

Howard bangs the hood twice and steps back from the truck. "I appreciate your concern, Stu."

There is nothing more Stu can do. He has to get back to his wife and head for higher ground. "Look, that water gets any worse, y'-don't ferget 'bout that boat, y'here?"

Howard waves as if to say "understood" and then turns for the porch. He can feel the water seeping through his raincoat and beneath his jeans. Stepping inside, he holds onto Coby's leash even though the dog is pulling to get free—he wants to spaz around the house, rolling around to dry himself. It's quiet inside except for the muffled sound of the wind and rain and the jingle of the tag on Coby's collar as he shakes. It's surprisingly comforting, at least for a moment. But then he feels a rush of fear, of guilt, of uncertainty. *Did I just turn down a ride to safety for this dog?* The decision is now baffling him, one he knows he would not have made a year earlier. Still, he made it with conviction and without hesitation.

With some struggle, Howard removes his drenched raincoat while still holding the leash. His shirt and pants are dripping onto the floor and rushes of chills shiver down his arms and legs. Coby, meanwhile, has matted hair that's soaked. He also looks much thinner, only about half the size from when he was dry. Howard holds the dog in place with one hand and reaches for a nearby rag with another, and then proceeds to wipe his paws. When the ordeal is over, Coby is running laps around the house in hyperdrive, only pausing to shake the remaining water from his hair. Howard sits in his chair, sets his glass on the table and picks up a book. The dull roar of the weather outside seeps into the house, but only as subtle background noise. The only other sound comes from Coby, who continues to run circles around Howard—and will do that until he is completely dry or until he becomes too tired to continue.

This all allows Howard to reflect on what just happened. Watching Coby spaz brings careless joy to his day, a respite from the chaos. It is the innocence that captures his attention. Sure, the whimpering in the doorway and the yanking on the leash bother him, but in those moments of freedom he doesn't see a dog—he sees himself; he sees Amber. That was their relationship—carefree, blissful. The opposite of where he now spends most days—guilty, alone.

A wet, cold nose nuzzling his hand snaps him from his thought. Howard pets Coby, who is pressing himself firmly against his owner. "You're a good boy," Howard tells him, "a good boy."

A good boy, he thinks, *who may get me killed*. That's a very real thought as the rain continues to pour in buckets. Howard sets the book down on the table and decides his time would be better spent taking inventory of his supplies. If—no, *when*, he corrects himself—he needs them, he needs to know what he has and where they are. He owns all the basics: a flashlight, a half-full box of matches, a thermal blanket, canned goods, a hunting knife that he has never used for hunting. Oh, and the pistol, with a full box of .22-caliber ammo.

Walking from room to room, he gathers these various supplies and piles them onto the kitchen table. He steps back, crosses his arms and stares at it all. It seems like a lot, and it seems like barely anything. If the worst were to happen, would these things really save his life? And Coby's?

A branch falls from an overhanging tree and crashes into the side of the house. It makes a terrifyingly loud noise that startles Howard.

His nerves are setting in now. If he looked down, he'd expect to physically see his heart beating out of his chest. As a remedy, he opens the cabinet. To his dismay, he has about three drinks left in his bottle of whiskey. He thinks there is another in the car, but he can't be sure. Now his hands are jittery. Without a glass, he walks the bottle over to his chair in the living room and sits down to take a drink, then a deep breath. That's his routine now—in anxious times, just breathe. *Just breathe.* He should get a bumper sticker made up.

But there's a reason it works. It's all cause and effect. Slowing his breathing helps him slow down his thinking. And when he can slow down his thinking, he can think about Amber. And when he can think about Amber, he loses his fear of death.

"I wish you were here," he says quietly to himself. His head is hanging and the bottle is barely caught in his limp, dangling hand.

Then the lights go out.

8

Holland, 1982

In which Howard was 28 years old

Howard spent weeks, months, years thinking about Amber. The one that got away. On free weekends, he would make day trips across the state back to Holland, sitting in bars or coffee shops or restaurants just hoping to run into her. He'd strike up conversations with locals sitting near him and casually drop her name, but he never got a bite.

Sex from that point felt meaningless—always chasing the high. Just like he did with Amber, he would have the occasional fling on a drunken Friday night, but that's all they ever were. He never asked for a number and if a woman left one, he immediately discarded it once she left. There were never formal dates and certainly never a second night together. He was crossing off bars throughout metro

Detroit, never returning once he had picked up a girl for the night. It was a sad existence and he was completely aware of it.

He had let relationships slip from his life. His mother had been gone since his young childhood. His dad was dead and buried. His lone friend, Willy, had given up on Howard during this depressive spell and returned to Pennsylvania looking for something better. But Howard never left. He continued living in Detroit. Continued working the contracting gigs, drinking more beer than he ever had before. Continued reading books into the early morning hours, until his inebriation blinded him and forced him to give up.

Twenty-eight years old. What was he making of his life? Too young to be washed up, clinging to memories of short-lived lovers from years past. He knew this, of course. But knowing it and doing something about it are two different things.

One fall Saturday, nearly four years to the day he first went to Holland, he woke up, climbed into his truck and drove back. It was a short-lived ritual he had established in the weeks after learning that Amber had moved, but he had finally abandoned it after months of no luck. Now, for no apparent reason, he found himself unable to resist the urge to return.

It was a dreary day, a gray sheet hanging overhead like four years of regret. Howard drove the streets aimlessly for a while, just trying to gain his bearings. Finally, after an hour or so, he pulled over downtown and bought himself a coffee. Sitting on a nearby bench, he stared blankly at the steam rising from the cup. It mesmerized him. And then he thought, *Who are you, Amber? Who are you, mystery girl?* Then: *Pathetic. Get ahold of yourself.*

Returning to his truck, he thought his time would be better spent reading. He reached for his passenger's seat but came up empty. Forgotten in the fog of the morning. *Oh well.* He blew on his coffee, took a sip, and then headed out along the street for a walk. There was a chill in the air but it felt new, comforting somehow.

As he turned the corner, he saw Uptown Booksellers, an indie bookstore with a brick facade and a big front window with hardcovers propped up on display. He stepped inside to browse but didn't get past the entryway before being stopped dead in his tracks.

There she was.

The same gentle smile, the dark hair that tucked around her neck. Those blue eyes. Only she wasn't there, not in the flesh. A large poster sat on an easel promoting a local author and her debut novel, *The Empty Hills of History*.

Howard stood there in shock. *By God, she did it. She wrote the damn book.* After he realized how long he had been standing there staring at Amber's picture, he finally snapped out of it. He glanced at the date on the sign. One week. Noon. She would be there signing copies of the book.

Howard would be there, too.

Perhaps the longest week of his life crawled by. He spent the days on the job, his heart racing and needing to step away for undisclosed breaths of fresh air. While many of his fellow workers needed smoke breaks, Howard needed time to calm himself. His coworkers must have thought he had a problem—which, of course, he did.

Finally, on Saturday morning, he awoke once more before the sun and made an embarrassingly familiar drive across the state to Holland. When he arrived at the bookstore, the lights were still off. The streets were completely vacant of cars. He would have to wait, so he parked a little way down the block, turned the corner to the coffee shop and bided his time reading a haggard copy of Hemingway stories that he'd tucked inside the glove compartment to never be without a book again.

As the morning glow morphed into a soft daylight, people began appearing on the sidewalks. They were drinking coffee, mingling, just out for some exercise. Howard watched them intently. He sat there that way at a lonely table in the window drinking coffee all morning. One after another. As noon approached, he glanced at the clock and then he folded his book on the table.

A small bell dinged with the opening of the door and he glanced up to see her. There she was. Flesh and bone. She had that same presence that she'd had that day sitting at the bar, but there was something different now. More mature. A confidence she didn't have before. Her face was just as beautiful, but four years had taken her from the edge of womanhood and thrust her into it. She looked in a hurry, went straight to the counter, ordered a coffee, and then left. She didn't look around, didn't notice Howard. It all happened too fast. He watched the scene play out as if he were watching someone else's life, like there was a pane of glass before him and he couldn't make contact with anyone on the other side.

When he snapped from his daze, he felt an overwhelming rush of how real this was. He felt sheepish in a way. He thought about whether what he was doing—all these years later, showing up out of the blue—was a huge mistake. Or, at least if Amber would be turned off by it. It didn't dawn on him until that moment that while he spent the last four years obsessed, he may have been no more than a forgettable blip in her life on her path toward authorship.

He waited another few minutes and then slowly made his way from the coffee shop down the street to the bookstore. It was a small space, but the manager had cleared some room in the back corner where a table was set up, along with several chairs for readers to sit and listen. Howard saw Amber near that table holding a copy of her book talking to one of the booksellers. He ducked behind a nearby shelf and snuck looks, the feeling of stalking not lost on him.

"Alright, everyone, thanks for coming," a middle-aged woman with short curly hair said. A small group of people all also holding copies of the book found seats in the chairs, while Amber stood off to the side. "We have an absolute treat for you all today. Holland's very own Amber McNamara is here to read from her debut novel, *The Empty Hills of History*. Ms. McNamara will also be sticking around afterward to sign copies. So, without further ado, I will turn it over to the author herself."

The woman stepped to the side and took a seat in a chair behind Amber that faced the rest of the group.

"Thank you, Susan," Amber started. Hearing her voice again softened Howard's heart. She went on to talk about how much she loved the bookstore, how she spent so much time browsing the shelves throughout high school, and how much the community has meant to her. Then she flipped open the book that had been tucked under her arm and read the first chapter to the nine mostly older women gathered in front of her. When she finished, the group clapped and then Amber took a seat behind the table, clicked on her pen and greeted each person individually, exchanging pleasantries each time.

Howard was still across the room, trying to hide his face, until the original group all had signed copies. When Amber was finally sitting alone, Howard took a deep breath, stepped out and walked directly toward her. He could feel a warm rush to his face and perspiration begin to form on his nose. For a moment, he stood in front of the table staring down at her. She hadn't looked up and he didn't know what to say. Then, as if in slow motion, her eyes rose to meet his and they both froze.

"Amber," Howard said in not much more than a whisper.

Her eyes betrayed her emotions. A terrified look washed over her face and tears welled. "Howard. What—" she started, but she couldn't finish her thought. She looked panicked.

"Amber," he said again calmly, understanding the situation he had put her in. "It's nice to see you again."

She glanced around and then stood up abruptly. She didn't know what to say.

"Can I buy you a coffee?" he finally asked.

"Yes, yes. Let's do that. Say 15 minutes?"

"Perfect."

He half expected her not to show. Sitting nervously at an empty table, he waited. Ten minutes. Fifteen. Twenty. His palms were clammy. And then the bell above the door jingled and he turned to see her. She appeared as beautiful as she ever had. He stood to greet her and they exchanged an awkward, half-hearted embrace. The smell of her perfume was like a shot of cocaine, thrusting him four years into the past.

Stepping aside, he raised his arm to allow her to approach the counter first. "We should get these to go," she said, and then turned to the barista and placed her order. He followed suit, and they waited in near silence until their drinks were ready. Howard held open the door and said, "After you," and they walked out onto the sidewalk.

They strode in silence toward the street corner and then onward until they came upon a city park where the trees had begun changing colors. They sat down on a bench. Finally, without looking at Howard, Amber said, "I'm sorry."

The words he didn't know he longed to hear. He turned to face her but she held her coffee with both hands and stared out at the trees. "It's just nice to see you again," he said. "Frankly, I wasn't sure I'd ever get to see you again."

She smiled politely, ever so briefly, and then dropped her gaze.

"So, what have you been up to? Writing bestsellers, I see."

"Not quite bestsellers. But I've been writing."

"I'm glad you kept at it. That's one of the things I remembered most about you."

She nodded. "You know, Howard, it was only one night."

The comment caught him off guard. "It was. But if I can be honest, I haven't stopped thinking about you since."

A soft red flushed her cheeks. "Howard..."

"Look, I don't want to come on too strong. I know it must already feel that way with me just showing up like this. But I wanted to see you, that's all. Catch up. Talk again."

"I'm flattered," she said, finally making eye contact. "I'm sorry. Let's talk, of course. So, are you living in the area now?"

"Me? Nope, still over in Detroit. But work brings me out here from time to time," he lied. "Saw your picture on the poster the other day, which surprised the hell out of me, and figured I'd make it a point to stop in."

"That's nice of you."

"And what about you? You still living in the area?"

She shook her head. "Actually, it wasn't long after we met that I decided I needed to take a chance. I moved to New York, got a few roommates and a job at a diner, and I kept writing."

"And now here you are."

"And now here I am," she repeated with a smirk.

A gentle silence hung in the air for a few moments, and then Howard said, "I'm sorry I didn't come back to see you. I tried—honest."

"It's okay."

"My father died."

"Oh. I'm so sorry."

"Don't be. He was a son of a bitch. But I was all he had, so I had to leave town for the arrangements. And then my boss had me working 'round the clock. By the time I knocked on your door, seems you were already gone."

"Yeah..." She sounded guilty, almost.

"It was completely my fault."

She shook her head and it looked like a tear might fall.

"Hey," he said, wrapping a comforting arm around her.

She rested her head on his shoulder for a moment before recomposing herself and pulling away. "What is going on here?"

"What do you mean?"

"I mean, like, we had a fling, what, four years ago? And now we're sitting on this bench like we're long-lost lovers. How old are you even?"

"I'm 28," he said. "And I'm not pretending anything happened that didn't. I know all we had was a fling. But, I don't know. It meant something—to me, at least."

Sipping her coffee as a distraction, she said, "So then, I feel like I have to ask again—what is going on here?"

"I don't know. I just wanted to see you again."

She didn't say anything.

"How long is your book tour?"

"It's not so much a tour as a few stops. I wanted to make sure I made an appearance here. This place meant so much to me."

"And then it's back to New York City?"

"That's the plan." After a moment she stood and said, "Listen, I have to get going."

Howard stood to meet her, a rush of fear overwhelming him, like he was letting the moment slip from his grasp. "Can I walk you back?"

She nodded and they headed toward the bookstore, all the while Howard trying to decipher the perfect thing to say. But the words weren't coming. His fears grew with each step, and when the bookstore came back into view his heart sank. Finally, without much thinking, he said, "What if I were in New York, too?"

"What do you mean?"

"I mean, what if I were in New York. Could I see you again?"

She seemed to be thinking for a moment, and then said, "If you, Howard, ever find yourself in New York City, I'd be happy to see you."

He smiled. His fear wasn't gone, but he felt hope start to creep in. "Deal," he said. Then, as she reached for the door, he added, "How will I contact you?"

"How *would* you, you mean? If you ever happened to be in New York? Here." She took out a pen and jotted down a telephone number on a scrap of paper. "You could call me if that day ever came." Then she leaned over and offered a gentle hug.

And for the second time, as quickly and mysteriously as she entered his life, she was once again gone.

9

Wolf Valley, 2002

In which Howard is 48 years old

He doesn't move for a long while, he just sits there with his head hanging, the dark filling in all the space around him, the rain and wind much louder now that the quiet buzz of an electrified house is silenced. You don't realize how loud the quiet is until the lights go out.

When he finally raises his head, it's dark in the room but not so dark that he cannot see. It'll get that dark, he knows, and sooner rather than later—it's the fall and each day is shorter than the last. The house is cold—that's the second thing he notices. With the furnace out, the heat just seems to evaporate from the home. He stands from his chair and lights a fire. Turning around, he sees Coby sitting nicely on the opposite side of the room, just staring at him. The dog is confused. "Where did all the lights go?" he can nearly hear him asking. Howard replies to his imagination with an audible, "I don't like it either, bud," and then heads to the kitchen to re-survey the supplies he has gathered.

Touching each item to recall his reasoning for adding it to the pile, he takes a thorough inventory. All the while, he is thinking, *What am I gonna do now?* and *I should have gone with Stu.* But then, *No,* he corrects himself, *you did the right thing. Stu asked you to leave Coby behind. Couldn't do that.*

Now Howard realizes he needs a plan of his own. In the naive part of his mind, he hopes that the power will come back on soon, but each time he glances outside that thought is vanquished. His first action is to preserve. *Preserve,* he thinks, *and then survive.* This, in his mind, means Amber's work. The copies of her books that he possesses are inscribed—these aren't the kind of books that can be replaced with a trip to Borders. If they were to succumb to the storm, they would be lost forever. Keepsakes, family mementos, destroyed. For whom is Howard saving them? That's a question that, fortunately, doesn't cross his mind. Let it be a selfish desire, fueled by love.

In the kitchen, there is a storage hatch to a crawl space under the floorboards. He pulls it up because he knows there are a few plastic bins down there—the best chance for preservation when a storm like this hits. But what he sees sends him scrambling: In the dark, faintly, something looks off. He can sense the ground is closer than it should be. Then one of the bins moves. It's floating. He shoots up and darts for the window. That's when he sees the river—or what used to be a river—has swelled into a lake and is just reaching his foundation. *Shit.*

Now in a panic, his vision blurs and he puts his hands on either side of his face, slowly curling his fingers into fists. Almost instantly he is colder. The storm is louder. He can feel his breathing quicken and for a moment he thinks his heart will give out. Out of the corner of his eye, he sees someone. When he looks, no one is there. His mind is beginning to play tricks.

Reaching into the crawl space, he grabs a floating bin and pulls it into the kitchen. The water is freezing and it splashes all over the floor. Howard dumps the bin's contents into the corner and briskly heads for Amber's study. Countless books line the shelves, but he knows where to start. He carefully retrieves copies of Amber's novels and places them neatly inside the bin. There's still room for more and he decides, rather than cherry-pick books from the rest of the shelf, to start emptying the desk's contents. Most of these books, he knows, can be replaced. Nothing that Amber wrote longhand can—and he wants to salvage anything that she may have had tucked away.

What he doesn't anticipate is the sheer weight of the bin. Once full, he lifts it and almost tumbles forward, like a magnet is trying to hold it against the floor. Instead, he decides to slide it across the house to the mudroom. That's where the pull-string is for the attic. The next task is daunting: somehow getting that bin of books up that narrow ladder. The only option is to go slowly, one step at a time. He sucks in his gut and musters a bout of strength to lift, set it down, and then do it again. Eventually, he has to step onto the ladder himself, which makes it much more difficult. Impatience drives him to skip the final three steps and lift it all the way onto the attic's landing. The box wobbles and for a moment he thinks it will tumble over on top of him, surely knocking him to the floor and causing serious pain. But he finds the strength to steady it and get it where it needs to go.

He has spent very little time up there. He fumbles for a pull-string light, bumping into things as he does. His head slams against a beam; he is too tall to stand. Finally—*aha!*—the string. He yanks it. Nothing happens. He has forgotten that there is no power. Working mostly by feel, he finds a tarp that was folded in the corner and spreads it over the bin to protect the contents. Coby is sitting patiently at the bottom of the ladder, and as Howard climbs back down the tail starts wagging.

What next? His mind is racing. So fast that he cannot think of a single next move. He knows he needs to find some stillness to think clearly. The rain is battering the roof and the windows and it's so loud that it feels like the house could crumble at any moment. Then it finally hits him: This is what he deserves. For what he said to Amber. For his actions. For his inaction. It is a manifestation of his guilt. More importantly, of his punishment. At that, he collapses onto the floor. His knees are shaking and his hands fall to his sides. *Just take me*, he thinks. Then: "Just take me," he says aloud. Coby nuzzles his nose under Howard's arm. It's not enough, not nearly. *Not after what I did, bud.*

That floor is where Howard remains for a long while. He doesn't know for sure—maybe an hour? Maybe three? But it also could have been fifteen minutes—he has lost all sense of time, what it means, how it's calculated. Finally, he rises back to his feet and looks out the window. The boat is floating in the middle of his yard. The rope is taught, so he knows it must still be tied to one of the stakes—probably being dragged across the lawn.

At this point, Howard is a desperate man, so he does what desperate men do. Back at the front door, he slips into his rubber boots and his jacket. "Stay here," he tells Coby. "I'll be back, boy."

One step outside and a gust slams him against the house. The blow disorients him for a moment. The front door is still open, so he reaches back and pulls it shut, almost pinching Coby's snout in the process. It takes him a second to realize he's hit his head. He checks but there's no blood. Now his back aches and he contemplates slipping inside and hunkering down, turning to prayer perhaps. But instead, he makes a desperate step from the porch. The grass is so saturated it's like trudging through sand. As he reaches the back corner of the house, there is now standing water. The yard has a subtle grade to it and with each step the water is higher. Howard can barely keep his eyes up, the wind and rain lashing across his face. When he strains, he can see downed branches sticking out of the water. One that submerged catches his boot and he falls. He's able to catch himself before going completely under. The water is rising, almost two feet deep at this point.

The boat is bobbing with the water, thrashing back and forth. Howard finally reaches it and places both hands on the side, trying to steady both himself and the craft. He uses the boat to maintain his balance as he shuffles along until he reaches the rope, and then he follows the rope until he gets to the stake. When he reaches underwater, he can feel the stake isn't secure in the ground but rather caught on a fallen branch. Howard is using both hands to untangle the rope from the branch, but it's all by feel. The water is so deep at this point that he can barely work on the knot and keep his head above simultaneously. Heart racing and growing frustrated, Howard struggles to free it. The wind is pushing the boat toward the house, tightening the rope against the branch. This is when Howard tries a new plan. He wades back to the boat and reaches inside. There's a storage box near the back that holds a serrated fishing knife. He seizes it and returns to the rope, sawing as quickly as he can. No more than a minute later, it snaps and the boat thrusts away. Howard starts off after it, high-stepping through the water, driving his thighs. The craft bottoms out in the yard before he can catch it.

Knowing that he may need this boat to save his life, he decides to tie it up to the light post beside the house. He walks around to the bow and digs his boots into the ground. It feels like it's stuck in the mud—no, it's literally stuck in the mud. But he drags on, going less than a foot with each pull. By the time he gets close enough to tie it up, he's out of breath and lightheaded. For a brief moment, he thinks he may be having a heart attack. But he catches his breath. When he stands up, he looks out at the yard and how far he's managed to pull the craft. For the first time since this storm began, he has a feeling of hope.

Turning back to the house, he sees Coby in the window, tongue hanging out of his mouth, looking like he's ready to burst.

10

New York, 1983

In which Howard was 29 years old

Howard belonged in a treehouse, hiding in the woods, reading books by moonlight or flashlight. He belonged in the tranquility of the forest, the thickness of the trees keeping even the slightest breeze from touching his skin, where sunlight reached only on the brightest of days. He belonged on a construction site, a hard hat on his head, a hammer dangling from his side, the weight of steel in the toes of his boots, the dust and banging and organized chaos of it all. Where he didn't belong was waking on a rock-hard mattress by the sharp reflection of rays on the windows of nearby skyscrapers, the bustle of people and car horns below beckoning from a city that never slept.

And yet there he was. New York City. A move, not a visit—that was clear. But temporary, not permanent—that was also clear. A mission—that's what he was on. If he were to achieve it, he would be in heaven. If not, perhaps a place a little hotter, a little further south. But regardless, he would never have to call himself a New Yorker—not that any of the folks walking around the streets would ever let him get away with doing that.

He spent his first day in a hotel room. He thought about walking the streets, but just getting off the flight and taking a cab into the city was enough to shock his system. A little rest would do the trick, reset him. But the next morning when he awoke, dressed and stepped outside to the smell of garbage and the warmth of an artificial humidity smacking him in the face, he debated heading right back inside.

It wasn't until his third day in town that he found the courage to pick up the phone.

"Hello?" Her voice was soft and unassuming.

"Hi, it's Howard."

She paused for a moment, and then said, "Oh, Howard, it's nice to hear from you."

"You too. It's nice to hear your voice."

They had spoken several times over the previous months since they saw each other in Holland at her book signing. The conversations grew in length and frequency until Howard felt comfortable enough to take a leap of faith. He found himself sitting in a New York City hotel room with no warning to Amber.

"I'd love to see you again," he said.

"I think that would be nice, but I really don't know when I can plan a trip back to Michigan."

"I was thinking in New York."

She let an audible scoff slip and said, "I can't picture you in New York. No offense. You just don't strike me as a big city guy."

"Well, that's the truth. But if you're in New York, then I want to be in New York."

"Okay then. It's a date. Do you have any time off coming up?"

"How's 8 o'clock?"

"Eight o'clock...? I'm not sure what you mean."

"There's a little cafe I saw on 10th. Damon's, I think it's called."

"Wait," she said sharply. "Are you—where are you calling me from?"

"A hotel room near I think it's called Washington Park."

"You're in New York right now?"

"I'm in New York right now," he said.

He could hear some heavy breathing on the other end, but no words.

"Amber?"

"I'm here." Then another moment of silence. "I wish you'd have told me you were coming to the city."

A wave of guilt rushed over him. In all of his haste, his planning, his ego-driven mind, rejection wasn't something that ever occurred to him as a possibility. "I'm sorry," he finally said after recomposing himself. He wasn't sure what else to say.

But then he heard, "Eight o'clock—see you there," and the click on the other end.

A taxi honk startled Howard as he stood on the hectic corner. Traffic moved past constantly. He had never been in a city so unrelenting. He had never felt so insignificant. On the walk from his hotel, he had stopped to buy his first-ever pack of cigarettes. Calm the nerves.

Slipping one from the pack, he lit it and took a long drag. The smoke attacked his throat and he coughed, and then he took another and watched the smoke leave him. A nasty habit. But it was the first instant of relief he had felt since arriving. Though some guilt accompanied the puffs, it was worth it. This city—he didn't know if he could do it.

And then he saw Amber. It was like she glided over the sidewalk, a glow around her. She didn't belong in a place like this. She was better than New York.

Howard snapped himself from his thoughts and managed to crush out the cigarette and wave away the lingering smoke before she stepped up to him.

He smiled and without a greeting, Amber said, "Not the healthiest habit."

"Sorry, I'm just nervous."

She smirked and stared into his eyes.

"It's good to see you," he said.

"What in the world are you doing in New York City?"

"It's kind of a long story," he said, holding out his arm. "I'd be happy to tell you over dinner."

After a slight hesitation, she said, "I'd love to hear about it," and walked inside.

They were seated at a small table near the window that allowed Howard a front-row seat to the bustle outside. Inside, the harsh odor of tobacco hung in the air. The cafe was almost exclusively small, round tables, and nearly all were filled. Couples chatted and sipped from petite, stemless wine glasses, the faint hum of Sinatra serenading the crowd. It wasn't the type of place Howard frequented, but his hours of experience in the city didn't permit many other options.

"It's nice to see you," Howard said again after a moment to breathe in their seats.

A middle-aged waitress in a faded maroon dress stepped up to take their drink order. Amber asked for a pinot noir, Howard a whiskey, neat.

Amber leaned back in her chair and crossed her legs. "You were going to tell me this long story about what brought you to New York."

She still had the softness of a summer tan and Howard had a hard time focusing on her words. "You don't want to hear about that. Tell me about what you're working on."

That piqued her interest, though she played coy. "What makes you think I'm working on something new?"

"Five years ago, that night we met, you were scribbling away in that notebook all night. The next morning, I saw a stack of those notebooks on your dresser. I find it hard to believe you're never not working on something."

"Very observant. Well, it turns out I *am* working on something."

"Care to share?"

She hesitated and then leaned forward, resting her elbows on the table as if she were about to open up, before exhaling and saying, "I never talk about ongoing work."

Howard laughed at her deception and complimented her. She seemed fond of herself. For a moment he was thrust back into that bar in Holland, the picture of the young woman in the sundress sitting on the barstool like an angel sent there for him. A minute later the waitress delivered their drinks. Amber took the glass and raised it to Howard's. With sincerity, she looked him in the eye and said, "Thank you for calling." Howard didn't say anything but he gave her a look that he hoped helped her understand he was grateful. It was not lost on him their lack of a relationship. On one hand, he felt like he'd known her for years. On the other, this was only the third time he'd seen her.

"What are you reading?" Her question broke the silence.

"What makes you think I'm reading something?" he asked, tongue-in-cheek.

"Touché."

He sipped his whiskey and then said, "I'm reading this new book by some up-and-coming author. It's decent but I think the title is a little too mysterious for my taste."

"What's it called?"

"Not sure if you've heard of it, *The Empty Hills of History?*"

If she were closer she would have smacked him on the arm. But the look she gave him said it all.

"I take it you've heard of it, then? It's decent. The author actually signed my copy. I only bought it because I got to meet her and she signed it. And because she's so darn cute."

"Just decent, huh?"

"Yep, decent. The same way Joe Montana is proving to be a decent quarterback."

The reference eluded her. She wanted a new response.

"Amber, I'm gonna be honest with you."

"I wish you would."

He took another sip first and then said, "Your book was one of the three best novels I have ever read."

She blushed and looked away. After a few moments, she said, "Just top three?" But Howard could hear the frog in her throat.

He leaned forward and reached across the table, placing his hand on hers. "I'm gonna need to see a follow-up before I am ready to dethrone Steinbeck or Hemingway."

Through glassy eyes, she tried to smile and whispered, "Deal."

Drinks turned into dinner. The two discussed books, the city, reminisced about their previous fling, and Amber told Howard about her literary journey, how she decided to move to New York and how tough it was to break into the industry.

"Seems to have worked out pretty well for you," Howard said.

She nodded. "Seems so."

The earlier cacophony of the restaurant had softened as patrons paid their bills and left. They hadn't even realized that night had fallen on the city and they were two of the remaining few in the place.

Amber finished the last sip of her drink and said, "Can I take you somewhere?"

"Where would you like to take me?"

She stood up, smiled and extended her hand. He slid a few bills from his pocket and placed them on the table.

What would have been darkness in most other parts of the world —and certainly in the places Howard wished he lived—the lights of the city ceased the night from taking its full effect overhead. Though less busy than earlier in the day, the sidewalks and streets were still filled with pedestrians and taxis in an endless stream of chaos. Trepidation bubbled inside Howard, a constant fight to remind himself that this is the cost of going after what he wants most in life. She must have seen the look on his face and said, "Welcome to the Big Apple."

He nodded and said, "So, where are we heading?"

"You like books—despite looking at you."

"Hey," he said in jest.

She laughed. "We're going to meet some friends of mine."

"Other writers?"

"Mhmm."

"Despite me liking to read—and you—I'm not sure I would fit in with that scene."

Amber waved down a cab with the flick of a wrist. It dawned on Howard that she didn't just move to this city—she fit in here. Standing there, in that moment, a thought flashed through his mind that perhaps they weren't as compatible as he'd led himself to believe over the last five years. But the thought was fleeting. He consciously reminded himself about the book, those words and what they meant to him. About the conversations they'd had about literature and life and philosophy. About what he felt when he touched her, kissed her.

Before climbing inside the cab, she reached back and grabbed his hand and pulled him along. Her touch ignited something in him. She uttered some street names that sounded completely made up but all he could think about was holding her hand.

For most of the ride, she looked silently out the window at the towering buildings and the bright lights. Howard just watched her watch them. Even after years here, she still looked like a kid experiencing it all for the first time. The ride was surprisingly long for how close the place seemed. When they arrived, Howard let Amber lead the way through a heavy black door—the paint chipping—and down a narrow staircase into a dimly lit basement bar with exposed brick walls and low ceilings.

Sitting at a table in the corner was an interesting cast of characters, none of which looked like anyone Howard had ever met before. They couldn't have belonged in the hills of Pennsylvania and certainly not on the construction sites in Detroit. Without hesitation, Amber slid onto a vinyl bench beside a woman who looked to be nearly twice her age. The woman had curly brown hair that sat over her ears and large, wiry glasses.

"What can I get you, doll?" the woman asked Amber.

Without acknowledging the question, Amber said, "Guys, this is Howard."

"Howard," a tall, skinny man of about thirty said as he stood from the other side of the table. He put out a big paw and said, "Welcome, friend. My friends call me Fitzy."

Howard shook his hand and then sat in an empty chair near Amber.

"He wishes!" another young woman shouted from across the table. She turned to Howard. "He thinks he's the next F. Scott Fitzgerald. You can call him Lance, like the rest of us do." She rolled her eyes.

"This is Piper," Amber said.

The younger woman reached her hand across the table. "And it is a pleasure to meet you, Mr. Howard."

"And this is Wendy," Amber said, extending a hand toward the woman with the glasses sitting beside her, who nodded Howard's way and raised her glass in a friendly gesture.

Settling back into their seats, they all looked around the table. "So, this is the gang," Amber said.

"Nice to meet you all," said Howard. "How'd you all meet?"

"What kind of time you have on your hands?" Lance said through a slick smirk.

"I'll be right back," Amber said. "Behave." She paused and looked around the table.

Once she was out of sight, Lance and Piper scooted closer to Howard. Lance said, "You a writer, fella?"

"Just a reader."

"A fan of Amber's here?"

"You could say that."

"I assume you've read her book."

"Mhmm."

"What did you think?"

"Pretty damn impressive," Howard said.

Piper chimed in, "Lance has a book, too. Have you heard of it? *The Man in the Summer Place*."

Howard shook his head. "Apologies but I can't say that I have. What's it about?"

Lance didn't look upset, but he also didn't speak up. Instead, Piper carried on and told Howard that the book was inspired by Lance's summer vacations in northern Michigan. It was about the social and economic divide between the locals and the people who summered up there.

"That is very Fitzgerald of you," Howard said. When Lance didn't respond, Howard added, "So, you're a Michigan man?"

"Originally," Lance said, finishing his drink.

"What about you?" Howard said to Piper and, glancing over her shoulder, indirectly to Wendy as well.

"I grew up on the Au Sable," Piper said.

"Grand Blanc," said Wendy.

Howard nodded and smirked. "The Literary Misfits of Michigan, all gathered here in the big city."

"That's our band name," said Lance.

Amber returned a few moments later and handed Howard a low-ball with whiskey. She had ordered herself something taller and clearer, but Howard suspected nonetheless potent.

"So, Howard," Wendy said, "what's your story?"

It was a basic question and yet felt like it couldn't be more loaded. No, maybe loaded was the wrong word. Explosive. He thought for a minute. He looked around the room at all the people packed in, the writers and artists and poets and dreamers. The misfits and failures and secret successes. They all didn't seem like they fit into normal society, but they all didn't fit in together.

Howard finally shrugged and said, "What do you want to know? Am I from Michigan, too? Not originally."

"Where are you from?"

"Somewhere in Pennsylvania you've never heard of."

"Hmm. How'd you meet this gal?"

He stole a peek at Amber, who stared back and said, "Yeah, Howard, how did we meet?"

"Well," he said, turning back to Wendy, "interestingly enough, we met in a bar. About five years ago, was it? Nothing too groundbreaking. I saw her from across the room and couldn't keep my eyes off her, so I went and said hi, and then we met up at a different bar later that night."

"Wait, how old were you even?"

"Eighteen," Amber said.

"And I was twenty-four at the time."

"Robbing the cradle," said Lance.

"It took us another four years to see each other again, though."

"For real?" said Piper.

Amber nodded and Howard said, "For real." When no one said anything, he added, "If she hadn't written her book, I wouldn't be sitting here right now."

"Shit," said Lance, "if she hadn't written that book I'm not sure any of us would be sitting here." The group laughed and finished their drinks.

"Tip them back," Piper said to Amber and Howard. "We're gonna head to O'Donnell's."

At the Irish pub a few blocks down, the lights were surprisingly brighter. Just like the last place, patrons were packed in tightly. A small band in the corner played traditional Irish music and sprinkled in the occasional Beatles or Elvis. Lance snagged the group a small round table in the opposite corner from the band and a steady flow of Irish whiskey made its way over, one round at a time. As the night wore on, Howard found himself closer to Amber's side, until their chairs met and eventually so did their hands. She slipped hers into his without so much as a glance in his direction and he sat there having to piss for what felt like hours because he refused to let it go.

Toward the end of the night, Howard found himself sitting across from Piper after the rest of the group scattered to the bar and bathrooms. He noticed a small tattoo on the inside of her right wrist. The ink looked fresh.

"What's your tattoo say?" By this point in the night, whatever filter he'd had between his brain and his lips was long gone.

She turned out her arm and stared at it. She took her left hand and felt it as if it were brail. For a moment, it looked like she was going to speak, but no words came out. Just as Amber returned with several shot glasses pinched between her fingers, Howard could see tears welling in Piper's eyes.

"Forget I asked," he said.

Amber quickly assessed the situation, handed a shot glass to Howard and said, "Drink up." He took it from her, threw it back and placed the glass back on the table. She did the same and then turned to Piper and said, "We need to head out. Tell the others we'll do this again soon. And I settled up at the bar."

Piper didn't say anything. She was still looking at her arm.

Amber grabbed Howard's shoulder and dragged him from his chair and out onto the street. A warm air from earlier in the day lingered outside, along with a fairly wretched odor. Once they were walking toward the end of the block, Amber said, "What did you say to her?"

"Nothing, I just asked about her tattoo."

He saw the look on her face.

"Obviously I know now that I shouldn't have. You left us there together so I was just trying to make small talk."

They crossed the street and Amber stopped him. "Look. Piper doesn't come from much. She had a baby when she was young and... well, she lost it. Didn't take long for her to fall off the wagon. She started drinking. Fucked her life up for a bit there—pardon the language. Then she decided to get straight and take up writing and moved to New York. I think that's about the time she got the ink, too. It's her son's name. *Was*, I mean."

"Damn. I had no idea. Why did she do that?"

"What?"

"Get the tattoo, I mean."

"Who knows why the hell anyone does anything, Howard."

They continued walking until they got to Amber's apartment building. By this point, they had put the tattoo situation behind them and were holding hands again. "Any interest in a nightcap?" he asked.

She stretched onto her toes and kissed him on the cheek. "Not this time, Howard." She saw the disappointment on his face. "Look, what we did all those years ago. I had never done that before. I didn't feel great about myself after that. Running into you again has helped, but I told myself I'd never let that happen again."

"Never what? Have sex?"

She smirked. "No, not have sex. But I'm never going to give it up on the first night again."

"I hardly would consider this is our first night."

"It kind of is."

He looked at her.

"I like you, Howard. If we're going to give this a try, I just want to do it right."

He sighed but then nodded and said, "You're right."

"How long are you in town?"

In that moment he realized that he'd led her to believe he was just visiting. He wanted to come clean. Honesty seemed like the best policy. "About that. I sorta bought a one-way ticket."

Her eyes grew. "As in...?"

"As in—well, let's just say I'm not just visiting."

She smiled and threw herself into his chest. They kissed and Howard wrapped his arms around her so tightly he could feel his sides with his fingers. When she pulled back, she said, "All the more reason to do this right, then."

He returned the smile. His heart was beating out of his chest and he had to tame the hormones that were rushing inside him. "Do you have plans tomorrow night?"

"Not anymore," she said with a grin.

"Then it's a date."

"This time, yes, it is."

The pale wallpaper was peeling and the flushing sound from the toilet in the unit above him was disturbingly loud. The carpet was long and shaggy and he could tell whoever lived there before him snuck in a dog, despite being against the tenant agreement. It was a small space, but it was all Howard really needed—a bedroom, a living room, a kitchenette and a bathroom, all squeezed into a few hundred square feet.

Howard found this place after about a week of living in the hotel. The hotel was nice for the price and he certainly enjoyed the lifestyle, but always knew it was temporary and quite frankly he didn't have the funds to sustain it. He briefly considered asking Amber if they could move in together, but he thought better of it. He'd never done anything as reckless as quitting his job and moving across the country for a girl, let alone a girl he barely knew and who hadn't given him any indication she wanted a relationship. When he let himself think about it, he spiraled into a hole of doubt, so he did his best to cast those thoughts out the window. Instead, he was just grateful that the old man running this building was fine with a month-to-month agreement, which was difficult to come by in this part of the city. He was close to Amber's place—only a few blocks— and that's all he really cared about.

His days were filled mostly with reading. It was a welcomed change of pace from all the job sites that stole many years off his life. The books whirled him back to his childhood—instead of being holed up in his closet or a treehouse, he was holed up in a quiet room in a noisy city, the dichotomy somehow helping to provide comfort. It also helped that the Literary Misfits of Michigan liked to talk about books, so the habit had the added benefit of helping him fit into the group.

And they had taken to him. Over his first couple weeks, they all got together several times. Other than Amber, Piper, Wendy and Lance were the only people Howard knew in New York. Of course, he was the only one of them who didn't write—or try to write—but he sure as hell liked to read.

A knock on the door startled him and he set down his book and looked at this watch. Through the peephole he saw Amber's smiling face and as he let her in she rushed past and hopped onto the bed. "Hello to you, too," he said.

"Have you heard?"

He looked at her with his eyebrows raised as if to say, "Well? Let's hear it."

She stared at him to build the suspense, a knowing grin across her face. She was sitting on his bed on her knees, but upright like she was ready to stand. "You haven't heard—good, I wanted to be the one to tell you." She paused but still had the look on her face.

"Well? You gotta just come out with it."

"You know my agent, Kim? Actually, I don't think you've met her, but I should introduce you. I've talked about her enough, though."

He looked at her. "You're killing me."

"Right, the news: My book was a finalist for the Pulitzer Prize!"

"Are you serious?" Howard sprung toward the bed, wrapped her up and pulled her to her feet. "That is incredible! How—I mean, when—I mean, well, I don't know what I mean. I don't even know the questions to ask."

"I feel the same way right now, Howard. I'm a bit lost with all this. But I know it's good news, I know that much!"

"I am just so damn proud of you."

"Thank you," she said sweetly. "This doesn't mean that I've won anything, but being a finalist is pretty good too."

"Does the rest of the gang know yet?"

"Maybe, I don't know. I wanted to tell you first."

"I'm honored," he said, still holding her.

"Jackie Crosby was my age when she won it, and she was the youngest woman ever to win, so I wouldn't have gotten that title anyway."

"Wow, Amber, this is all incredible." Howard thought about this for a minute and they sat down on the edge of the bed. "So is your book going to say 'Pulitzer Prize Finalist' on the cover now?" Howard smiled at her and she smiled back at him and then they kissed again and fell onto the bed.

Howard knew that Amber's book was good—great, even—but he didn't know it was *Pulitzer Prize great*. Certainly, if he were a voting member he would have given it the prize, but his bias was so strong that he had no perspective about how others received it.

The next several weeks were a whirlwind. Amber was escorted from one wining-and-dining event to another. She rubbed shoulders with the literary elites of the city. It was amazing to Howard to see how much attention a runner-up could get. It made him wonder about the kind of treatment the winner was receiving. It also made him wonder about his place in her life. While he understood that these events were focused on her and her book, he was surprised that she hadn't brought a plus-one to any of them. Surely, she'd been offered the opportunity. Afterward, she would call him and they would meet at a bar or her apartment or, sometimes, she would even stop by his place. She'd be wearing a dress, usually something light and flowy, and she smelled sweet and sometimes still had the warmth of excitement on her skin. On the good nights, the cocktails would lead to undressing and Howard loved those nights, but he also felt distant in the morning when Amber woke up and walked out the door. But they never made love. He prayed for that day to return, but they were taking it slow—"Doing it the right way," as Amber kept saying.

As the weeks passed, he began to think more about how he fit into her life. He had now been in New York for a couple of months and, despite the rekindling of a physical relationship, had yet to cross the threshold into steady boyfriend territory. Something, at some point, had to give. He needed income. He needed to find a job if he was going to remain in the city—or, on the flip side, perhaps needed to move out and go back to his old life.

Something gave on a Tuesday morning when he met Amber at a coffee shop. When he walked in, she waved toward him and he went over and sat down. "I got you a coffee," she said, nodding toward the cup on the table, steam rising.

"What's up?" he asked, eager to get to the purpose of the meeting. Because make no mistake, that's what this was. Despite the several weeks of growing closer, the pretense was clear—"I have been crafting my upcoming schedule around all this Pulitzer madness and I would like to discuss it with you."

Amber leaned forward over her cup and held it with both hands. "My agent scheduled me a new tour, to re-promote my book with the reprinting of 'Pulitzer Prize Finalist' on the cover."

"Congratulations," Howard said plainly. "I hoped they were going to give you that distinction."

"Thanks." She looked away and then back into his eyes. "I'm going to be gone for a month, maybe more."

"A month? To promote a book that's been out for almost a year?"

"That's just how these things work."

Howard thought for a moment. "What comes after that?"

"I don't know, really. At some point I'm going to have to finish another book, that's part of the deal with my publisher."

"Are you still going to be living in New York?"

"That's my plan. When I'm here, at least."

Finally, Howard said what they'd been unwilling to say: "What does all this mean for us?"

Amber looked away again. She let the question hang in the air for longer than was comfortable. "Howard, I never expected you to move to New York."

"Oh."

"No, that's not what I'm saying. I never expected you to move here—it caught me completely by surprise—but I'm glad that you did. I have loved getting to know you better these couple of months."

"So have I." It was going slower than he'd hoped when he up-rooted his life and took a chance on them in New York, but still pleasant.

"I just can't give you a steady relationship right now. A few months ago, I never would have been able to picture how every-thing would change. I'm sorry."

"So...what? What does this mean? Just give it to me straight."

She took a deep breath. "If you are still in New York when I get back from the tour, I would be happy to get a drink. But I'd under-stand if I knocked on your door and your apartment was empty."

Howard felt a pain in his gut and he was paralyzed. After all he'd sacrificed. Amber stood from the table, kissed him on the cheek and walked out the door. Howard watched her dress swish in the wind and then disappear.

All of Howard's things fit neatly in the two bags that he'd brought them in, except for a small pile of books that he'd decided to leave on the kitchen table for the next tenant. Throughout the packing process, he didn't shed a single tear; he was closer to punching a hole through the wall. It was an animal-like emotion that overcame him—the risk he took, the progress that they'd made, the hope that she'd given him. He went out on a limb, felt the hand of safety, and then the branch broke and he tumbled to his demise.

He never said goodbye. Amber disappearing through the front door of the coffee shop was the last he'd seen her or talked to her.

Before leaving his apartment for the final time, he jotted down a simple note for her, on the off chance that it would find its way into her hands. He knew that would only happen if she were to come by soon after he left, for the landlord would likely fill the vacancy quickly.

Climbing into the driver's seat of a small Ford that he'd rented on the New Jersey side of the river, he gripped the wheel loosely, took a deep breath and thought to himself if he was making the biggest mistake of his life. But as he sat there, he replayed the coffee shop conversation in his mind—*this was her decision, not yours.* That's what he told himself. *For all you've given up, for all you've risked. This was her telling you no. Not the other way around. Don't confuse that. Put it in drive and go.*

Howard Lynch left New York City as suddenly as he'd arrived only a couple of months earlier. As the skyline faded into the distance behind him, he tried his best to turn the page on that chapter. *I may never see you again. Goodbye, old sport.*

Within hours, in the dwindling light of the evening, he saw a familiar highway sign and his memory led him toward it. Without realizing it, he was idling beside a creek in the hills of Pennsylvania. He sat there and stared out at the water trickling by. He could hear it click against the rocks, no single drop the same as that day so many years ago. He closed his eyes and tried to breathe the feeling from his lungs, his heartbeat, his limbs. He could still feel it. He didn't know what led him back to this spot. This water, so much that started that day. So much that has never ended. He wanted to get in, lie on his back and let the current carry him somewhere new. Maybe submerge himself and go away.

In the spring of 1983, it would have been easy for Howard to take his own life. Dying was easy. He didn't pity the dead. He envied them. It was the living that were stuck in hell.

11

Wolf Valley, 2002

In which Howard is 48 years old

Howard is sitting in his chair. He can feel the breakdown coming. His heart is racing and he stretches the collar of his shirt and presses his hand to his chest. The contrast is blatant: outside, chaos; inside, an eery calmness; and within himself, more chaos. Where there is darkness, the smallest sliver of light will thrive. Where there is a crack, water will find a way inside.

Within hours, the rising river makes its way to the foundation, then around the house to the front yard. And in what feels like an instant, in the house's darkness, Howard sees something out of the corner of his eye—movement. It's one of those moments that feels almost hallucinogenic, because there can't be anything there. When he turns his head, he sees nothing. But he doesn't turn back. Instead, he keeps his gaze across the room, staring blankly and using his periphery to detect motion.

That's when he sees the shimmer on the floor. It is subtle at first, nothing worth noticing. But it grows, and by the time Howard stands to walk over to it he can see the water coming in. He's not entirely sure where it's coming from—everywhere, it seems. There is already a thin layer covering nearly all of the kitchen floor and it's clear that it's rising. Coby runs over and splashes in it. When his paws feel the cold he jumps and then loses his mind—dashing and sliding around the kitchen.

"Hey, get over here!" Howard calls.

Coby freezes and looks at the man.

"Now!"

The dog relents, but with the same spirit he had splashing around, eager for the next move. Now it's time for Howard to freeze—*what the hell now?* It's late afternoon. The rain is still coming down in buckets. As he thinks about next moves, the water flows into the living room and it's now crossing the entire house. It's freezing. It's invasive. Any semblance of security is gone. He doesn't think about the regret of turning down Stu's offer because he has fully transitioned into survival mode.

The boat is their only chance.

Howard pulls on his waders and jacket and then packs his pockets with a few necessities: a water bottle, a knife, granola bars. He takes a deep breath. "Ready, bud?" Coby is looking up at him with an eager look that says, "I'm following you!" Just as Howard reaches for the doorknob, he pauses, thinks better of it. Then he looks out the front window. Despite the water at their feet inside, it is significantly higher outside. Opening the door will be opening the floodgate—literally. Knowing he just dodged a bullet, he heads to the side window with a plan to climb out, reach back for Coby, and then carry the dog as he wades to the boat. But as he looks out the window through the blowing rain, he stops dead.

The boat is gone.

Was it the wind? Did Howard not tie it up well enough? Surely someone couldn't have stolen it? This realization hits Howard hard. For several moments he just stares at the rippled water where the boat should be. But he knows, as painful as it is, he has to figure out a way to survive now. Fleeing is no longer an option.

There is only one place in the house that can get them away from the water—the attic. It's the last place Howard wants to go, but he knows his options are running out. First, he splashes his way into the bedroom and gathers blankets and pillows, and then he takes them to the pull-hatch and tosses them up. Then he heads for the pantry and grabs anything he can to sustain them—water bottles, snack nuts, canned soup, dog food. Just before heading up, he snatches a bowl for Coby. All of this has taken several minutes— pretty efficient gathering in Howard's mind, but when the water is rising all around you, any efficiency is too inefficient.

Coby's paws are soaked and he is shaking. Howard knows the ladder will be too treacherous for the dog, so he bends over and scoops him up two-handed and scales up to the attic. It's cold up there—years of inferior insulation going ignored. Howard always thought it could wait until the next season. Now it's just a new regret. Setting Coby down, he assesses the situation. Food, blankets. But what are they missing? Towels, Howard knows, because he has to dry Coby or he'll freeze. Candles and matches, too.

"Wait here, buddy," he says before climbing back down to retrieve the remaining supplies. His rubber boots keep the water from getting to his feet, but it is above his ankles now. The dog looks down from the attic and whimpers. When Howard returns, he wraps Coby's paws in small towels and then covers him in a blanket. He pours some water into a bowl and rubs his head. "Here you go, boy."

Fortunately, Amber was a candle person. Howard finds an entire box full of them—of various sizes and scents. Most of them are significantly melted, but there are a few new ones, too. He clears an area of the attic to rest, moving boxes and bins to the side, and then arranges the candles in a circle around them, lighting each with as few matches as possible. There is a window that looks out toward where the road used to be—it's all water now. The view is terrifying. A murky lake surrounds the house as far as Howard can see, cresting up to the bay windows of the neighbor across the street and reaching the bed of his pickup in the driveway. Worst of all, there is no sign of life. Howard takes a long breath and settles in for what he knows could be hours, days—or worse.

To Howard's surprise, the candles warm the space quickly. It's not quite a furnace or wood stove, but the relief is relative—and highly appreciated. Coby is lying on the wooden floorboards, still wrapped in the blanket, sleeping. Howard is curled up under a blanket as well, but he can't sleep. He is listening to the rain on the roof over their heads. Each drop sounds like it's going to strike him. If he closes his eyes, he can almost feel them soaking his blanket. Where he has positioned himself is deliberate: he has Coby by his side and a clear view through the window and down what used to be a street. He thinks the rain might be slowing, but he doesn't let himself believe it. That's a thought that can drive a man insane.

The sun would be nearly set now, but the clouds muffle its brilliance, instead casting a dull darkness over the valley, like God is turning down the dial on the day. In the faint distance, something sparkles on the water. Not the dimples of rain, but symmetrical, growing ripples. As Howard studies the darkened water, he suddenly sees a light. It flickers across the surface and then pans upward and sideways. It's moving side to side now, deliberately. From down the road, it finally comes into view: a boat. It nears and Howard can see there are two men aboard wearing reflective life jackets and peering about. They don't see him—with the rain and the wind and the darkening sky, they are looking for something to catch their eye, not merely movement. Movement is everywhere. Thrashing sounds are everywhere.

The dichotomy is alarming—the calmness of Coby sleeping in the attic, and yet the hope of rescue races Howard's heart. He startles to his feet and the peace is broken, because Coby is by his side as they peer out. This window has remained idle for decades—if it has ever been opened. Howard ensures the lock is unlatched and crouches for leverage, but it's jammed. He removes his hands, shakes them out, then lowers himself so that he is pushing upward with the full force of his body weight. He grunts. His right foot slips on the dusty floor but the window breaks free. Opening it the rest of the way strains him, rusty metal rubbing against rusty metal, warped wood against warped wood.

The act of opening the window is enough—that is exactly what the men in the boat are looking for. Howard leans out, waves and shouts, "Over here!" He sticks one leg outside, but his boot slips on the wet asphalt and he almost loses his balance completely. The boat is making its approach to the house and he instead decides it's best to remain where he is. Thoughts are now flooding his brain. Relief—someone to save them, for their options have all but run out; hope—that this will deliver them from this hell; regret—that he should never have put himself and Coby in this situation to begin with; anger—with God, mostly, and also with himself; exhaustion— that soon he can let go. It's the first time in days he has felt some of these emotions. Some, the first time in months.

He looks at Coby, who is trying to decide if he wants to jump up on the windowsill to look outside. "We're gonna make it, boy." A firm rub of the dog's head and down his back soothes him.

The boat is nearing the house now and Howard can see from his vantage point the terrifying reality that the men are not much below his own elevation. Perhaps only just beginning to relent, the rain is still falling and speckling the water around them. With a flick of his arm, Howard waves the men over, his legs inside the house but his upper body ducked and leaning outside.

"You okay, sir?" one of the men shouts through the rain.

Howard gives the okay sign with his hand. "We're gonna make it."

The man at the front of the boat is tall and thin, evident even through his rain jacket and vest. He's clean-cut and barely looks old enough to belly up to the bar. There's a rope in his hand and as the boat glides up to the house he slowly rises and puts out his arms to soften the impact. Then he uses his hands to walk the bow along the edge of the roof until he gets to a spot along the gutter where he ties up. For a moment Howard thinks that that gutter won't hold and that the current could rip it right from the house, but then he quickly understands that this isn't an operation to avoid damage to a drowning house.

The second man, the one in the rear and steering, is barrel-chested with a handlebar mustache. The hood on his jacket is barely covering his head, which is shaved on both sides and long on top. *There must also be some tattoos under there*, Howard thinks. This is the man whose deep voice bellows, "Just you in there?"

Howard is already climbing out of the dormer window for the roof, more carefully this time. He steadies himself on the sloped surface and then reaches back to gather Coby. "Me and the dog," he says over his shoulder, trying to out-shout the rain. Coby hops his front paws up on the windowsill and Howard grabs him around his body and pulls him out like a toddler.

"Sir!" the mustached man shouts.

Howard can hear the urgency in his voice. He squints through the rain, trying to make out the expression on his face. Coby is shaking and still wet from earlier.

"Are there any other humans inside?" the man asks.

"Just me and the dog," Howard repeats.

Before he can take a step, the man says, "The dog stays."

It's a cold command that freezes Howard in place. "Just me and the dog," Howard says again, as if the man didn't hear him the first two times. "I can't leave him."

The other man, the first man, the skinny one, is remaining silent. Howard glances in his direction and the look he sees on the man's face says that he's seen this movie before and is terrified of the ending. "Sir, this boat is heading back to the shelter set up at the community center," Mr. Mustache says through a strained voice. He is trying to offer a stern command without shouting but the environment makes him toe that line. "This boat is instructed only to retrieve humans. Put the dog back inside and come with us."

Howard is still frozen in place. He's not leaving Coby. But he also knows that this may be their only chance at rescue for days. "I can't leave the dog," he tries to say calmly and then bends his knees to better balance as he starts down the roof.

Just then the man pulls a pistol from under his jacket. "Sir, I will not tell you again."

Howard's heart might explode.

"The dog is going back inside that house," the man continues, the pistol trained directly at Howard's chest. "The only question is whether you're going back inside with him."

For what feels like minutes, Howard just stands there staring down the man's barrel. The first feeling is rage—not fear, though that will come. He's being asked to make the impossible decision. Leave a helpless, vulnerable animal in a flooded house to survive on his own, or remain behind with him and risk his own survival. It's the second time he's been faced with this unanswerable question. He knew the answer the first time but chose the alternative anyway, a sliver of hope persuading him. He knows now that that choice would have killed Coby because he never dreamt his home would flood the way it has. His fear now is that the same fate will prevail— he saves himself at the peril of his friend. The dog that Amber brought home. One of the few things he has left in this world that seems to matter. *But nothing matters if you die in the process*, he thinks.

Finally, without saying a word, he turns back toward the house and slowly sets Coby inside the window. The candles are still burning and he wonders if he should blow them out. He also knows his own pistol is tucked under one of the blankets. He considers climbing back inside for it, putting a bullet in the man's head and taking Coby to safety. Instead, he lowers the window. Coby is on the other side, one paw on the sill and another on the glass. Through the window Howard can hear that familiar whimper, the one that used to annoy him because he didn't want to help; now he couldn't.

He turns back to the man, who has replaced the gun in its holster. "No dog," Howard says slowly, his voice shaking, and then descends the roof. The skinny man extends a hand for help but Howard refuses it, instead scooting to the edge of the roof and hopping the foot or so down into the boat.

"Good decision," the skinny man whispers so only Howard can hear.

"When can I come back for him?"

The mustached man pans from the back of the boat, "When this rain finally stops for good."

As they push off from the house and the boat pivots to head back where it came from, Howard finds the courage to let his eyes land on the window. Coby is there, staring. Then barking, shuffling his paws from one side to the other. His bark is loud and his head lurches backward with each cry. He's telling Howard that he made the wrong choice. He's telling him that he can't survive without him.

It's a bark of betrayal. It's a feeling Howard already knows.

He tortures himself by watching Coby fade away, the distance and darkness two sinister evils, until he's left with regret, his most familiar hell.

12

Detroit, 1990

In which Howard was 36 years old

Howard had to wear a sweatshirt while mowing the lawn this time of year, but he didn't mind it. The sun was still shining and there were worse things. He knew better than most.

As he headed back toward his garage he saw his neighbor, Frank, step out his side door.

"Frank!" Howard shouted as he raised his sunglasses on top of his head. "Frank, can I ask you a favor?"

A rugged man with heavy arms and a permanent sneer on his face, Frank was a very particular person with a very particular set of skills. "What can I do for ya?"

"Hey, you still got that chipmunk trap?"

"Of course. You having a problem?"

"A problem, you could say that. Misty was walking into the garage this morning and a squirrel jumped on her damn shoulder. Scared her half to death. Think it's living in there."

Frank looked shocked for a moment and then burst out laughing. "Jesus, man. You gotta kill that fuckin' thing. Let me grab the trap for ya."

Howard rolled his lawnmower back around into his garage and then inspected the space while waiting for Frank, who walked in shortly after carrying a small wired cage.

"Here ya go," Frank said. He gave Howard a quick tutorial on how to use it and then asked where he wanted it set up.

"I'm thinking over here." Howard crouched down near the corner of the garage door. There was a strip of weather seal missing from the bottom edge and he suspected the squirrel was squeezing in through the gap.

After Frank set up the trap and poured a pile of seeds in the middle, Howard gestured over to a fireplace that stood between the garage and the breezeway on the other side of the wall. Howard stepped onto a small ladder and hidden behind the top of the chimney block were several small holes that the squirrel had chewed in the paneling. "I think this thing has been nesting in the ceiling of the breezeway."

"Ah, you've got shit luck, if that's the case."

"Why's that?"

"You probably got a whole litter living in there."

"Seriously?"

"About all you can do is trap 'em and kill 'em."

"How do I do that?"

"Well," Frank said, then put his hands on his hips and looked around. "Trapping's the easy part. You'll have a squirrel in that thing by tonight. Then you take your pick. Hammer works. Or fill that wheelbarrow with some water and just—" He made a plop sound, acting out dropping the trap into the water. "Or, there's always poison, but that can take a while—and be nasty."

Without much thought, Howard said, "I think I would drown them." As he said it, he felt a twist in his gut. No, it would need to be something else—poison, maybe—but he'd decide that later.

"Good man. Well, let me know if you need any more seeds." Frank turned and left the garage.

Late that evening, Howard went out into the garage and heard the metal of the cage rattle. He lifted the large stepping stone from the top that he'd used to keep it in place and saw a full-grown red squirrel inside. Without the weight of the stone, the squirrel's thrashing inside left the cage nudging across the pavement. Howard put his boot on top and then crouched down and looked closely at the animal. He expected to feel animosity. Instead, something different. It was terrified. It was alone. If it was a mom, it was probably petrified that something would happen to her babies. This all flashed through Howard's mind and suddenly the brash toughness that he'd espoused earlier vanished. He knew he couldn't kill this creature. Knowing releasing it nearby would lead back to square one, he lifted the cage into the bed of his truck, drove about 20 minutes into the darkness of the country, out well past where the suburbs ended, and pulled off to the side of a dirt road. In the bright of his headlights, he opened the cage and watched the squirrel dart for the woods.

When Howard returned, he set the trap back up just to be safe, but the moment he stepped from the garage to the breezeway he could hear scurrying overhead. Baby squirrels. His fear, what he'd tried to convince himself was unlikely though obviously the opposite was true. He'd orphaned squirrel babies. When he crawled into bed that night, Misty kissed him on the cheek and said, "How'd it go?"

"Got the mom," he told her. "But there's more."

"Oh. What are you gonna do about those?"

"I don't know. Hope they come out tomorrow, I guess. Or I'm going to have to figure out a way to scoop dead squirrel babies out of the ceiling."

"What a mess." She kissed him again and then rolled over. "Thanks for taking care of that."

Howard lay there staring at the ceiling fan. He felt evil.

The next morning Howard checked the trap but it was empty. He wrestled with the moral crisis the rest of the day, spiraling between *you're a monster* and then *it's just a damn squirrel*—until Misty got home from work and said, "You caught one."

Howard flew out the door and into the garage, flattening himself to the pavement to see under the stepping stone. It wasn't one squirrel—it was three. And they didn't look so much like babies as they looked like adolescents. A wave of relief overcame him. *Thank God.*

Once again, he decided he'd relocate them that night in the darkness, as close as possible to where he let the mom go. When the time came, he went to retrieve the trap, removed the stone and saw a chaotic mess of furry movement. *Wait a minute.* He counted as best he could. One. Two. Wait. There were five in there now. He felt even more relieved than before and headed out into the country. When he returned, he set the trap up again but prayed he wouldn't catch anything. The next morning, nothing. Thankfully. So he replaced the rubber weather stripping on the bottom of the garage door and sealed the holes in the wall by the chimney, hoping that his squirrel problem was over, feeling grateful for sparing their lives.

On his drive to work the next morning, he felt a sluggishness in his truck and it was making a sound he hadn't heard before. Instead of driving to the work site, he pulled into a mechanic garage in town and had them inspect it. He called his boss from a payphone and told him he'd be on his way as soon as he got the "all clear" on his truck.

A man in a greasy blue jumpsuit came out and waved Howard back with him. The smell of oil and exhaust went straight to

Howard's head, but he followed the man to where his truck was hoisted.

"See this," the man said, pointing up under the engine.

Howard looked. Some wires looked frayed. "What am I looking at?"

"You like to feed birds? Or you have a mouse problem that you know of?"

"Not exactly," Howard said.

"But you got some kind of problem, I can see it on your face," said the mechanic. "Look, when I bring the truck down, you're gonna see a whole lot more damage like this under the hood. You got yourself a rodent problem."

You're telling me. If any of those squirrels somehow made it back to his garage, he swore he'd fill up the wheelbarrow.

Howard found his house in a newspaper ad a few years earlier. It wasn't anything to write home about, but it had a one-car attached garage, a little yard and a finished basement. He and Misty shared a bedroom in the back of the house, and then he had the second bedroom set up with a small TV, a couch and a bookshelf of all his favorites. Despite having the basement and the living room, he felt that he needed a room with a door where he could escape.

The room also had a small writing desk. By no means was he writing fiction or any kind of lengthy prose, but a few years earlier as a coping mechanism he took up journaling. When Howard returned with his newly-fixed truck, he went straight into that room, sat at his desk, scribbled his frustration with those damn squirrels, and then dropped the pen and sat back. He opened a drawer and pulled out a thick envelope and set it on the desk. He stared at it. It was thinner than it used to be. It was going in the wrong direction. A week ago, he was ready to go to the jeweler, but the truck set him back. *Those goddamn squirrels.* It would probably be another month or two.

He went into the kitchen and took a beer from the fridge. Misty walked through the door. "How's the truck?"

Howard forgot for a moment that he'd called her at work that morning to tell her about the issues. "Fixed, I suppose. Wasn't cheap though."

She stopped dead and looked at him. "How much?"

"A lot."

"How much, Howard?"

"$925."

"Shit." She opened the fridge and grabbed herself a beer as well. "Do we even have that kind of money?"

"I scraped it together." He didn't think she knew about his savings, but he had a hunch she was expecting a proposal soon. She could do the math on how this situation would impact her prospects. He watched her concerned expression. She was leaning against the cabinet with her hand on her hip. She wore a baggy golf shirt tucked into beige pants—an unflattering look for a woman as tall and thin as her, but then Howard never understood fashion anyway. "Come here," he finally said to her, putting his hands gently around her waist and pulling her close. "We'll be fine." Then he kissed her.

Misty was wild. She liked to get rowdy on Friday nights and had a hot streak that landed her in the back of a cruiser not once but twice. She made Howard laugh and she made him comfortable with being uncomfortable. But perhaps best of all, she understood who he was and what made him tick. That's why, when he was down from the squirrel saga, she surprised him with tickets to a local art theater.

"Where are we going?" he asked as he buttoned his favorite shirt. It was black with a subtle pattern and it itched a bit in the collar, but he wore it on nights like this because he liked the way he looked.

"You'll see."

He threw on a light jacket and they headed toward Royal Oak and parked downtown, and as they rounded a corner onto Main Street Howard saw a small line gathered outside an art theater. "What is this?"

Misty just smiled, took his arm and pulled him forward. The playbill encased in glass on the sidewalk advertised Preston Guy reading from his new book titled *With the Wind the Way* and being interviewed by a local journalist named Sandy Herron.

"Who the heck is Preston Guy?" Howard said in jest, and a mortified Misty shushed him and pulled the tickets from her pocket. In reality, Howard knew exactly who Guy was and had read three of his books over the years.

The theater, which had a few hundred seats, was about a quarter full when they arrived. They sat about fifteen rows back, right on the end, and watched patrons fill in around them until nearly half the seats were taken. It had an ornate ceiling and heavy curtains that hung on each side of a low stage. Directly in front of them sat an older woman with short, gray, curly hair, and Howard could smell what was surely the scent of her house wafting his direction. As the lights overhead dimmed, spotlights lit up the stage, revealing two chairs and a coffee table. They watched an older white man, whom they knew as Guy, and a middle-aged black woman, Herron, enter the stage, wave to the audience, and then take seats.

After some quick banter, they jumped right into the interview. Howard looked around the room and marveled at the fact that not a single other person looked like him. The audience was primarily older and heavily female. There weren't many blue-collar, 36-year-old men in the crowd. But Howard was comfortable with that fact. Being bookish was the one thing that made him different and he learned to embrace it years ago.

As Guy and Herron went on, a stagehand ran out from the side and hustled a third chair beside them. The audience gasped and then Herron said tongue-in-cheek, "What could be happening here?" while Guy added, "Do we have a surprise guest?"

Both knew what was happening and, in contrast to the two people already on stage, out walked a younger woman with dark hair and a flowy dress. The crowd clapped and some rose to their feet. Howard knew the second he laid eyes on her who she was: Amber McNamara. From his vantage point, she hadn't aged a day—even though she was now around 30. She had the same smile, the same charisma, the same frame and the same effect on Howard. His heart rate spiked. He felt a warm sensation under his arms. He fanned his shirt as calmly as he could.

"Folks," Herron said as she stood to greet Amber. "Please welcome our surprise guest, a Michigan native, Pulitzer Prize Finalist and the author of two New York Times Bestsellers, Ms. Amber McNamara."

The crowd rose to their feet in applause. Howard remained seated, tunnel vision trained on Amber, as Misty joined the rest in standing and clapping. She looked down at Howard and motioned with her head for him to stand but he didn't see her. When the audience sat back down, Misty took Howard by the arm and whispered, "You okay?"

It snapped him from his trance and he said, "Yeah, sure. Sorry. I'm okay."

"This is a neat twist, huh?"

He said nothing.

Sitting in the third chair, Amber joined the conversation on stage, first by complimenting Guy over and over about his newest release, and then the conversation—toward the end but before Guy stood to read a passage—turned briefly to Amber's works. She discussed her first book, *The Empty Hills of History*, the one that put her on the map, as well as the inspiration for her second novel, *A Stranger on Charles Street*, about a man who shows up in New York City to confront a long lost love.

"Let me just say what a treat it is for all of us to have you as a surprise guest tonight," Herron said to Amber. "Tell me, would you call *A Stranger on Charles Street* first and foremost a love story?"

Without hesitation, Amber said, "Isn't life one big love story?"

"What inspired you to write this particular story? Where were you when the inspiration struck?"

"I'd be lying if I didn't say it was semi-autobiographical. I suppose I'm a bit like Hemingway in that sense. 'Write what you know,' isn't that what they're always saying? I don't want to dig too far into it, for personal reasons, but this story is very close to my heart. I'm just happy that I was able to share it with all of you." She looked out at the crowd and Howard thought for a moment that she was looking right at him.

When Guy stood at the lectern to read from his book, Amber sat on the stage and the look on her face was unsettled. Howard could see it clearly from his seat in the back. She had won awards, made money, received acclaim—and yet...

When the event ended, both Guy and Amber sat behind small tables in the lobby with a stack of their books and signed copies for guests. Nary a guest left without at least one book tucked under their arm. As most of the audience left for the signing, Howard and Misty initially remained in their seats. They eventually made their way to the lobby to join the rest of the patrons, but Misty could tell something was off.

"Can I buy you a signed copy?" she asked.

He shook his head. "Let's just go," he said.

She tugged his arm. "Howard. I bought these tickets because I thought you'd enjoy this. It seemed like a great event. You have to tell me what's wrong."

"Nothing is wrong," he said, and then kissed her on the forehead. "This was great. Should we go get a cocktail?"

They stepped onto the sidewalk and night had fallen in the time they were inside. People bustled about, mostly headed to dinner and other evening plans. The theater let out in front of a busy intersection that led into the heart of the downtown strip. But Howard's head was spinning. He felt the chill in the air and realized he had left his jacket inside the theater.

"Shit."

"What?"

"I'll be right back," he said.

He left Misty standing in front of the marquee and went back inside. Most of the lobby had cleared by this time. Guy was still signing books for his last few fans and Amber was standing off to the side talking with a couple people. Howard slipped through the room and back into the theater. His jacket was bunched up in his chair and he grabbed it and slipped it on, but when he turned to head back to the lobby he froze because he was face to face with his past.

Amber stood still. Her hands were folded in front of her, her posture straight. They were the only two in the empty theater. Yet it didn't feel empty, not in this moment. It felt like thousands of eyes were trained right on Howard.

"Howard."

"Amber, it's nice to see you," he said, although he couldn't feel the words leaving his lips. There was so much to say. So much that had gone unsaid over the years. He was flashing back to that day in the coffee shop in New York, to packing up the apartment and leaving town.

"Howard," she said again, more delicately this time. She took a step forward and embraced him, and then pulled away but kept her hands on his arms for a moment. "It really is. What are the odds?"

He didn't know what to say.

My girlfriend bought me these tickets.

She's waiting for me outside.

What the hell have you been up to for the last seven years?

Why didn't you ever call or write?

Where are you living now?

Are you dating anyone?

Why did you break my heart?

I love you.

He said nothing.

"Listen, I know there are probably a million things running through your mind right now," she said. "I feel the same way. You think we could get coffee this week, while I'm in town?"

I have a girlfriend.
She's waiting outside.
She bought me these tickets.
You broke my heart.
"Howard?"
"Saturday morning work?"
She smiled. "Saturday is perfect."

Howard spent the next day and a half grappling with the lie that he was going to tell Misty. He was meeting an old friend—that wasn't a lie, actually, not technically. They hadn't spoken for years. He might even use Willy's name—that was the lie—knowing that he was long gone and likely wouldn't be showing up in his life anytime soon to spoil it.

What Howard really needed to grapple with was not what he was telling Misty. Rather, it was the lie he was telling himself—that he didn't have feelings for Amber anymore, that meeting with her was a courtesy for old time's sake. It was a lie, he hoped, that he would force himself to believe if he thought about it frequently and deeply enough.

That Saturday was like any other in the mid-fall in the Midwest: leaves had begun changing colors and littering lawns, shades of orange and yellow and red sprinkled throughout the green overhead. A chill in the air, not enough for a coat, but enough that you couldn't leave home without long sleeves. The sun shined more than people who weren't from the region would believe, and the misbalance of sunglasses and the biting breeze was somehow the most comfortable feeling of any season. As Fitzgerald said, sometimes life starts new in the fall.

When he first stepped outside, he took a deep breath of crisp air and closed his eyes, and when he was standing outside the coffee shop he did it once more, reminding himself of his life one final time before he grabbed the cold metal door handle and pushed. In that instant, he heard, "Hey."

He released the handle and turned to see Amber walking up. Before he could even get a look at her she threw herself into his chest and hugged him tightly.

"Howard," she said softly as she pulled away. She looked like she was trying to gather her thoughts for the right thing to say. Her eyes were a bit glassy and her face flushed.

"Hey," he said. "It's okay."

She smiled sweetly and nodded.

"It's really good to see you again. Let's go inside and get coffee." He pushed the door open and held it for her.

They found a table in the back corner near a fireplace. Amber had her latte and Howard his black coffee, and for the first minute or so they sat there in silence looking around the room and then glancing at one another. Finally, Howard said, "So, two bestsellers now?"

"Mhmm," she nodded. "I keep getting lucky."

"You don't write a bestseller from luck. And you sure as shit don't do it twice. You're really talented, always have been."

"Have you read my second one?"

"I have."

She looked like she was waiting for his verdict but didn't want to outright ask.

"And it was brilliant."

She smiled.

"A little sad, though," he added. "The guy didn't get the girl."

"Well, perhaps it's not that he didn't get her. Perhaps it's just that he didn't get her *yet*."

"Are you saving that for the sequel?"

She shrugged, a little sheepish. "I only ever talk about myself and my books. Tell me, what have you been up to? It's been, what, seven years? Feels like a lifetime."

"A lot has happened in those seven years." He went on to tell her about everything that transpired since that day in the New York

City coffee shop. How he drove through his childhood town, about coming back to Detroit and begging Lester Pitford for his old job back, about moving from one apartment to another before settling in his current house. And, finally, about Misty—how they met, their current status. He didn't use her name. He just said he'd "met a girl" that he'd been dating.

"How serious is it?"

Howard shrugged and sipped his coffee. "I don't know, it has its moments, I suppose."

"Has its moments," she repeated. "Howard, what does that mean? Really, truly, I am interested and want to know."

He stared at her. He knew the truth. The truth was the simplest thing: he was days from buying a ring until his financial setback, but his plan to buy the ring hadn't changed. At least not until the other night when Amber walked back into his life. She was about the only thing that could change his mind. She'd always been the only thing that could do that. But he didn't want to say that to her. His scar wouldn't let him. "Well," he said slowly to buy more time. Then he gathered his thoughts and said, "She lives in my house with me. We have been dating for about two years." He stopped there, and it felt abrupt, even to him.

"And? Is that it?"

"And that's it."

Amber leaned forward and said, "Howard, let me tell you what I've been doing for the last seven years. I did the things I told you in that coffee shop all those years ago. I went on book tours. I sold a lot of copies and had an interesting time traveling the country. Then I went back to New York and spent many lonely nights writing in the dark. Eventually, I sold my second book and then did it all over again with the tour and the signings. And it's all great—it's certainly the career I always wanted. But it's not the *life* I've always wanted. I haven't kissed a man. Heck, I haven't even been on a single date." She stopped talking and a faint red appeared on her face and she looked away.

Howard reached across the table and set his hand on hers. A tear appeared in her eye and it fell when she blinked.

"Here I am all 'woe is me' when I got everything I asked for," she said through a sniffle.

In a measured voice, Howard said, "Amber, tell me what you want."

She blinked another tear and then looked around the room. "This is getting too dramatic for a public coffee shop," she said through an embarrassed smile.

He waited.

"I don't know if..."

"Amber. Seven years ago, we sat in a coffee shop after I had given up my life here to be with you in New York, and you chose your career over me. Now—impossibly—you showed up in my town and you asked for this conversation and I was willing to have it with you, but you need to tell me exactly what it is that you want."

A light chorus of background music played in the room and the steady hum of other patrons gave them the illusion of privacy. Amber looked like she had what she wanted to say. It was sitting there on the tip of her tongue, but she refused to let it escape. Sending it out into the world would make it real.

Howard gave her plenty of time to respond. He waited patiently as she looked around, looked down, took another drink of her coffee—anything but make eye contact. Eventually, he exhaled, picked up his coffee and stood.

Amber grabbed his sleeve and he stopped. "Please," she said, and he sat back down. "Howard, you are the only person I've ever been with. And, honestly, I don't have any interest in being with anyone else."

"I need you to be clear about what you're saying right now."

"I'm saying that I want to give it another try. I know I blew my chance, I know I don't deserve another one. I've just spent the last seven years regretting walking out of that coffee shop. I wish desperately that I could go back to that moment."

Those were the words. Howard had heard them in his dreams. He recited them to himself in his mind. For years all he wanted was Amber back. But then he moved on—or thought he had. He went through a series of flings. He met Misty. He decided to settle down with her. And now the words finally come. However, rather than the elation he would have expected, he felt butterflies in his gut and he began to realize that it was the feeling of anger. Anger at the missed years, the missed memories, the regret. "That doesn't seem entirely fair. You're saying you want to unpause our past and pick it back up from where we left off?"

"I know it's not fair and that's not what I'm saying. I know you have a girlfriend now. You have every right to tell me to get lost, and I'll walk out of this coffee shop and we'll pretend this conversation never happened."

"You know that's not what I meant."

"But if there is even a part of you that is willing to keep this conversation going... That's all I'm asking."

"This conversation," he repeated as a stall tactic. "This conversation." He looked around the room and then closed his eyes. At that moment he wasn't thinking about Misty. He wasn't thinking about his job or this new life he had going. He was thinking back to the last coffee shop that he sat in with Amber, about what this was and could have been. But he also let himself glimpse the future, if ever briefly. "Can I have your number?"

She lit up. "Yes, here." She dug through a small purse and pulled out a pen and a notepad, scribbling her number and tearing off the page to hand over.

He took the paper, looked at it and said, "616?"

"I'm back in Holland."

"No more New York?"

"No more New York. If you want to talk again, I'd be happy to make the drive."

Howard smiled and finished his coffee.

One week later, Howard found himself sitting on the stool of a local bar holding a small glass of whiskey. In his hand, he was staring at the slip of paper that Amber had handed him. He ordered another drink and sipped it slowly, not talking to anyone else and not doing anything but staring at the number. He had long since memorized it. Then he finished the drink in one gulp.

After the bar, when the sun was setting, he pulled up his jacket tight to his neck and walked the half-mile or so from town to his house. This time of year went beyond just a chill once the sun disappeared. Misty wasn't home so he grabbed a beer and a cigar and went out to the back patio and lit it up. He stared into the empty sky and watched the smoke leave his mouth. He thought maybe some of it was his breath as well. It was mesmerizing. Fall in Michigan was one of a kind.

The sliding door opened and Misty poked her head outside. "What are you doing out here?"

"I didn't think you were home."

"I just got home. Still, it's freezing out here."

Howard relaxed and took another puff from the cigar. "I like it."

For a moment, Misty was gone and then she stepped outside in slippers and a robe and closed the door behind her. She sat beside Howard and said, "What's going on with you?"

"What do you mean?"

"I don't know, you've just been acting weird since we went to that book event," she said, resting her head on his shoulder.

Even through the strength of the cigar and the beer he could smell her sweet perfume, the one that he always loved. "I'm fine." He looked at her and she looked up at him without removing her head from his shoulder. "Honest, I'm fine."

She let that hang in the air and then said, "Okay, then. Good." And she stood and went back inside.

Immediately, he also stood, chugged the rest of his beer, and then he walked around the side of the garage, down the street and up to a nearby convenience store. When he got there, he crushed out the nub of the cigar and tossed it in the parking lot. His quarter scratched the metal slot as he slid it into the payphone. He dialed the number without looking at the paper.

It rang. And rang. And rang. Finally: "Hello?"

"I want to see you again."

"Howard?"

"I want to see you again."

"Where are you right now?"

"I'm at a payphone. I want to see you again. When can I see you?"

"Good, good. I mean, I'm flattered. Just—are you okay?"

"I'm okay, yes. When can I see you?"

"Well," she paused to think. "I have a book signing at an event in Howell tomorrow morning. Do you know where that is? I think it's about halfway between Holland and you."

"Howell, got it. I'll be there."

"Wait," she laughed, "you need more details than that."

"Oh, right."

She told him where the event was, what it was called and what time it would be appropriate for him to show up. She ended with, "And Howard? I appreciate you calling me. I understand calling from your house might have been difficult."

"I'll see you tomorrow." He hung up the phone and walked back to the bar.

As his truck idled in the parking lot, he watched the wipers skim away the fog that continuously reappeared on the windshield. Although the event didn't start until 10, he slipped out of bed before dawn, dressed and left the house without Misty waking. He hadn't even had the courage to lie to her. He just left. Now he waited on the promise of a blue sky to burn away the fog and dry the glass.

Steam rose from his cup and he blew on it and sipped, blew on it and sipped, blew on it and sipped. It was the only way he could think to sober up. In truth, he hadn't slept but a few winks. He was nervous. And he was excited. But mostly nervous.

From his car, the engine long turned off, he sat and watched as people began arriving. The event was at an indoor market set up in the large gathering space on the main floor of the old Opera House, which had long since been used for many things, none of them opera. He was a block away and felt both embarrassed and creepy.

Throughout the morning, he saw more people coming than going. A sizable crowd had gathered inside that Howard could see through the large glass windows along the front of the building. Finally, he saw a woman who looked like Amber meet a man on the sidewalk, watched them shake hands, and then she was escorted in the side door. That's when Howard climbed from his truck and slipped in the front door and hung in the back of the room. For a historic building, it looked newly renovated, with high ceilings, fresh hardwood floors and exposed brick along the two side walls.

Amber took a seat behind a table on the opposite wall from Howard and the crowd naturally filled in around her. He watched her glance around the room and he thought she was looking for him as subtly as she could manage. The chorus of voices quieted to a whisper and then she stood and made a few charismatic opening remarks before returning to her chair. Stacked in front of her were copies of each of her two books and a large sign hung behind her with a larger-than-life photo promoting the signing for the critically-acclaimed Michigan author.

As people moved through a line, Howard watched them make small-talk with Amber, take photos with her, get their books signed. She was a real-life celebrity, he was starting to realize. He felt his face get warm and for a moment thought that this was a major mistake, that he shouldn't be there, that he had no business being with a girl like Amber—beautiful, talented, could have any man she could possibly want.

The morning wore on and the crowd slowly shrunk. As it did, Howard's position became less concealed and that's when Amber finally glanced up and noticed him standing there. She smiled with her eyes and his nervousness went away in an instant and all that remained was excitement.

By the end of the event, he pushed from the wall he was leaning against and walked up to the table. With a smirk he said, "Ms. Mc-Namara," and then held out his hand. "Big fan. Huge fan."

She took a book from the remaining lot, signed it *To my biggest fan* and then handed it to him and said, "Now you have to buy it," with a smirk of her own.

"Gladly." He paid the man a table over who was sitting in front of a cash box. "Is this wrapping up?"

The man looked at Howard and then over to Amber, who had stood and had her hands on her hips. "She's all yours," he said.

Outside the Opera House, they walked side by side down the sidewalk. Any remaining clouds had drifted away and the sun shone brightly. People were out and about, but it certainly wasn't a busy town like Royal Oak; it was even a little quieter than Holland. They matched each other's stride and Howard was acutely aware of their hands nearly brushing as they walked. He wanted so badly to take hers in his but he refrained.

"So," he said.

"So. Thanks for coming out here. I know it's just another little town along Grand River but I've been here once before and it's charming."

They continued walking and eventually came to a large lawn with a beautiful, historic courthouse set back upon it, overlooking the main drag.

"Yeah, seems like it," Howard agreed.

For all the history they had—for the night in Holland all those years ago, for the months in New York, for the other day at the theater and coffee shop—words just felt impossible to come by for Howard at this moment, and clearly the same was happening to Amber. There were benches out front of the courthouse and she sat on one and he joined her. From the shade of the building, they looked out at the lawn and at the occasional passerby.

Turning to face Amber, Howard finally said, "Can I just be honest with you?"

"Please."

"From the night we first met, I spent five years thinking about you each and every day. Truly. But you broke my heart in New York, and then I spent the last seven years trying to forget about you."

A painful look came over Amber's face.

"It didn't work, of course," he continued. "But I did my best. And now you're here again, and I really just don't know what to think. You're saying you want to be with me again. And Amber—that's all I wanted to hear from you. The best thing in the world. But it scares the shit out of me right now—if I'm being honest."

"I understand, Howard," she said, resting her hand on his. "I completely do. And I'm sorry. God, I'll tell you that every day that you let me be with you if that's what brings us together. I'm sorry. I made a massive mistake."

It was nice to hear, but it somehow didn't solve the problem. He looked down and tightened his eyelids, trying to think. But then he felt her come close and her lips pressed lightly against his cheek and he turned his head slightly, eyes still closed, and met her lips with his. When they pulled apart he opened his eyes and she was staring back at him, so much hope on her face, the same feeling he had in his heart.

They sat for a little while longer in silence, just listening to the breeze and the birds and the cars. Then: "Excuse me? Pardon me, I'm sorry."

The voice came from a young woman who had walked up without either of them noticing. She had two little kids in tow.

"Hello," Amber said.

"I'm so sorry to bother you, but are you Amber McNamara?"

Amber looked at the woman, and as if she didn't have a care in the world, said, "That's me."

"I thought I recognized you! Sorry for the excitement, but I'm a huge fan. Both of your books are incredible. I was so bummed I missed the event this morning, I couldn't seem to get these two dressed and out the door."

"No trouble at all. It's very nice to meet you. And thank you for such kind words about my books, I'm really glad you enjoyed them." Amber turned her gaze to the children. "And who are these two little ones?"

"This is Oscar, who's five, and Laney, who just turned three."

"You don't look old enough to have a five-year-old," Amber said before returning her eyes to the kids. She didn't see the embarrassed look on the woman's face when she said that, but Howard did. He also noticed she wasn't wearing a wedding ring. "Are you two having a fun day and behaving for your mother?"

The children shyly wrapped their arms around their mom's legs and didn't say anything, but nodded.

Amber stood and said, "Sweet kids."

Howard was still sitting on the bench just taking it all in. He had never seen that side of Amber, delicate, nurturing, soft with little ones. It was like an epiphany. He wasn't just infatuated with this woman. She could truly be someone he could share his life with.

"You're sweet," the woman said to Amber. "Well, we won't take up any more of your time. It was such a pleasure to meet you. Enjoy our little town."

They watched the small family walk back across the courthouse lawn. The further away they got, the more animated the kids became, bouncing and tugging and running and laughing. It was beautiful.

Amber sat back down beside Howard. She opened her mouth to say something but he spoke first. "Okay."

"Okay?"

"Okay," he said again. "Okay." And then he smiled at her and they kissed.

"Okay," she repeated, a little more energy in her voice.

"Okay."

"Okay!" she shouted through glassy eyes.

But as they kissed a third time, the excitement began to dissipate and when she pulled away he could see a look of concern wash over her in an instant.

"What is it?"

"Well," she said softly. "It's not nothing, but it's not anything groundbreaking."

"Just tell me."

"I am going to a place called Wolf Valley next week. That's the plan anyway."

"Oh. Where the hell is that and why are you going? And, more importantly, can you just, uh, not?"

"I'm going there to work on my next book," she said. "It's kind of in the middle of nowhere. I'm so sorry. I should have brought this up sooner, but honestly, I didn't think you'd want anything to do with me so I didn't even think about it." When Howard didn't say anything, she added, "Come with me."

He looked at her.

"I'm sorry," she said again, and then stood and paced the grass. "I knew the second it came out of my mouth that it wasn't fair to ask you that. You've already—"

"Okay," he said.

That caught her by surprise.

"Okay?" The scared tears edging her eyes turned into happy tears.

"Okay."

He grinned and walked over to her, leaned in and kissed her again. The middle of nowhere sounded like paradise.

13

Wolf Valley, 2002

In which Howard is 48 years old

The skinny man is holding a high-beam flashlight in his right hand, shining it parallel to the water and toward houses and buildings and out into the abyss. But they don't see anyone. Howard is shaking, both from anger and the cold rain. And, of course, guilt. The image of Coby sitting in the window, the look on his face, the pain and desperation in his bark—that is burned into Howard's mind. It's all he can see. A living nightmare.

Out on the water—what used to be streets—Howard tries to shake his concentration from one tragedy to another. His eyes are now being diverted across a black, sometimes reflective, expanse. This is the first he can see the damage that has unfolded across the community. Sure, he knew how bad it was near his house, but something about it—perhaps the river, perhaps the ignorance—felt personal and local, like he was the only person being tortured. But the damage spreads much further than that. Entire houses are swallowed in the flood. Rooflines poke through the surface as if begging for air. At first, Howard is so stunned by the sight that he doesn't quite realize what this all means. But then he thinks about being trapped in that attic with Coby. Without this boat, he would still be there. There are other people trapped in attics, alone or with family or pets. Or worse. When time washes these waters out of this valley, it will reveal the true damage, something that can only be imagined in the darkest corners of minds.

As the boat trickles through the rural community and makes its way toward the town, the rain begins to slow—as if being taunted from above—and throughout the ride, as quickly as the storm came upon them, the drops slow until Howard stares at his arms and doesn't see a single new splatter. They are heading back in the same direction from where the boat originally came.

The sounds of the engine and the small wake are all they hear until the barrel-chested man finally says to Howard, "Don't know what all the resentment is, we just saved yer life."

Howard lets the comment sink in. He is trying to restrain himself. He is trying to be the bigger man. He is trying to be positive and convince his mind to switch into survival mode—and stay there this time. *You can't help Coby if you're dead.*

All this restraint proves to be a fool's errand. If he had his pistol, he knows he would use it. "I don't see it that way," he finally says.

"We ain't savin' yer life?" the man asks.

"You're killing my dog."

The man scoffs and says partially under his breath, but loud enough for Howard and the skinny man to hear, "Imagine puttin' yer dog's life ahead'a yer own."

Howard snaps back. "You ever lost anyone you cared about? I mean, really, truly cared for?"

"Well, sure—"

"The fuck you have."

If words could kill.

The two men share a stare, and then no one says anything for the rest of the ride. The mood hangs in the air. It's a humidity that sticks, clings to you. No respite, no escape.

The boat putters through the town, ripples fanning behind until a nearby building kills their momentum. Howard has been bent over, elbows on his knees, staring at his fists and trying to regain his composure. *This goddamn town. This goddamn town is going to kill me. And my dog. Why did Amber bring me here?*

These thoughts are futile, he knows. Self-deprecating. Torturous. All to say, their purpose is to further punish himself. It's an eternal sentence he believes he deserves, and he will dole it out alongside God, who has been doing a fine job of the task himself.

The thin man says, "Here comes the shelter."

Howard looks up and the scene is apocalyptic. Though the rain has stopped, or at least paused, residual humidity hangs in the air. It is dark all around them and the clouds overhead keep the stars and moon from offering any light. In the distance, Howard sees the shelter. He hears the rumble of generators and there are low, dim lights that cast a subtle shimmer over the water. It's enough to notice the buildings that surround them, the expanse of the disaster. The skinny man flashes the singular headlight on the boat to let people ahead know they are coming in. The water stops about a hundred yards from the building, which would either be part of the parking lot or the surrounding lawn, Howard thinks.

Over his shoulder, the mustached man clears his throat. "Listen, I know yer pissed at us," the man says. "But we did what we had to do. Yer not the first person we saved who had to make that choice. That's not countin' the couple folks who made the wrong decision."

Howard looks up. "So others chose to stay with their dogs?"

"One was a dog. One was a cat, I think."

There was a silence.

The man tries to make eye contact but Howard won't look at him. He goes on anyway. "Y'understand, those folks might die because of that call?"

Howard's indifference to the comment was evident.

Finally, the skinny man says, "I'm Pinky. Well, folks call me Pinky, at least. Pinky Stevens." After a slight silence, he continues, "And that's my cousin, Jerry Gunderson."

Howard glances at the men and then says, "Howard."

"Just figured we'd give you a heads up to what yer gonna see at the shelter since we're volunteers helpin' out an' all."

"Are all the other volunteers also just people looking for an opportunity to pull guns on their neighbors?" Howard doesn't know where the comment comes from, but he's glad he says it.

The look on Jerry's face tells Howard he's juggling thoughts—should he respond to the comment or let it be? After a moment he tries to pick a middle ground. "Well, Mr. Howard, this shelter'll be full of volunteers jus' lookin' to help you out, is all."

That simmers Howard's frustration and the boat glides to a stop where the water finally shallows to nearly knee-deep. He can see now that they are positioned over an expanse of grass and there are stakes planted all around, just a little ways off. Pinky hops out of the boat as it jerks to a stop and jogs up to one of the stakes, rope in hand, and loops it around.

"Alright, this is yer stop," says Jerry.

Howard looks back at him. "My stop?"

"We gotta head back out. There's more folks like you still out there."

It's a notion that Howard's mind never considered—that he was one piece in a much larger puzzle. It had been too easy, given all of his personal trauma and struggles, to live like he was the only man on the planet in need of help. When he comes to this realization, he nods and climbs out of the boat.

The walk up to the shelter is the last torture he needs at this point. The lawn is a gradual incline for several dozen yards, and then a steep hill splits the grass from a parking lot sitting above. Those lights that looked so dim from afar are now brightening and Howard is thankful for the gradual adjustment to his vision. A wave of foolishness washes over him—he barely remembers this building existing in the however-many-years that he's lived in this valley. Now it's going to help save his life. But that thought stops him. *Save your life*, he thinks again. *Your life. Meanwhile, Coby is alone in the cold and dark, abandoned.*

At the front door, a man is waving a flashlight in Howard's direction. "Come on in, fella!" the man shouts.

Howard crests the hill and stops for a moment to put his hands on his knees. Then he continues toward the man.

"You made it now. Come on in here, friend!" the man shouts again, this time stepping aside and holding open a door for Howard. Howard doesn't say anything but nods in appreciation and walks by. The man gives him a firm pat on the shoulder as he passes, which causes Howard to flinch.

The entryway is spacious. It's easy to picture this place being a community center. There are bulletin boards with flyers tacked to them. To the side, there is a reception area, though no one is sitting there. Howard has a quick thought that there should be someone sitting there asking entrants, "How may we help you survive this storm today?" But he shakes it off and keeps walking. A few people are sitting on the floor, spaced apart, propped up against the wall, with their eyes closed. They don't exactly look like they're in tatters. They look like regular people, wearing regular clothes, who are all having a really terrible day. Beside them are backpacks or duffle bags filled with who knows what—essentials, heirlooms, anything that had been handy.

He isn't sure exactly what he should have expected—a hustling and bustling rescue shelter or a calm place of refuge. Perhaps it's the time of night, but this place is far closer to the calm refuge than anything he would consider hectic, which surprises him. He has never been in the middle of a natural disaster before, but he thought it would be a bit more like the Hollywood shows.

He pushes further inside the community center and into a long hallway. There are doors on either side. Most of them are shut, a few are open. Only the occasional overhead light is on, powered by the generators outside. The dark corridor gives Howard an uneasy feeling. He can't see very well, but he can tell the rooms are mostly empty. Then, toward the end of the hallway, he comes to a set of double doors. These are propped open and before he even gets to them he knows this is the gathering place. He can hear hushed talking and the faint echo of a larger space. When he turns the corner, he sees the gymnasium.

Inside, people are huddled in small groups or sitting isolated. Families with little children kneel in a circle and fold their hands in prayer. A few people are there volunteering, trying to help however they can. One man is breaking down a case of water bottles and then begins handing them out to the patrons. Howard thinks that Stu is probably in here somewhere with his family, but it's a large room and it would take some looking. The faint light in the vast space gives it an eery feel. For a moment Howard thinks he is living in a dream. There are some blow-up mattresses scattered around with extension cords running over the wooden floor, but mostly it's a mess of blankets and sleeping bags and pillows. Many people have nothing but the clothes on their backs and maybe a rosary. One thing that is loudly missing: pets.

Howard stays near the perimeter of the room and doesn't say a word to anyone. He is just watching—and observing—as he follows the wall toward the back corner. At the far end of the gym is a stage with curtains partially drawn. He climbs a couple of stairs and peeks behind the curtain, mostly out of curiosity. In the darkness, he sees a shape that catches his eye. He trains his eyes on it for a moment, hoping they will adjust to the dark. Then he sees some movement and realizes that the shape is an old woman. She is curled up in the corner with a blanket over top. But the movement didn't come from her; it was the small dog in her lap. The dog looks as weary as the other refugees in the shelter as it nuzzles its head into its owner.

The scene nearly startles Howard, who then, only a moment later, begins feeling some anger bubbling in his gut.

He takes a few steps forward and reaches out to touch the woman. A quiet voice says, "She'll attack if I tell her." When she looks up at him, her eyes appear as though they don't have much fight in them.

Howard ignores the comment and instead says, "I'm so sorry to bother you. How did you get your dog in here? I was told pets were forbidden."

The woman takes a moment to respond. She looks more like she is gathering her breath than her thoughts. "I couldn't live with myself if I left her."

He knew the feeling. "But, how?" he asks, nearly pleading at this point.

"How what?"

"How did you get her in here?"

"Son, there's a reason I'm curled up here behind this curtain. I'm staying out of sight."

"So you just hid her under a blanket?"

The woman scoffs and gestures behind her. "Back door," she says proudly.

Still trying to penetrate the darkness with his vision, Howard squints backstage looking for a door. The woman notices.

"It's back there, trust me."

He thinks. "What would happen if they saw you with a dog back here?"

"Ain't no one gonna find me," she says.

"Hypothetically."

"Okay, hypothetically? They'd kick me out of here. Or worse."

"Worse?"

She exhales. "There was a man in here this morning. Came in with his pup. So they says, 'Gotta leave, no dogs allowed.' So the man says, 'I'm not leaving.' So the chubby guy with the strange hair has this gun in his waist and he threatens to shoot the dog."

Just picturing the scene, Howard is furious. "I know that guy."

"With the dog?"

"With the gun."

"Mmm."

"He pulled that gun on me not too long ago when I tried to bring my dog with me."

"Where's your dog now?"

"Back at my house."

The old woman is trying to sit up. There's a piece of bread in her pocket and she pulls it out to feed bits to her companion. "Don't know how you did that."

The guilt overcomes Howard like it's happening again in that moment. "I don't either," he admits. Then he lets the silence fall over them. That's how they stay for several uncomfortable minutes. Finally, he says, "Think you could help me?"

The plan is simple, but that doesn't make it easy. Howard is going to go back and try retrieving Coby to bring him to the shelter. The woman has shown him where the backdoor is and they have worked out a special knocking sequence that he will use once he returns, and she will let them in. Then it's just about concealing the dogs backstage. She is supportive of the plan, which is essential.

Simple plan. Difficult plan.

Howard decides to wait an hour or so before venturing out, looking for a way to trek back toward his home, and saving Coby. He knows it will mean crossing some lines. He's just ashamed he hasn't crossed them sooner.

14

Wolf Valley, 1991

In which Howard was 37 years old

On warm summer evenings while Amber was shut in her study writing, Howard liked to make himself a whiskey cocktail and walk down to the river. Not long after they moved in he had to cut down a tree along the banks and would use the stump as a stool. The bugs were usually hell but he wore long sleeves, even on the hottest nights, and dealt with it for as long as he could bear. Sometimes it was minutes, sometimes hours. Some nights he felt as if he could meditate them away. Nonetheless, it was an escape that was just for him, where he could watch the water trickle past and listen to the clicking of the current against the rocks. Fireflies and frogs and the occasional owl started a chorus at sunset, and Howard sipped his drink and took a deep breath. For its simplicity, this was the only life he wanted to live because when he was ready to walk back up to the house he knew he'd find a beautiful woman devoted to her craft and ready to greet him with a kiss on the lips. Life didn't get much better than that.

This was a routine that Howard established in the first days of living in Wolf Valley. Amber dove immediately into her novel upon their arrival and finding the house, and so in the evenings, before he opened his book to read, he decided to take a walk and get some fresh air. It continued into the winter months—which weren't nearly as harsh as the ones he experienced up in Michigan—and then right on into the spring and summer. And now he was eager for his favorite season to be back upon them. Regardless of what the calendar said, he always knew autumn had returned when he awoke and felt the bite of winter in the morning and the kiss of summer in the afternoon.

When he returned from the river, the flood light on the back patio had turned on, and after stepping inside for a refill and to grab his journal, he returned to the outdoor table. Another aspect of the cooler evenings that he loved: they chased away the mosquitos, at least to a degree. He stared at the journal for a moment. He felt it in his hands. He became sentimental and observant when he'd been drinking. Maybe it was the canvas texture or the way the pages warped over time, but it now had character that it didn't a year earlier when he first bought it—at Amber's urging—in a small shop in town the day after arriving in Wolf Valley. "We can traverse this land together," she told him. "Plus, it'll be fun to look back at these days. It's our first adventure together."

And she was right. About it all. It was an adventure, and he was infinitely glad he had been trying to document it along the way. He flipped open to the first page and read aloud in a whisper, as he tended to do.

"September 17, 1990 — Arriving in Wolf Valley."

The weather was gloomy, he wrote. But the smile on Amber's face lit up the day. She hadn't stopped smiling since they'd gotten in the car. It was a long drive from Michigan, but it could easily be done in a day. Howard spent the whole time behind the wheel. They took his truck and left her car back in Holland. They each had a bag packed and a small stack of books. Who knew how long they'd be gone? Howard still didn't even fully understand why she needed to go there to write, and because she said she never talked about her projects while they were in process, he just went with it.

The day before, Howard had broken up with Misty. He wasn't even entirely sure what he was doing, and the news came out of left field to her. There was some swearing and a lot of tears. Something surely was broken. But Howard threw some clothes in a bag and slept on the couch, and he was gone by the time Misty woke the next morning. "Take your time finding a new place to live," he had told her, "because I'm going to be gone for a little while." He didn't tell her about Amber, but she knew. It was the only thing that made sense and Misty was no dummy. She probably just wished he had the balls to tell her. He wished the same.

The first thing they did when they arrived in Wolf Valley was stop in a small diner so they could eat and Amber could pull out her notebook and officially write her first words. Howard grabbed her camera and took a photo of her, pen in hand, contemplative look on her face. That first night they stayed in a hotel but hoped to find a short-term rental soon. Howard was just going with the flow, eager to see where this adventure would take them.

"October 3, 1990 — Finding a house."

Two weeks in a hotel, even in a place like Wolf Valley, can start to take a toll on a wallet, Howard wrote. After about a week, they started taking morning or evening drives through the valley looking for rental properties. They had found a few places in the little towns, but Amber wanted to be out in the country and Howard agreed. One day, Amber met a realtor who showed them a few more properties. There was some promise but nothing stole their hearts.

"I have one other I could show you," the realtor said. "This has been a rental the last few years but the owner is tryin' to sell it right now. Havin' a hard time, as you could imagine. Interested?"

"Are they willing to let us rent?" Howard asked.

"Could be worth throwin' their way."

The realtor took them out to the house. It was a one-story brick ranch in a quiet, forested neighborhood where the houses were far apart and the driveways were mostly gravel. It was near the end of the lane and backed up to the river across an open yard. Inside they had a couple bedrooms and a study with glass French doors that Amber was excited to turn into her writing room.

"It's perfect," Amber whispered into Howard's ear when the realtor was in the other room.

"I know, it's great," he admitted. "But the owner is looking for a long-term deal here."

Amber gave him a look.

"Is that what you want?"

Her look softened and Howard could see the glean in her eye.

"Babe," Howard said, putting his hands on her waist and pulling her close. "Are you looking for a long-term deal?"

She blinked and then put her head into his chest. "I want a long-term with you."

"October 29, 1990 — Making it real."

Boy, Howard wrote, all that can happen in three weeks. He knew pretty much from the moment they moved in that Amber wanted to buy the place. Of course, she had more money than he did. When her books sold, they *sold*. But he also knew that she wouldn't just come out and say that she was buying it. It would be a decision they had to arrive at together. They sure were moving toward "long-term" awfully quickly.

The house had its flaws, certainly—that's the nature of rental properties—but Howard had also spent his entire adult life renovating houses for other people. Why the hell not start a project of his own? Still, even though this was exactly what he always thought he wanted, it felt like it was all moving fast. Very fast. He was spending his days reading, meandering about the community, while Amber stayed in the house and wrote. About three weeks into the arrangement, she sat down beside him on the couch and said, "What do you think?"

"About what?"

"About the house. I think they want us to make a decision."

"You want to buy it?"

"I mean, don't you?"

He looked at her. "You know what this means, right? This means that we're in this together for the foreseeable future. Do you think you can commit to that?"

"I can commit to a lot more than that," she said with a smirk.

And so they went back to their realtor the next day and started the process. Of course, Howard still had his old house back in Michigan. Over the last month, he had lost any semblance of the notion of ever returning to it—that wasn't his life anymore, and even if he and Amber returned to Michigan, he doubted that house would find its way into the plan. Hell, even if he returned to Michigan without Amber, he still didn't want that house to be his safety net. Too many memories. So, simultaneously while they were buying the house in Wolf Valley, he was selling his house in Michigan. He just hoped that Misty wasn't still living in it.

The last remaining big ticket item on his list was to find employment. If they were sticking around, he needed to do something useful with his time. He scoured the newspapers and looked at the bulletin boards in the local diners and post office. But in the late fall, as winter approached, most folks weren't looking for an extra hand—they were looking for handouts or for people to keep out of their business. Howard searched but to no avail. In the evenings he'd be quietly disappointed or even frustrated, but was careful not to upset Amber with his struggles.

This went on for weeks, until, finally, around the same time they decided to buy the house, he met a man named Wendell Williams at a local hardware store. Wendell was skinny but sturdy, the blue-collar life worn into his leathery skin. As Howard was preparing to check out, they struck up a casual conversation. "You seem to know a lot about this stuff," Wendell said.

"I spent the last 15 or so years doing home remodels for a company up in Michigan."

"What brings you to Wolf Valley?"

"A girl."

The old man smirked. "Tale as old as time," he said. Then, "You ever lookin' for work, you give me a call," and then he slipped Howard a business card with his name and number on it. And that was that. What it would lead to, he still had no idea, but work was work. He needed to keep busy, and the only way he ever knew how was either with a book or a hammer.

"November 19, 1990 — Finally."

They did it, Howard wrote. They signed the papers. This house, he looked around, was now home. It didn't feel real. It still felt like he was living in some type of fantasy and that at some point someone would knock on the door, say, "Alright, you've had your go at it, time to head home," and then he'd be escorted to an old pickup that would drive him back to Michigan. But the knock never came and Howard woke up each day thanking God that it didn't.

The first night sleeping in the house after officially becoming the owners felt different. They had opened a bottle of cheap champagne and poured a couple of glasses, after which Howard opened a bottle of whiskey and proceeded to drink nearly half of it. He stirred that night at the thought of this new life with Amber. He was giddy with excitement.

The next night, having drank far less, Amber walked up to him in the kitchen and kissed him gently on the cheek, then the lips. "Let's go," she whispered, taking his hand and walking toward the bedroom. Howard's heart was racing. His mind ran in a hundred different directions. Since that night 13 years earlier, that first night together, they hadn't been intimate. Well, they had been intimate, but they hadn't been all-the-way intimate. There were nights back in New York when they came close—to the point where Howard had to restrain himself from pushing too far. But it never happened. And then since getting back together, since vacating their old lives in a moment and moving to Wolf Valley, since sleeping full-time in the same bed, since buying a house together—never. Until that moment.

In the bedroom, she spun and pressed herself against him and whispered, "I'm ready again." It was all Howard needed to hear. They made love that night. It wasn't anything like the first time. It was gentler. It felt as unfamiliar an act as it did 13 years prior, but in the way that trying something new with the person you love feels exciting and fresh and not scary and strange. When they were done, they lay on the bed breathing heavily, the warmth of their skin still touching. Howard could feel the rhythym of her breathing and for a moment it felt like their lungs were moving as one, as if they had somehow come together and could no longer be separated.

And then they made love again.

By the time fall rolled around and they had been in Wolf Valley for a full year, they had settled into their new lives without even realizing it. To them, living in Wolf Valley—despite the jobs and the home purchase—somehow felt like a temporary but exciting chapter. And yet, a year later, there they were. It was becoming more permanent by the day.

In that year, Amber had written nearly a complete manuscript. She told Howard that something about being in Wolf Valley, something about the tranquility and nature motivated her.

"Is that why you wanted to come here in the first place?"

She would always smirk at that question but she never answered it. Howard didn't mind, though. He had gotten everything out of the impulsive life overhaul that he could have ever wanted.

Amber spent the better part of each day at the desk she'd set up in her office. It sat in the center of the room and faced the French doors that looked out to the main living space in the house. Behind her was a floor-to-ceiling, wall-to-wall shelf with books of all kinds —classics, contemporary, novels from friends and even copies of her own. It was nearly filled. Every shelf. Every drawer of her desk. Amber was a meticulous writer. Everything had a place. Everything was purposeful.

"What about that top shelf?" Howard said leaning in the doorway.

Amber, still sitting behind her desk, turned and looked up. "Just like everything else—purposeful."

"You're really not going to put anything up there?"

"I'm reserving that for my greatest achievement," she told him.

"What, a Pulitzer?"

She gave him a look and then went back to her work.

Howard was just thankful that Amber had been able to put together a new project. If she'd hit writer's block or lost her motivation, who knows what would have happened to this adventure they were on. The way he saw it, the longer she could keep putting pen to paper, the longer he could pretend this was truly his new life and not just a failed experiment. For all of the happiness and decisions they had experienced and made over the last year, in the back of his mind he still thought it was a house of cards that could come crashing down at any moment. That's the way Amber lived her life. He knew her well enough now.

Still, he had been working for Wendell for nearly a year and Howard had found a life he could envision living for decades. Admittedly, he was a creature of habit—once he established a routine, he liked to stick to it. That didn't mean he was immune to sometimes making irrational decisions—hence, moving to Wolf Valley with a woman he hadn't seen since she broke his heart seven years prior—but he adjusted to situations quickly and learned to accept them as his new reality.

Amber, for her part, also seemed to be a bit beholden to her routines. When she found momentum with her work, she stuck to it religiously. That's what had been happening in the last few months heading into autumn. After work, Howard took to grabbing a beer from the fridge and sitting down to watch the news on TV. He'd peek over at Amber through the glass doors, who never looked up from what she was working on. It went that way late into the evening when Howard would eventually switch from TV and beer to books and whiskey.

"I don't get it," he said to her one evening.

Amber had just emerged from her office and sat down next to him on the couch. "I think I'm going to shower," she said, completely ignoring his comment.

"I really don't get it," he said again.

"What?"

"When I wake up in the morning—and I wake up *early*—you're already sitting at that desk. When I get home after work, you're still sitting at that desk. Nights like tonight, you don't stand up until ten o'clock. I just don't get how you can do it."

The look on Amber's face was contemplative, trying to figure out if Howard was complimenting her focus or criticizing her inaccessibility. "It's a gift—and a curse."

"It's something." He wrapped his arm around her just as she tried to stand up, and he pulled her back down beside him. "I'm proud of you."

She smiled. "Thank you. But it's been a really long day so I'm going to go shower."

"I'll be waiting in the bedroom for you," he said with a devilish smile.

She rolled her eyes and walked out.

Saturday rolled around and Howard woke and went into the living room to find Amber already sitting at her desk. This was normal, but her weekend writing sessions were usually short—sprints rather than the marathons she ran during the week—and he took a quick drive into town to grab a newspaper and a coffee from the Shell station. That's where the old-timers convened and sometimes Howard liked to pop in and shoot the shit.

When he returned, she was still working—feverishly, it seemed. He respected the hell out of it but also missed her. It was a weird thing to feel, he thought, to miss someone who never left the house. But there he was, separated by two glass doors, watching the woman whom he never really seemed to have—even when he had her.

With a softness, he tapped on her office door and waited a few moments before she acknowledged him. She looked up without changing the expression on her face. Howard motioned toward the handle and she nodded.

"You up for a little hike?" Summertime in the valley could be unbearably hot at times, so this time of year when the milder weather rolled in Howard wanted to take advantage of it.

"Now?"

"Now-ish. I can wait a bit if you need to finish up what you're doing."

"I won't be done for a while."

"What's a while?"

"It's probably better if you just go without me."

Howard looked at her thinking about what to say but eventually just gave her a pleasant look and said, "Don't work too hard," and then put on his boots and left.

The morning was still cool and the sun hadn't burned off the fog that liked to moisten the valley before the heat of the day. This was one of the most underrated aspects of living down here, Howard knew. It was one of the secrets that he was afraid would get out and then people would come flooding to the area in search of the bliss that he experienced every day for the last year.

The trail that he liked to walk ran along the river, starting on the grassy banks near his property but heading upstream into the trees. Near the dam, the path winds away from the water to climb the terrain, and this was the part that usually kept Howard from reaching the trailhead. But on that morning he was feeling motivated—or, rather, he knew he had plenty of time and was in no rush to return home.

As he emerged from the trees, he found himself on an overlook that peered down into the valley and at the river below. It was breathtaking. The tops of the rolling hills surrounding the area were fluffy and green and the occasional pasture that spotted the land offered an inviting contrast. It was a painting. Howard took a deep breath and walked over to the edge where a thick wooden railing had been constructed. Glancing around, he knew this was going to be the place. He was all alone but he removed the small box from his pocket, crouched to a knee and held out the ring.

"Will you marry me?"

He said it aloud. He wanted to hear the words. And when the time came, he hoped he'd hear himself say them again.

Another week had come and gone, and Howard returned home with the Saturday morning paper in hand. He was surprised, however, to see Amber's office empty. He checked the bedroom but that was also empty. He shrugged and went out to the back patio to read the paper, and that's where he spotted his girlfriend off in the distance sitting by the river.

Amused, he walked down quietly and stood over her shoulder. "Beautiful morning," he whispered.

She flinched, jumped off the old stump and smacked him on the arm.

"Hey!" he said jokingly.

"Not funny!"

He managed to add an "I'm sorry" through his laughter, which seemed warranted given that she had been unable to restrain her own. "I expected to find you cooped up in your office," he said once they had calmed down.

"I'll bet you did."

He crouched and dipped his fingers in the water. "River's cooling down. Fall's finally here."

"Okay, Mr. Outdoorsman," she said rolling her eyes.

"I happen to know everything there is about the outdoors."

"I'm sure you *think* you know everything."

"Let me take you on a hike and prove it."

She looked back at the house. "Give me an hour? I was just taking a break. I need to get back and finish something."

He sighed. "Okay. How's the book coming?"

"Almost there," she said as she turned to head back to the house.

Howard watched her walk to the door, while he hung around by the water and felt the ring in his pocket. The longer he kept it in his possession, the more anxious he became. It was burning a hole. He just hoped it didn't fall through.

"Ready?"

"For?" Amber had just stepped out of her office. Howard had been watching the door like a hawk.

"For our hike."

"Oh," she said, and then sighed and sat down on the couch. "I don't know if I'm up for it."

"But you said..."

"I know. I'm sorry. I didn't expect to work this much today."

"I don't think you understand how cool this hike is."

"I find that hard to believe."

"I'm telling you, it will blow your mind."

"Give me a little preview." She tucked her leg under her, making it easier to turn and face him. She waited with embellished anticipation.

"Well, we spend all this time down here in this valley, but I found a trail through the woods that leads up the mountain and overlooks this place."

"Oh really?"

"Yes, really. And it's not too hard, either."

"Huh." She thought about it. "Okay, give me a half hour."

And he did. But thirty minutes later, he found her asleep on the couch and didn't have the mind to wake her. So he waited longer, and when she finally awoke he said, "Ready now?"

Another sigh. "Howard, I just don't think I have it in me today."

"One hike. Please. It'll take an hour."

"A full hour? Yeah, I definitely don't think I can do that then."

She meant it lightly but Howard took it personally. He walked out of the room. A moment later he returned and grabbed her hand and said, "Will you please stand up?"

"I'm not going on the hike with you."

"Amber," he said in a measured tone, "I need you to stand."

She looked into his eyes and then did as he asked. "Are you okay?"

He ignored her question and, once she was standing, bent to a knee and pulled the ring from his pocket. His heart was pounding and he couldn't feel his legs. His nerves killed any semblance of a speech he might have had planned in his head. Instead, he simply said, "Amber McNamara, will you spend the rest of your life with me?"

Tears instantly welled in her eyes and she nodded and covered her mouth and said "Yes, yes, YES!" and then he slid the ring onto her finger and took her into his arms and they kissed. He didn't want to ever let her go. He could feel tears of his own landing on her shoulder, and he held her tighter.

When she finally pulled away, she said, "I love you," and then, "Let's go on that hike."

15

Wolf Valley, 2002

In which Howard is 48 years old

Outside the shelter, there is no movement. In the distance, the sparing lights that the generator is powering offer a faint shimmer on the surface of the surrounding water below. Howard can make out the silhouettes of some nearby buildings in the distance as well, but mostly it's an endless black sea.

He remains steadfast in his plan. The woman inside the building has positioned herself close enough to the door backstage to be able to hear Howard's knock, though far enough away not to draw any suspicions if anyone sees her back there—though they both know that is far from a primary concern. People aren't terribly worried about conspiracies to sneak pets inside, not when friends and neighbors and loved ones are hungry or missing or dying or injured all around town.

While there is still considerable cloud cover overhead, which keeps the stars from shining through, the rain has stopped. Howard can still feel the dampness in the air, the moisture that floats all around him as a sea of its own. On his way out of the shelter, the man at the front door says, "Where ya headed, fella?" But Howard just gives him a polite nod and makes his way around the side of the building, disappearing into the night.

Now, this is where he stands. He needs a boat. Something that will get him back to Coby. He will wait as long as it takes. If he has to wait until daylight, so be it. If he has to wait until the next night, so be it. It's a decision he knows is an hour or so too late, but better late than never, he tries to tell himself. It's a coping mechanism—he's acutely aware of that—but he's allowing it to work. There, with his back pressed against the cool brick of the building, he slides down to the ground and looks out at the vastness. He is invisible. The town barely exists. This rumination of nonexistence settles over him like a weighted blanket. But in these moments of presumed solitude comes the one thing Howard cannot outrun, cannot escape—his guilt returns.

All at once—it's Coby. It's Amber. It's that night. It's this night. It's all those childhood nights. He feels his chest tightening. Labored breaths. He falls to the side and brings his hand to his heart. The episode is distracting from the memories that caused it. The thought of death, about his heart stopping and rapid breaths instantly ceasing, is somehow better than the weight of his past. Lying on the pavement, he feels the roughness on his face. He rubs it in, deliberately, wanting the pain. Eager for it. And then, as quickly as it all began, it stops. The night is still, and the chaos of his mind begins to fade, leaving him with an uneasy calmness.

The thought that terrifies him more than all the others: *maybe this is all supposed to be happening.* He pounds the concrete once with a closed fist and tries to snap that from his mind. It's not fair. His survival, over Amber's, over Coby's, was not part of any master plan. That would be a sick plan from God.

But surely Coby was in his life for a reason. Surely Amber bringing him home was part of the plan. But he never wanted a dog. But he and Amber never lived the life they thought they would. The dog couldn't be part of the plan. But then he was. He hated that dog at first. But he grew on him. He thought about Amber. It was her dog. He owed it to her. He would at least do that: care for the dog. But he hadn't—Coby was at home trying to survive on his own. But Amber knew Howard didn't want a dog in the first place. She should still be here.

Guilt is cyclical.

Only one thing can snap Howard from the spiral: the faint hum of an engine. He shoots up to his feet and scans the water. Without seeing the boat itself, he sees a single light in the distance splashing over the still water. When he steadies himself and concentrates for a moment, he can tell it is moving toward the shelter. The switch in his mind flips and he flattens himself against the wall, waiting, watching from the shadows.

From this far, he can't tell if it's the same boat he was on before. He looks for the hair, the skinny guy. *What was his name—Pinky? What the hell kind of name is that?* As the boat approaches, it follows a similar path as when Howard arrived earlier. The apron of light cast from the building skirts onto the water and the craft slips into it, close enough that Howard can get a better view of the boat. He can't quite tell who is maneuvering it—a man with two smaller figures, it looks like—but he knows for sure it's not the two who dropped him off. Without moving, he watches them as carefully as he can from this distance. After the boat pulls up to what is now serving as a shore, a child jumps off holding a rope. He runs to a nearby telephone pole and ties it up, slinging it around the back and using his weight to pull it taut. He then returns to the boat where a man is helping an elderly woman. He nearly has to lift her and set her down gently onto the wet ground. The boy is now standing there to offer a hand of his own. The two of them—the man and the boy—help her, slowly, carefully, up the hill and to the shelter.

Howard is still pressed against the brick wall. He watches this scene play out in slow motion, his heart racing. Previously, his only thought was to sneak down the hill, untie the boat, push off quietly and leave. Save Coby. But now he has the chance and he freezes. The image of the man and the boy is stuck in his mind. In another life, that's him and his son on the other side of this tragedy, helping others instead of being enveloped in the devastation. It's a fleeting thought. Then: *What if they come back? What if that man and boy have others to go back and save?* He can't do it. He hates himself, but he can't do it. He slides back to the ground and thinks about Coby, all alone in the cold and dark and damp. And he cries.

It's not a sleep that Howard startles from, because he cannot sleep, but more of a trance. Once again, it's that familiar hum. He sits up and looks around the corner. This time there is no mistaking what he sees. It's the two men returning with an empty boat.

They aren't particularly calm about it, given that it's the middle of the night and true tragedy has unfolded around them, and they aren't particularly quiet either. By the time Howard stands—still with his back firmly against the wall, lurking in the shadows—he can hear them. Pinky is out of the boat tying it up, though he looks to have half-assed it. Jerry switches off the motor and hops off, making a splash in the shallow water. It's an arrogant jump. He could have missed the water altogether, landed safely on the dry ground, but he chose to make the splash.

The two men are talking and making their way toward the shelter. Howard can hear them now, faintly.

"Ain't that there's no one left, just ain't gonna find 'em," Jerry is saying.

When they get to the door, the cheery man greets them, though he is far less cheery at this time of night. "Probably the last of us til morning," Jerry tells him.

The man sighs, relieved. "Thank God. I need to lie down."

Howard is peeking around the side of the building and watches the three men go inside, the door closing tauntingly slow behind them. Then he waits. One minute. Two minutes. Ten minutes. *This boat. This is a boat you can take. This is a boat you deserve to take.* At least that's what he tells himself. *You'll be back before anyone notices.*

Where the boat is tied up, the light is dim. From the front of the shelter, it would be difficult to identify someone without them bearing a distinctive characteristic. Howard uses this fact to his advantage, sliding down the hill, moving to the water's edge, and then tracing it back toward the boat. He heads straight for the rope and unties the makeshift knot—rudimentary at best. He expected more from Pinky. But as he goes to push off and hop in, something catches his eye. Something etched on the side. Three words: SWEET SUN DAYZ. He freezes. *How in the hell did those two assholes end up with this boat?* For a moment his mind is a mess. He flashes back to his yard, to the bobbing craft. Then it vanishing. *Did they steal it? Did Stu come back for it, but not for him? Did it break free and drift downriver?* The questions are unanswerable, he knows, but they are so unsettling that he is distracted from the task at hand.

"Can I help you?"

It's a vacant shout that comes from up the hill. He glances with his periphery to make sure the man isn't upon him but doesn't turn enough to allow anyone to get a good look at his face. In one motion, he pushes the boat into the water and rolls inside.

"Hey! Sir!"

The voice gains volume for a moment as the man chases down the slope, but it is ultimately stifled by distance. And within minutes, Howard is alone in the dark.

Rather than use the ride home to demean himself, Howard tries to be productive. He knows this town well enough to maneuver in the dark, though he believes there are likely to be sunken branches and cars that could impede his route. He keeps his eyes trained on the water and the objects protruding from it.

Once he can crank the engine to life, he raises it to a low rumble—quick enough to evade any pursuers but slow enough to avoid any crashes. There is a small cooler on the boat and he opens it. Inside is a half-full water bottle, a pair of gloves, a first aid kit, some twine, a hunting knife and a flashlight. After all the lights from the shelter have faded behind him, he flicks on the flashlight and shines it over the water.

It's a smooth ride. With the rain stopped, it's eery how quiet the scene is. People on the outside can't imagine the calm that follows a chaotic event like that. But Howard is thankful for it because he can retrain his brain on Coby. He knows—or at least prays—that he's still in the attic. He hopes the water hasn't crested over the roofline. There are concerns about total structural collapse, but Howard casts those from his mind—too soon to think about that. Instead, he makes a plan: tie up to the gutter, just like Pinky had done. Scale the roof and get in through the window. Grab Coby and head back to the shelter, enter through the backdoor and hide. It seems simple enough.

As he turns down what would be his street, he feels shivers run down his spine. It's the cold, the bite that has been hovering in the air, but it's also the fear about what has happened to this neighborhood. It was always a quiet community, but now it is worse than quiet. He sees Stu's home, a two-story farmhouse that sits on a partially raised piece of land across the road. The water barely looks like it's made it to the front door, compared to other homes that are nearly completely submerged on Howard's side of the road. The sight both disgusts him and terrifies him.

He is nearing his own house, but he hesitates to shine the flashlight on it. There is an attic window—the one he closed behind him and watched as he left Coby behind. He doesn't want to look at that window again. For fear of what he might see. For fear of what he might not see. Still, he has a chance at some sort of redemption, however small. And if it saves a life, it will have been worth it.

Despite the rain having stopped hours ago, the water level seems to continue rising. Running the flashlight along the dark surface, his house finally creeps into faint view. His breath catches and he darts his flashlight ahead. The scene terrifies him. By this point, his first floor is entirely submerged. His home is all roof and a window—a window that is supposed to have a dog in it.

Gliding gently to the gutter, Howard ties up where he remembers Pinky tying up. He pulls the rope as tight as he can so that the boat is pinned to the house. Stabilizing it, he takes a lunge onto the asphalt. His foot slips and he braces himself against the gutter before trying again. He is securing the flashlight with his teeth and the light bobs recklessly into the night and the trees nearby. With urgent caution, he ascends the roof, latching himself to the dormer window.

"Coby," he calls gently, so as not to startle him. Then again, a little louder, "Coby. Buddy, I'm here." But he doesn't see any motion.

Throwing open the window, he steps inside. It's freezing—as cold as outside, perhaps colder. "Coby," he whispers. He looks around with the flashlight but he doesn't see his dog. The candles have stopped burning. One of them is knocked over and a puddle of wax has dried on the wooden floor. The pistol is still half-concealed by a blanket, and the pile of Amber's books is sitting nearby. Then, across the attic, he notices the hatch is open. He walks over to it and looks down. It's a blackness of water, the ladder suspended in it, a rush of cold air pouring upward. His heart races and he tries to keep his mind from thinking the worst. "Coby!" he shouts this time, distress in his voice. He can hear it, feel it. His throat is dry and he gags.

At this point, he isn't sure what to do. If Coby went down that hatch, it would be nearly impossible for him to survive. But where else could he have gone? The window was closed, unbroken. *Where are you, bud?* Panic has now completely set in. He looks back down the hatch at the water. *Impossible.* And though he doesn't want his mind to go there, he knows that regardless of which type of mission this ends up being—rescue or retrieval—he owes it to Coby, the one he left behind, to go down there after him.

Even with the flashlight, it's nearly pitch black all around him. Forcing the ladder downward, he waits for it to make contact with the floor below so that it's stable. Then a quick thought: *Is this suicide?* He stands upright and decides to be smart about this. The attic is filled with boxes. He begins rummaging through them looking for something useful, something that can float, something that could give off light. First, he finds holiday decorations. Christmas lights, tablecloths, ornaments. Then more decorations, this time Halloween and Thanksgiving. There's a box of old tools, but he shuffles through it and doesn't find anything worthwhile. Another box of blankets and bedding that he missed last time. One with old books. Eventually, he stumbles upon a box with exactly what he is looking for: a life vest. It's in rough condition and his eyes, seeing strictly by the glow of the flashlight, almost miss it in his frantic search. When he pulls it out, it's hard to tell it's even a life preserver—the orange has faded to an off-white, and it's riddled with tears and scrapes. The strap that wraps across the front is missing and he wonders for a moment why on Earth he ever kept this thing.

Slipping it over his head, it smells of mothballs and mildew. Then he remembers in the box of tools that there was a roll of duct tape. He scrambles for it. The roll is so old and worn that he's lucky it has any adhesive left. He scratches his finger along the side until his nail catches and he begins peeling a strip. Flashlight back in his mouth, he wraps the tape around his torso. Once. Twice. As much as the roll will allow. He knows it will start deteriorating fast in the water.

Now he's standing over the hatch once again. He takes a deep breath and then carefully begins descending the ladder. Through his boots, he can feel the cold of the water. First, his legs disappear with each step, and then he freezes when the water line hits his thigh. It's almost enough to paralyze him, but the adrenaline shoots through his limbs and he presses on. The water is now hovering at the bottom of his life preserver and Howard decides to pivot the flashlight in his mouth so that it is aimed straight ahead. It will strain his jaw.

Then he lowers himself gingerly into the water, his breath catching when it hits his lungs, and moving slowly enough that when he pushes away from the ladder he can keep his head above the water.

After a moment of floating, kicking his legs and treading his best, his head not far from the ceiling, he moves into the kitchen. "Coby," he tries to shout, but his lungs feel like they have shriveled. The act is futile. If Coby is down here—and where else could he be?—the worst has happened. But that's not what he is letting himself think about. This is a mission with a strict objective. *Operation: Karma.*

In the darkness, he barely recognizes that he's in his own house. He could be anywhere in the world. For the first time in a year, he moves past his liquor cabinet without feeling the urge to open it. That's something he will realize later, not now. Now, he grabs the flashlight from his mouth and holds it over his head while he takes a deep breath and dunks himself under. He tries to open his eyes but there's no hope for seeing anything. When he finds the surface again, it's with a heavier heart. *What the hell are you doing?* He is allowing his guilt to influence his actions—a dangerous game. *If Coby's down here, you don't want to find him. Not like this.*

His treading takes him into the living room and he does a quick scan of the surface. Nothing but the ripples that he's making. The only furniture that even reaches above the water level is an old grandfather clock in the living room and, in Amber's study, her oversized bookshe—

He stops dead and nearly sinks. Something is there. He steadies the flashlight toward the bookshelf and his eyes see a brown mass curled on the top shelf—the only part not submerged. He doesn't trust his eyes but begins swimming toward it anyway. "Coby," he states more than he shouts because he doesn't believe that that's what he's seeing. But by the time he makes it through the office doors, he can see for sure—it's his lost pal. *Please be alive*, he prays. *You can't leave me like this.*

Coby is curled into a ball with his back to Howard, seemingly trying to suck out any warmth that may be left in these walls.

As Howard reaches the bookshelf, he grabs hold of the structure and then rests a hand on Coby. His fur is freezing and wet, matted to his skin. Howard is feeling for a sign of life. But within a moment, Coby's head slowly perks up. The two seem to be on the same page—it can't be possible that they are finding each other right now.

Howard expects to see some sort of relief in Coby's eyes—that was at least the feeling flowing through him right now—but instead what he gets is anguish. The dog isn't far from death.

"I'm here, boy," he says as he runs his hands down his side. "I'm here. I'm not going anywhere without you."

Standing on one of the lower shelves for support, Howard does what he knows he has to do. Carefully, he slides his hands under the dog and lifts him over his head and rests him across his shoulders in a fireman's carry. Coby feels heavier than ever before, a dead mass. He's making no sounds or movements, but Howard can feel the soft breathing of the dog's belly against the back of his neck, and that's all he needs.

Howard says a little prayer and pushes away from the bookshelf. The momentum is enough to make it to Amber's desk, where he can stand and ready himself for the rest of the trek. His next move has to be flawless: lowering himself gingerly from the desk so as not to sink them both, while simultaneously kicking his feet to re-establish his tread. But in moments like these, despite exhaustion and the darkness and the freezing water, you find yourself capable of things you never thought possible.

Suddenly, to his surprise, he's moving swiftly through the living room, holding both his head and Coby above the water. The flashlight is bobbing in his mouth and spraying chaotic light around the room. Howard moves quickly and finds the ladder, lifting them both back into the attic. Somewhat surprisingly, just pulling himself from the water to a dry surface instantly feels warmer. There are blankets scattered around and Howard gathers as many as he can. With most of them, he wraps up Coby—some for dryness, the majority for warmth. The rest he throws into a big pile and carries out to the boat. Then he scoops up his dog and, as if holding a child in his arms, cautiously descends the slippery rooftop until he feels his unsteady footing on the boat.

Nestled into the blankets with only his head poking out, Coby closes his eyes and Howard once again prays for forgiveness of his betrayal.

And once again, he leaves the pistol lying on the attic floor.

16

Wolf Valley, 1992

In which Howard was 38 years old

Marriage proposals bring out the most intimate details of people's lives. That was a lesson Howard learned shortly after he slid the ring onto Amber's finger. Not long after, while at home cooking dinner, Amber said, "I can't wait to marry you."

It was one of those little moments that sticks in your memory for a long time. The way she said it warmed Howard's heart. "I can't wait to marry you too. Should we start talking wedding plans?"

"Something small," Amber said.

"Small is good."

"No... *small*. Just us, I was thinking. On that bluff at the top of the hike?"

"There's no one you want to invite?" He turned the chicken over and then checked on the asparagus. "None of the Literary Misfits of Michigan? Or Kim?"

"Nope, not even them. I'm sorry if that's not what you were picturing. Is there someone you wanted there?"

It hadn't dawned on him until then how lonely his life had been up to that point. He hadn't seen or heard from his mother since he was a small child, his father was dead, Willy long gone from his life. It also dawned on him that while he had virtually no family—perhaps a distant aunt he'd never met—he knew almost nothing about Amber's family. This was now his fiancée and for a brief moment he looked at her as if she were a stranger.

"No family?" he asked softly, afraid to strike a sensitivity.

Amber let out a breath and then went to the cupboard to get plates to set the table. "I know I've never really talked about my family with you. Truth is, I don't even know who my parents are." She glanced in Howard's direction and must have seen the concern on his face. "It's okay," she said, standing up. She smiled softly. "Don't burn the chicken over it."

Howard flipped off the stove. "They're about done. But, babe, what do you mean? The night we met you told me your parents were super religious."

"I mean I never met my parents. I grew up in foster homes when I was really little and then I was adopted, but those people—Jackie and Fred—never felt much like parents to me. They were nice enough, but—I don't know, I don't keep in touch with them. They had plenty of other kids in the house to worry about. That's just how it goes in the system."

"I'm sorry." He pulled her close.

"Don't be, honestly. I'm fine. I have you and my books."

"You always will."

"So." She lifted her head from his chest. "Just us on the bluff?"

"Sounds like heaven."

That's what they did. They hired a local to officiate and Howard's boss Wendell served as the witness. It was a clear day in the fall, the kind where the air is warm but the breeze is cool and the trees look like they are clinging desperately to the summer but without much hope. Howard wore a new pair of black jeans with his nicest cowboy boots, a shirt and a sports coat on top. Looking as radiant as he'd ever seen her, Amber wore her signature flowy dress, just below the knee, in a new color for her—pure white.

One of those gentle breezes was playing with her hair when they said "I do" and Howard took her in his arms and kissed her. Wendell snapped a photo that they later hung in the living room—the trees like broccoli in the distance, the river peeking out below, the blue sky hovering over it all. It was perfect.

If not for the terrain, Howard would have scooped Amber off her feet and carried her all the way back to their house and laid her right down on the bed.

"What now for the happy couple?" Wendell asked.

"Mr. Williams," Howard said without his eyes ever leaving Amber's, "I'm taking my bride home." And that's what he did. They had driven up the mountain so that they weren't hiking in their wedding attire, which was all the better for Howard—a quicker dash back to their house.

"Don't you want to take me somewhere romantic?" Amber said teasingly once they were back in the truck.

"Darling, I would be more than happy to take you somewhere romantic. In about an hour."

She laughed and kissed him on the cheek, her hand resting on his thigh. His truck rumbled down the dirt road and she left her hand there without saying a word. The ring on his finger was rubbing against the steering wheel and his skin but he was delighted at the thought of wearing it every day.

"Mrs. Lynch." It was a whisper that landed just so.

Howard turned his head for a brief moment and smiled.

"Eyes ahead, husband. These roads can be awfully treacherous."

In the late evenings, the sun didn't often make it all the way down into the valley and peek through the windows of their house, but that's exactly what it was doing on their wedding day. Amber was tucked under the sheet and Howard was sitting up just staring at her. The sheet was thin and fell neatly over her figure and he couldn't take his eyes away, even after making love twice. He wanted to get up and get a drink—after all, that day was something to celebrate—but he wasn't going anywhere until she moved.

When she did, she wrapped the sheet around herself like a towel and shimmied from the bed.

"Come on," Howard said. "Give me something."

"Like this?" she said, turning and dropping the sheet as seductively as she could.

"Like that." He smiled and motioned for her to come back to bed but she playfully squawked and ran to the closet.

"What are we going to do to celebrate?" Her voice was muffled from inside the closet.

"I think we already have a pretty good plan in place."

"For real!"

"Okay, okay. But maybe we can continue this plan later." He waited for a snarky comment but none came. "Should we head into town? Go to that one restaurant—Yvonne's? Can't get much fancier than a place called Yvonne's in these parts."

"Yvonne's it is."

"And then—"

"Shut it!"

Married life for Howard and Amber was no different than unmarried life. There was no honeymoon—Amber was close to completing her manuscript and couldn't risk losing her focus, she said. Every morning, Amber headed into her study and Howard pulled on his boots and drove to a worksite. Most evenings upon his return, he would find Amber either still in her office working or sometimes down by the river reading or just thinking. It was a quiet existence, but one that they both cherished.

Watching Amber's writing process was fascinating to Howard. For her first book, other than the jottings he witnessed in bars that day in Holland, he didn't even know she had written let alone published a novel until he saw her face on a poster years later. Even for her second book, he wasn't around for the writing process. But this one—whatever it was she had been poring herself into—he watched her day and night. The papers on her desk scattered and organized and scattered again. The ink refills, the piles of books that came and went from the shelves. And yet, all through the process, she remained glued to her seat. That seemed like the most challenging part about writing a book—keeping your ass in the chair. It certainly would have been Howard's downfall if the roles were reversed.

Still, a quiet life, with its obvious benefits for an introvert like Howard, could be overdone. Quiet is nice; lonely is not. And after just weeks following their wedding, that was the feeling he had begun to tumble toward.

One evening, Howard was sitting on the couch with his arm around Amber. She had collapsed beside him shortly before, after a long day in her office, and he had a glass of bourbon in his hand and another waiting for her on the coffee table. Seinfeld was on the TV, though the volume was turned low like they both preferred it. The show cut to a commercial and Howard said, "Do you remember that young mom who came up to you after your book signing that day back in Michigan?"

"Mhmm," she said, taking her first sip of her drink. "What about her?"

"Well, it's pretty quiet in this house."

She sat up and set down her glass. "Are you about to ask what I think you're about to ask?"

He shrugged.

"Howard."

"I don't know. I just feel like it's something we never talked about."

Amber looked away for a moment. The air was still. The TV in the background was the only sound. "Let's talk about it then."

"Look, I can tell this isn't something you want to talk about."

"No, that's not it."

"At least not right now. I get it."

"Howard, I'm gonna smack ya. Just ask it."

"What are your thoughts about it?"

"What are yours?"

"Honestly, I'm not even sure why I brought it up. I think it's the whiskey. I haven't really given it much thought."

"Hmm. Well, if I'm being honest, I *have* given it some thought."

He looked at her with a piqued interest. "Have you?"

"I have."

"And?"

"If *you* want to try...then *I* want to try."

The way she looked at him told him she was being genuine. He pulled her back close and hugged her tightly, kissed her on the top of her head. "I love you, you know that?"

"Well that's good, because I love you too," she said, looking over her shoulder and kissing him through her smile.

Over the next couple of weeks, Howard and Amber made love daily—the way a husband and wife love each other when they are subsumed and infatuated. With everything they had. They made love in their bedroom. On the couch. On one occasion in a moment of buzzed breath, on the patio against the brick wall. And, yes, on one other rare and unexpected occasion, Amber drew Howard into her office and made a new use out of her desk.

It all felt like zero to sixty. From imagined to married. From afar to embracing. From strangers to lovers. It was a fast, furious and short time in Howard's life. After making love one evening, Amber rolled off of him and collapsed in the bed. Howard draped a sheet over her body and could hear the wheezy breaths of sleep before he could even slip on his loafers. He made his way to the kitchen, poured himself a drink, and then stepped out onto the patio and lit up a small cigar. In more of a seep than a billow, he opened his mouth and watched the smoke leave him. The aesthetic of it calmed his mind and he sat back and thought about what his life was rapidly becoming. And for the first time in years, he thought about his parents.

Howard faintly remembered his mother having positive qualities, but those memories faded over the years, pushed out of his mind by the singular memory of her walking out on him, the note he found on the table. And his father—whatever credit he deserved for sticking around was negated by the sheer neglect and trauma and shame that ruled over the boy's childhood.

You might be a father soon.

The thought, once exciting and motivating, instantly stopped him in his tracks. His breath quickened and fear washed over him. *You might be a parent soon.* It was chilling. He had no role models in this area of life. The thought suddenly terrified him.

That's how he sat for the rest of the night. He finished his cigar and stubbed it out on the concrete, and then he threw back the whiskey and set the glass by his feet. He sat there and watched the evening glow turn to a midnight blue until finally he was sitting in a blackness. At some point in that blackness, he slept.

His eyes thrust open at the sound of the patio door opening. Amber stepped outside holding a plain white coffee mug, steam rising from it. The morning was dewy and Howard could feel the cool moisture all around him. This late in the season, it was foolish to allow himself to sleep the entire night outside.

"Hey," he said in a groggy voice.

"Hey yourself."

"Sorry, I must have fallen asleep out here."

Amber ignored the comment and handed him the coffee.

"For me?"

"Mhmm." She had an odd smile on her face.

Howard took a sip and then glanced up at Amber, whose expression remained. "Good coffee," he said.

She continued to stare.

"You okay?"

She didn't say anything.

He held out the mug and looked at it. The coffee was fine—good, even—but it was still just coffee. Finally, he turned the mug in his hand and some writing came into view from the other side. WORLD'S BEST DAD.

Holy shit. His eyes shot wide and he stood up. "Amber."

"Uh-huh," she nodded as tears came to her smiling eyes.

He set the mug down and she jumped into his arms. They embraced for a long time and when they finally peeled apart, they both could see the puffy red edges in the other's eyes. And then they embraced again.

Finding out that he was going to become a father was probably the only news that could have simultaneously excited and frightened Howard, the two extremes pulling his emotions in opposite directions until he just needed to sit down.

"What are you thinking about?" Amber asked as she walked into the living room later that evening.

The question snapped Howard from his trepidations and he looked up at her. "Oh, I'm just thinking about how we are going to convert that other bedroom into a nursery."

She sat down at his side and put a hand on her belly. "He's in there."

"You think it's a he?"

She shrugged. "I don't know. Maybe she's in there. But I feel different knowing it. Good different."

"Good different," Howard repeated. "The best."

For the next few weeks, as autumn cooled into early winter, Howard thought about one thing: what kind of parent he needed to be. The thought consumed him. He spent long nights remembering the trauma that his parents inflicted upon him as a young boy. A mental checklist of sorts, he was trying to recall everything *not* to do with a child of his own—how *not* to act, how *not* to talk to their mother, how *not* to set an example. Instead, he wanted to be the opposite of what his parents were to him: affectionate, patient, present. As he engaged with this exercise, all the fears he'd initially felt about parenthood seemed to drift away.

He crawled into bed one night, leaned over to Amber, and said, "I have a whole new outlook."

"What do you mean?"

"My parents were terrible parents."

"Uh huh," she said sounding skeptical of where this was going. "And?"

"And—they didn't show me how to be a good parent, but they sure as hell showed me how to be a bad parent. So I at least know a bunch of stuff *not* to do with our kiddo."

"Howard, don't stress about this. You are going to be a GREAT parent. That's all that matters."

"The way I figure," he continued on his original thought, "whatever's the opposite of what they did—that's probably the right way to do it."

She leaned over, kissed him, and then turned out the lamp and pulled up the covers. "Sounds like you've got it all figured out."

Maybe not all figured out, but at least a plan to help him rest easy at night. And that's how it started—his head hit the pillow beside hers and they were both out. But at some point in the black of night, he was awoken by a painful scream. His eyes shot open and he thrust himself out of bed. As his vision adjusted, he could tell that Amber wasn't lying beside him. Another scream. Howard ran out of their room and into the bathroom. That's where he found his wife, curled up on the floor and rocking in pain.

"Oh my God, are you okay?" He fell to the floor beside her, unsure exactly what he needed to do.

She didn't speak but her pain was audible.

"Amber, please let me help you." He saw blood on the toilet seat and a few drops on the floor.

Her teeth were clenched and her eyes were red and swollen against a ghost-white face. "You can't help."

"Please."

"Go."

He hesitated. He stood and looked at her. His heart could barely take it. But then he left and went back to the bedroom and waited on the edge of the bed with the lamp on. What felt like hours passed, and the entire time he sat there like a statue, his heart racing, the occasional muffled moan from down the hall stabbing his ears.

Finally, he heard footsteps and he sat up more attentively. Amber appeared in the doorway and he jumped up. "Are you okay? Jesus, Amber, are you okay? What was going on?" He went to take her hands and noticed she was holding a small box.

She wasn't crying anymore. She had no expression to speak of— she was stone. "I'm sorry," she said.

Howard looked confused. "Sorry? Don't be sorry, I just want to know you're okay."

"Howard," Amber said, realizing that he wasn't fully grasping what had happened. "Howard, I'm sorry. I lost the baby."

"What—I mean..." He wasn't sure what to say. His mind was running in a million directions. "Are you sure? We can see a doctor in the morning. I'll take you to the hospital right now."

"Howard." She held out the box. "This is our baby."

Without even a moment to comprehend it, tears began flowing down his cheeks. And when his started, that's when hers returned. They didn't speak another word for a long time, but he took her into his arms and they stood there in the doorway crying into each other. The house was silent except for their labored breathing.

They pulled apart and Amber said, "We need to bury it."

"Okay," Howard said as he stared off into the distance.

"Howard."

"Okay." And then, "Right, okay," as if it finally clicked. He slipped on some shoes and grabbed a flashlight, and then he went outside to the shed for a shovel. Amber met him out back and they walked slowly and silently across the yard toward a thick tree with low overhanging branches along the riverbank. For a brief moment, Howard could hear the river but he couldn't yet see it in the darkness. Death had come for him. His sins of rivers past had returned. *This is what you deserve.*

Howard handed Amber the flashlight and then began to dig. The instant the metal hit the dirt the floodgates opened and he was openly sobbing. He couldn't control himself. Tears flew from his face and he felt like a child again. He was blinded by them. With each thrust into the earth, he hoped he was hitting the same hole. And then he felt a soft hand on his shoulder and he dropped the shovel and wiped his eyes.

Amber lowered herself to the ground and gently rested the box in the hole. "We should say something."

Howard was still choking on his emotions.

"Rest easy, little one," she said. "You are with the Lord now. And though we never had the chance to know you in this life, we look forward to meeting you someday."

Howard couldn't believe what was happening. In the dark of the night, this all felt like a dream, like he would wake up in the morning and discover none of it happened. But when morning arrived, his face was stiff from the salt of dried tears. He climbed out of bed and went to the kitchen and splashed some water on his face. Looking out the window, he could see the tree and the branches and the disturbed soil where there used to be grass. Before he could splash his face again, he felt more tears pushing at the backs of his eyes.

Instead of coffee, he reached for the whiskey.

17

Wolf Valley, 2002

In which Howard is 48 years old

Their time apart could be measured in hours, not days, and yet it feels like it has been an eternity. Howard won't let himself break contact with Coby now. He is steering the boat with one hand and gently resting his other hand on the dog's side. He's not going anywhere this time. "Never again," he says aloud so Coby can hear his voice. "Never again. Y'hear me, boy? Never again."

They have just pushed off from the house and the boat slowly spins to head back in the direction of the shelter. Once they are a safe distance away, Howard pulls the cord and after a few tries hears the rumble. He adjusts the choke until it's steady—the only sound in the night. With clouds overhead, he still can't see anything without the help of the flashlight. As they float down the road, Howard replaces his hand on Coby's side and does something he has done very little of over the last year: he prays.

"Thank you, God, for watching over this dog," he says audibly. "Thank you for saving his life. I wouldn't have had the strength to come back for him without you."

He pauses and shines a light on Coby. He can see the gentle up and down of his breathing.

"I was pissed at you. Really pissed. You took Amber from me." Another pause. "But thank you for keeping Coby in my life."

He ends, hesitantly, with, "Amen, I suppose."

The prayer feels uncomfortable, yet appropriate. At the very least, it's another opportunity for Coby to hear his voice, which he hopes provides even just a basic level of comfort to the despondent dog.

Suddenly, Coby's head shoots up.

"What is it, boy?"

But Coby seems to ignore him. Instead, the dog struggles to his feet and takes a couple steps over to the side of the boat. His head is now hanging over the edge and he's on high alert. He barks. Once at first, then again. And again. Then louder.

Howard repeats, "What is it, bud?"

The barking continues. Coby finally looks over to Howard and whines urgently, then looks back toward the darkness and barks again. Howard is shining the flashlight toward where Coby is barking but he doesn't see anything except a dark house. More barking, and louder. Howard can hear the desperation in the signal now, so he decides to at least maneuver the boat in that direction.

Slowly, the boat begins across what likely would have been a front yard toward the house. The blanket starts moving—Coby is trying to wag his tail.

"What's going on with this house, Cobes?"

As the boat comes to rest against the gutter, Howard ties up and watches Coby, who is wagging his entire body back and forth, looking like he is ready to hop right onto the roof.

Howard puts a hand on the dog's back. "It's okay, buddy, I'll check it out."

Before taking a step from the boat, Howard shines the flashlight over the entire house to get a better look at it. It's one he's driven past hundreds of times, yet never stopped to notice. Unlike his brick ranch, this is a two-story wooden farmhouse that must date back to the nineteenth century. A pale yellow with white shutters framing each of the windows, the owner has evidently cared for it. No longer visible, Howard can remember a wrap-around front porch with a swing in the corner. The house is on the same side of the street as his but far enough down the road that the river has already bent into the woods, so this house has a deep back lawn that eventually turns into trees. That was the thing Howard always noticed about it, he tells himself now, that of all the houses on this road, it had one of the worst views because the river runs away from it. But for the life of him, he can't think of who lives here—or why on Earth his dog would be leading him to it.

Coby is eager to hop onto the roof, but Howard holds him back and tries to settle him. He can only imagine the trauma that Coby has endured and he is not going to allow him to endanger himself even further. The boat is rocking gently and Howard lifts Coby, sets him off to the side of the boat and re-wraps him in the blanket. "Stay here, boy. I'll go check it out."

Flashlight in hand, Howard steps off the craft. He thinks he's standing on the awning over the porch. Taking a few steps, he reaches an upstairs bedroom window that looks like it could be original to the house—the glass is warped and cloudy and he can barely see through it. The air is still and he looks it over briefly. Without much to grab onto, he holds firm to the wooden frame and tries to slide it upward, but it's stuck—perhaps from decades of being painted shut. Shining the flashlight down the side of the house, he thinks this is pointless, but Coby lets out a painful howl that re-engages his attention.

In the still of the early morning, Howard stands stoically for a moment. He looks at Coby and back at the house and out over the flooded neighborhood. That's what it takes—a moment of silence. Howard remembers that as a child one of the neighbor kids told him when everything suddenly goes silent it's because an angel is flying by. That's what this feels like now. And that silence is needed for Howard to hear just the faintest sound. At first, he thinks he's hearing voices in his head, convincing himself that Coby's whines must have purpose. But then he pauses and hears it again. He's not entirely sure what he's hearing, but he thinks it's coming from inside the house.

Pressing his ear to the glass, he listens intently. Quiet, then—*uuggggghhhhh*—a low crescendo of moaning. He shines the light inside but he can't see anyone, just shelves and boxes packed, a twin bed pressed against the opposite wall.

"Is someone in there?"

Another silence, then another moan. He hurries down to the next window, about twenty feet away, and shines the light inside. This room looks more like a functioning bedroom than the last. It's a bit disheveled, but there is a larger bed against a nearby wall, a dresser, a vanity—and what appears to be a person. Howard tries to wipe the lingering moisture from the glass so he can better see inside. He attempts to slide the window open but it feels lodged—not glued shut like the first one, but unwilling to budge.

"Is anybody in there?"

The question is more of a statement, because unless his eyes are deceiving him—which is entirely possible at this point—he can see someone inside. This person is sitting on the floor near the door, his or her back propped up against the wall. He thinks it's a woman, but that's something he can't quite be sure of. Bracing himself, he tries the window again. It gives a little, but it still won't open. He's straining himself, putting his entire body behind it.

"I'm here to help," he shouts through labored breath.

He has distracted himself with the window for long enough that he doesn't notice the woman stand and walk toward him. She's just on the other side of the glass, and when Howard takes a breath between attempts she startles him.

Through the pane, he hears, "Let me unlock it."

Under normal circumstances, he would be embarrassed, but instead, he takes a step back while the woman flips the latch, and then the two of them jointly put their hands on the window and slide it upward. Howard recognizes her immediately. He has seen her around before. He thinks he can remember her stopping by the house after Amber passed, but those days are all a blur now. *What was her name?* She told him, he knows that, but he's forgotten it. Along with so many other things.

The first thing that comes out of his mouth is, "Are you okay?"

"I'm okay," she says, but Howard isn't blind. He can see with his own two eyes the state she's in: raggedy nightgown hanging from one shoulder, hunched over, bags under her eyes. She barely resembles the woman who stopped by the house all those months ago. Some of these things come with age, he knows, and she's certainly getting up there. Just the fact that she has survived this long on her own seems miraculous.

"I have a boat. I can take you to the shelter. There's food and water."

The woman hesitates. She looks concerned.

"This is bad, ma'am."

"Call me Edna."

"Sorry—Edna. This is bad. This flooding goes throughout the entire valley."

After a brief moment, she finally says, "Well I certainly can't go anywhere looking like this."

It feels like a stubborn hill to die on—literally—but Howard accepts it. "Do you need me to come in there and help with anything?"

"That's very kind, Howard, but just give me a moment, please."

So Howard steps away from the window and walks back in the direction of his boat. Coby is still standing and wagging his tail, but he's managed to remain aboard instead of lunging for the awning to meet his owner. Howard crouches down and pets the dog, rubbing behind his ears. He looks out over the water. The sun hasn't quite emerged yet, but he can tell morning isn't far off.

A few minutes later, Edna comes back to the window. "Howard," she calls in a grandmotherly voice.

He turns and jogs back to the window. "Here, let me help you, Edna." He offers her a hand and helps guide her through the window. It's a delicate process given her age and frail state. In one of her hands, she is clenching an envelope. A loose necklace is dangling down her shirt with a large cross at the end. The transition is slow, and when Howard gets her all the way onto the awning he reaches back and closes the window.

On the boat, Coby is waiting with enthusiasm. Edna steps down and falls onto one of the planks that serve as a bench. Howard is quick to follow and wrap her in a blanket. "Brought these for the pup, but it seems he's okay with sharing," he says. Now pressing himself against Edna's legs, Coby looks up at Howard with thankfulness.

The morning glow will soon arrive, but it's still dull and low as they push off from the edge of the roof. Edna looks comfortable now. Howard waits until they are away from the house and leaving the neighborhood before trying to engage the woman in conversation.

"Did you see any rescuers come by the last day or so?"

She shakes her head no.

The response doesn't surprise him. *Those two jackasses.*

"This has been a nightmare forty-eight hours or so," he says. Edna is still petting Coby, not even looking out at the destruction of her town. "Glad we found you, though." He thinks about that comment. "Shoot, I can't even take credit. Coby here found you. He barked like a wild pup toward your place until I took us over there to check it out. And glad he did."

For another few moments, a silence lingers. He tries to think but his mind is still spinning from everything that has just transpired. Two lives saved. Maybe three, he thinks.

Then Edna says quietly, almost under her breath, "Are you a religious man, Howard?"

The question catches him a little off guard. "Not really," he says.

"Have you ever been?"

"Once upon a time. Stopped believing in the Man Upstairs a while ago."

"It might be time to believe again."

"Why's that?"

She gives Coby a couple of gentle pats and then pulls the blanket tight around her. Looking Howard in the eye, she says, "If there's no God, then there's no heaven."

He gives her a skeptical look.

"And if there's no heaven, there's no guardian angels. And that can't be the case, because the three of us here all sure have a guardian angel watching over us."

Howard ponders the notion. Then he thinks about Amber, and a tear fills his eye. For as long as he's avoided the church, the sudden idea that his late wife is somehow orchestrating their survival from above overpowers him.

Edna stands, slowly and cautiously to maintain her balance on the moving boat, and steps toward Howard, placing a hand on his arm. "Yes," she whispers. "It's her."

18

Wolf Valley, 1999

In which Howard was 45 years old

With a damp towel around his waist, Howard wiped the fog from the bathroom mirror and stared at himself. He barely recognized the man he saw. Gray flecks dotted his hair, and the skin on his face and chest was becoming loose. He had shed weight and years of a humble, quiet life in Wolf Valley appeared up and down his body. Forty-five yet he thought he looked fifty and felt even older, at least on certain days. His hands had a slight shake and his back was chronically sore.

"Admiring yourself?" Amber stepped into the bathroom and disrobed. "You better have left me some hot water." Twisting the nob, the faucet gushed and she held her hand under it to feel the temperature. "You got lucky."

"I've always taken short showers." He said it aloud but he knew it now was a lie, or at the very least misleading. He used to take short showers, sure. But as the years and the stress of life wore on, he discovered the shower was the place where he could best clear his thoughts. Five minutes turned to ten which turned to twenty or more. On occasion, he had emptied the hot water tank. Perhaps she was right, he got lucky this time.

He watched her knelt over feeling for the right heat before she pulled up on the lever and sent the water to the shower head. She was still gorgeous for her thirty-nine years, still slender. For all the damage the stress of the last seven years had taken on Howard's body, it seemed she was mostly spared—despite her physically carrying the trauma.

After their first loss, they waited a little while before trying again. And then, when they became pregnant a second time, they experienced nearly an identical end. They waited even longer after that one, and then they went through it all for a third time. After that, they decided that they were no longer "trying"; if it happened, it happened. And it did—all of it—for a fourth time. That was nearly a fatal blow to both of them. With each loss, the life seemed to drain from Howard's eyes. He had become a six-word Hemingway short story. *For sale: Baby shoes. Never worn.*

Perhaps the only thing that kept them going was Amber's writing. Throughout those seven trying years, she had completed and published two more books, both of which went on to more critical acclaim and some minor awards. Better than that, though, they sold well—alleviating at least the financial burden. Howard continued to work but less often. He retreated into a more solitary life. When an argument broke out one night, Amber said, "All this has made my books better," which Howard wrongfully took as her being grateful for the miscarriages.

"How could you ever say that?"

"You know what I mean."

"No, I don't," he said and then spent the next two nights drinking on the patio and sleeping on the couch.

They made up after that, and things were by all accounts going fine, but there was a gaping hole in their lives now—one that Howard was beginning to fear would and could never be filled. He was beginning to get restless in Wolf Valley. They had left for short trips over the years, but they had yet to take any kind of extended leave together. Amber, for her part, had done two short book tours and had gone to some book-related events in random cities around the country, but Howard usually elected to remain home.

That changed when Amber received a call from her agent, Kim Barnes, about an event her publisher was hosting the following month in New York. They wanted her to be there to say a few words.

"What do you think?" Amber asked. "Should I go?"

Without any hesitation, Howard said, "Not only should you go, *we* should go."

Her face lit up. "You want to come with me?"

"Don't you get a plus-one for these types of things?"

"They're usually offered, yeah."

"So how 'bout it?"

"I'll call Kim."

A few weeks later, they drove a couple hours to the nearest airport that could get them a direct flight to LaGuardia, and, on a cool and overcast afternoon, they boarded a plane.

For all of the pain and heartbreak that his short time in New York City had brought him, and for as much as he never truly fit in, when he set foot on those streets again he felt an immediate nostalgia. Like a long-lost friend had put an arm around him during a moment of panic.

"I hate this city," Amber said as they stepped out of a cab in front of their hotel.

"It's growing on me."

"In the hour that we've been sitting in traffic?"

"Just on the whole."

"I never pegged you for a New York man."

He couldn't help but grin. "Neither did I, to be honest. But, I don't know, those few months when I briefly called it home—just feels familiar. It's comforting, you know? Good to be back, is all."

She shook her head. "It seems you and I have switched positions."

He pulled her tight against his body as they walked into the lobby. "Now that is something I am all in favor of." She pushed away his advance and he playfully accepted the rejection. "To be continued," he said.

They didn't have much time before the event, so they quickly changed and headed back out into the New York City night—Howard in the only suit he owned and Amber in one of her signature dresses. The event was being held in a banquet room with high ceilings. Round tables with eight chairs around each filled the space, and at the front of the room stood a single podium on an elevated platform. When they arrived, people were standing and mingling in the back of the room and the adjacent lobby.

"Wow," Amber said.

"Uh-huh."

"This is bigger than I expected."

Howard saw her expression and turned to face her. "You are going to do great," he said. "Plus, there's an open bar."

"Why don't we hit that first."

Howard ordered a whiskey and Amber a glass of Chardonnay. As they returned to the crowd, they were immediately greeted by a middle-aged woman with big hair and a boxy frame.

"There you are!" the woman shouted.

Amber hugged her and said, "It's nice to see you again," as she pulled away and took a sip of her wine.

"And this must be Mr. Howard," the woman said extending a hand.

"Yes. Howard Lynch."

"Kim Barnes."

"Yes, sorry," Amber said. "Howard, this is my agent, Kim."

"Well, it is nice to finally meet you, Howard. Amber has told me so many great things about you. Now, if you could only get this one —" she said nudging Amber's side "—to move back from the middle of nowhere then we could do this more often!"

He smiled politely at the comment, but he could see from the look on Amber's face that she wasn't able to restrain her feelings as well. Kim, though, was oblivious and instead looked around the room.

"There's someone," she said in a drawn-out voice that sounded like she was trying to buy time, "that I wanted to introduce you to..."

Amber looked at Howard.

"Ah, yes!" Kim said, looping her arm around Amber's. "I'll bring her right back," she said to Howard and then pulled Amber through the crowd.

Howard quickly finished his drink and went back to the bar for another. He peered around the room at all the people. They were gathered in small groups mostly, with dozens of conversations happening simultaneously, him standing on the periphery of their lives as no more than a bystander. He took a sip and then walked over to one of the tables and looked at the nameplates that were set neatly before each place setting. The names were as strange as the faces scattered throughout the room, but they intrigued him. Names like Reginald and Marilyn and Francis and Nicklaus and Clement and Geraldine. *Who in the world were these people's parents and where did they come from?*

For as much as Howard loved to read, this was not his scene. His navy suit was faded and flat, a hand-me-down from an old colleague years ago, no doubt already multiple decades old at that point. Howard wasn't sure he out-aged it. He wished to be back in the valley, back in his house near the river where his problems seemed large but his insecurities felt small. Here, in the real world, those things were reversed.

Looking down at his glass, he realized he was already almost done with his second drink, so he threw it back and then navigated his way across the room to the other bar to get his third. He told himself he would sip this one slower. But the elixir was helping his nerves.

He wandered toward the front of the room where he found a table with nameplates that read AMBER MCNAMARA and HOWARD LYNCH. He set down his glass and then took a seat. It didn't bother him to be one of the only people in the entire room sitting down. It felt appropriate. However, it didn't take long until waves of people began searching for their own nameplates. It seemed that some sort of announcement must have gone out that the show was about to start.

A man in a tweed jacket and wire-rimmed glasses sat down across the table from Howard and gave a deliberate and embellished head nod his way. Howard returned the gesture in the same exaggerated manner and then briefly hoped that it hadn't looked mockingly. So he stood up and walked around the table and stuck out his hand. "Howard Lynch."

"Jeffrey Walls," the man said.

"Nice to meet you, Jeff."

"Jeffrey."

"Jeffrey—I'm sorry. I'm here with my wife, Amber McNamara." Even though she had legally changed her name, she still published under McNamara and for some reason, it made Howard uncomfortable every time it came out of his mouth.

"Ah, yes, Ms. McNamara. I was hoping we'd get to meet her tonight."

Howard glanced up and saw Amber rushing back to the table. "And it looks like here she comes now."

"I'm sorry," she whispered in Howard's ear as she gave him a quick embrace.

"Amber, this is our table-mate, Jeffrey Walls."

"Mr. Walls, it's a pleasure," she said in a hurried voice.

"The pleasure is all mine, Ms. McNamara. I've loved every one of your books."

"I'm honored. Truly."

They all took their seats and the room settled. A large man with a deep voice walked onto the platform at the front of the room and stood behind the podium to give welcoming remarks. This was something he had clearly done many times before. Howard finished his drink and wondered if it would be rude to sneak off to the bar for a fourth, but then thought better of it. And he was glad he did because only a moment later the man at the podium announced Amber's name and the room rose and clapped and Amber timidly made her way up front to shake the man's hand.

There she stood—all alone before the group of what Howard guessed to be a couple hundred. She gripped the podium with both hands, took a deep breath and smiled. "Thanks, Jerry," she started. "Forgive me if I seem nervous. I think there are more people in this room than in my entire town." She got a few chuckles for that. "It's amazing to see what can happen in life if you learn to string a few words together, over and over, over and over, over and over—in just the right way."

She went on to give a short but beautiful speech. She thanked the people who had gotten her to this point, the readers of her books, Kim and her editor, Lorraine, and her publisher. She talked about her upbringing, the risks she took to make this career happen, the challenges she faced and overcame, and what inspired her to write what she wrote.

"I believe everything happens for a reason," she said in conclusion. "And I intend to prove that with my next book—whenever that day comes."

The crowd once again rose to their feet and Howard joined them. His eyes had become misty as he watched Amber, and then he peered around at all the applause. These people loved her. And in that moment, he couldn't have been prouder of Amber Lynch.

"So, when is this next book coming?"

"I'm working on it," she said.

They were in a cab back to their hotel and a light autumn rain began to patter the roof. They listened to it in silence for a moment and then Howard said, "You were incredible tonight."

"Thanks. I was pretty nervous."

"Incredible," he repeated, putting his arm around her and kissing her head.

She gave him a halfhearted grin.

"Is this the kind of thing you do every time you travel?"

"I don't travel that much."

"Okay, well when you do travel?"

"Not really," she said. "Usually I'm not speaking. And if I am, it's just reading a chapter from my book to a room of middle-aged women. This was entirely different. Hence the nerves."

"Well, you were incredible."

She let out a restrained laugh and said, "Yeah, so I've heard."

The cab traveled toward Midtown and they looked out the window at all the lights and people. "Hard to believe we lived in this place," he said.

"I lived here years."

"I don't know how you did it."

"It wasn't so bad."

"Want to do it again?"

She turned and looked at him to better judge the seriousness of the question. "No," she said plainly. "No, I don't."

"You never think about leaving Wolf Valley?"

The rain picked up now and they watched people scurrying faster down the sidewalks and ducking under scaffolding that seemed to be on nearly every block. "Permanently? No, not really. But I take it you have."

She said it as a statement, not a question, but Howard answered anyway. "Sometimes. More recently. Don't get me wrong, I don't think I'd want to move back to New York, but Michigan? Maybe.

Somewhere else? Maybe. Honestly, I'm surprised it hasn't crossed your mind."

"Why's that?"

"Just—just with all that's happened the last several years. Pretty much the whole time we've lived there."

"I can't leave."

"Can't? Or won't?"

"I can't leave, okay? Do you remember when I first asked you to come with me to Wolf Valley? I told you I needed to go there for a book I was working on."

"Yeah, I guess. So was it for *The Last Good Neighbor?* Or *Once Angels Retreat?*" He named the two novels she'd released since moving to Wolf Valley, both of which sold well.

But she shook her head. "No, neither. It was because of the book I'm working on now. I've been working on it for years, on and off while I finished those two."

"Okay, so what's it about?"

"I can't tell you."

"Can't?" he asked again. "Or won't?"

"Howard. Leave it alone."

The cab pulled up to their hotel and they both climbed out in silence. Howard paid the driver and they went up to their room, changed and fell asleep. In the morning, they headed to the airport and flew home.

It wasn't until they returned to Wolf Valley that Howard realized just how much he truly needed that short getaway to New York. Stepping back into their home was like returning to a recurring nightmare that you hadn't realized you were in until you woke up. Well, Howard had awoken for a time and now he was back.

Amber went straight to her study, closed the door, set her bag down beside her desk, and then went right back to writing. She didn't even glance up. Howard took his bag to the bedroom and then went straight for the whiskey and the back patio. He brought a small radio with him and listened to 70's and 80's country—one of the few stations he could get on a semi-reliable signal down there.

Late that evening the phone rang. Howard and Amber played chicken for walking into the kitchen to answer it. After the fourth ring, Howard stood up and went inside. "Hello?" He probably sounded a little disgruntled as he peeked around the corner to Amber's office, where she sat working as if the phone never even rang.

"Howard, it's Wendell. Need a hand on a site tomorrow. Can I count on ya?"

"We just got back from New York a couple hours ago."

"That's great. Can I count on ya?"

An exasperated breath and then, "I'll be there."

"Wonderful to hear. I'll have Steve call with the details."

"See you tomorrow."

Since Amber's latest book, Howard had been working less and less often—taking on small projects with Wendell when he was needed, but spending more time in a self-imposed solitary confinement by the river. Waking up, making a canteen of coffee, starting his truck in the foggy morning—the dew coating the toes of his boots—filling his lungs with that cool, moist valley air. This was what he needed.

He followed the handwritten directions to the site. It was a house on a bluff overlooking the river. The vantage point was fascinating to Howard. All those years looking up to the bluffs, and these homeowners spent the same time looking down to the valley. The project was for a new two-story deck that came off both the living room and the upstairs master bedroom. It was a large project and there were a few guys already there when he pulled up. He grabbed his coffee, shook a few hands and went to work.

By lunchtime, the heat of the day was starting to settle in. Even this late in the fall, up on the ridge where you couldn't hide from the sun, sometimes an unseasonal warmth arrived and Howard had the unfortunate luck of agreeing to a job on just such a day. He was sitting under the shade of a tree in the front yard taking a rest. He'd already finished his sandwich and then he lay back and tried to close his eyes for a few minutes when another worker sat down beside him.

"How's it going, Howard?" the man asked. His name was Terry Spears and he and Howard had worked many jobs together over the last handful of years.

"It's going, Terry."

"I don't see you around these jobs so much anymore."

"Been cutting back."

"That wife of yours raking in the dough?"

Howard gave him a look. "She does alright."

"Let me tell ya, it's tougher when ya got kids. I been takin' every job that's offered since the kids started comin'." Terry was a family man, Howard knew this, with three older daughters and a young son at home.

"Terry," Howard said deliberately, contemplating if he wanted to engage. He thought for a moment and then said, "The kids thing is complicated." As the words spilled from Howard's mouth, he realized that he had never spoken to anyone about the difficulties they'd suffered over the last several years.

"How d'you mean? You and Amber thinkin' of havin' kids still?"

"It's been a sore subject in the house."

"Y'all not on the same page, I take it."

"We've been on the same page," Howard said sheepishly. "Got close a few times, but they never stuck, if you understand me."

Terry fell silent for a moment, looking around. When he turned back to Howard, he said, "I'm real sorry t'hear that, pal." He patted him on the shoulder. Then he said, "Y'know, there's other options. Ever look into adoption?"

At that moment Howard realized exactly why he had never spoken to anyone about this before. He didn't want a brainstorming session, didn't want any advice. He just wanted to utter his grievances aloud, make them real. Now he wished they were still invisible. "I'm not sure that's an option for us."

"No? I'd be happy to put you in touch with someone. Hell, our oldest was adopted. Cheryl wasn't sure she could go through the childbirth thing, so we adopted. Only for her to change her mind and, shit, then we had three more of our own."

"It's not really that. I think adoption is great—I do. Amber was adopted, actually." When he said that, he felt an immediate knot in his gut like he'd just let spill a family secret. "Don't tell that to anyone," he added. "But I respect the hell out of it and especially folks like yourself who do it. I just feel like I need a kid of my own blood, you know?"

"Well, Howard, I get that. But I think you'd be sorry if you didn't at least give it a shot. If a family's what y'want, then it's possible, my friend."

"Thanks, Terry." His voice was flat. Terry went back around the side of the house and Howard lay there smelling the grass and feeling the breeze and the sweat beading on his forehead and the regret for even entertaining that conversation.

When he walked into his house that evening, the exhaustion that comes from infrequency hit hard. By the time he had slipped off his boots and opened a beer, he could barely keep his eyes open. Amber was still sitting in her study hard at work, and Howard watched her intently as his eyelids began to slowly collapse.

For the entire afternoon, he continued to replay his conversation with Terry. *Why did you open up to him*, he kept asking himself. But his circular logic then would transition to, *Because you have no one else to talk to*, before going back to, *But then this is what happens when you open up—you make yourself vulnerable*. This went on even with his eyes shut and nodding off to sleep.

Moments later, his leg twitched and he jolted himself awake. A little beer spilled from the can and he could smell the stale dampness on his sleeve—perhaps the strongest reminder that he had a problem brewing. The next thought came to him in an instant, like an epiphany: Call Willy. If Amber was the only person he could still trust in his life, Willy would have counted as the first. They were inseparable for years before it all ended so abruptly. *How did it get to that?* All those years later, he couldn't claw back the memory of where their friendship had soured, or why.

The rest of his evening was spent digging through old boxes and bins looking for a contact book—he knew he had one lying around somewhere. When he finally found it—stuffed in the bottom of a box in the attic—he sat down next to the phone in the kitchen and dialed. There were several numbers jotted down beside Willy's name. He tried the first. This one was in Michigan. No luck. So he tried another, and then another, and then another. It was a series of "Who?" and answering machines.

Finally, the last number on the list, back in Pennsylvania, yielded a helpful response. "That guy moved to California years ago."

"Do you know where?"

"Not sure anyone knows that."

"Why do you say that?" Howard could feel the desperation in his voice.

"The guy wanted to disappear. Seems like he did a pretty good job."

The click on the other end was a dagger, a finality to something that Howard had lost many years earlier but didn't realize until that moment.

As the sun dipped behind the hills lining Wolf Valley, Howard stood on the back patio nursing his seventh beer, a glass of whiskey already sitting on the table beside him waiting its turn. He watched as the golden light filtered through the trees above. Earlier in the evening, when he was still sober enough to use the bathroom inside instead of pissing in the grass, he stared at himself in the mirror. His face was now weathered, bearing the weight of years of tumult. When he stepped from the bathroom, he could hear Amber's typewriter clacking away in her office—the daily reminder of the distance that had been growing between them.

This is what brought him back out to the patio, with the beer and the whiskey, to watch what remained of the day disappear. Just as the final beams of sunlight burned into the hills above, Amber emerged from the back door. She was shaking out her fingers, and then she glanced at Howard but said nothing. The tension that had been festering was finally bubbling to the surface, a silent testament to the joint trauma repeated miscarriages had inflicted upon their marriage.

A few moments of silence passed and Howard wondered why she had joined him on the patio at all. Finally, he said, "Amber, can we talk?"

She paused, and whether consciously or not, her hand began to wander toward the doorknob, as if immediately understanding that her presence was a mistake. "What about?"

Howard took a deep breath. He could feel the alcohol in his blood, taste it on his lips, smell it on his hands. "About us. About this," he said gesturing toward the house and then out toward their yard and the river. "Something has to give at some point, doesn't it?"

Amber's expression began to harden. "I'm not sure I understand."

"Yes, you do."

She took a moment to collect herself and then said, "What is it you propose we do?"

"I just don't know how to help you," he admitted. "Or us. Every time things start going well we get stabbed in the heart. And then you're back in that study pecking away and I'm out here liquored up."

"Seems like one of those two things is healthier than the other."

Reactive anger started twisting in his gut.

She saw it and immediately raised her hands. "Okay, okay—I'm sorry. That wasn't fair. I'm sorry." Her eyes softened.

"I just feel like I'm losing you. Like *we're* dying with each loss."

"You're not losing me. I'm just—just dealing with all of this in the only way I've ever known."

"The problem is that 'the only way you know' is shutting me out of your life. You won't let me in that room. You spend every waking minute in your office, and you won't even tell me what it is you're working on that's so damn important that we had to move to this God-forsaken valley in the first place. You treat me like a stranger half the time—in our own home."

Howard saw a cold look in Amber's eyes then, a look he had never seen before. "My writing—this book—is the only thing keeping me sane right now. It's the only thing I have control over. It's the only thing that's helping me heal."

The silence that followed was deafening. Howard stared off into the night, his eyes blurred with unshed tears and booze. His relationship with Amber was the only thing in his life that ever made him feel needed, and Amber's words cut like a dagger to his heart. "I'm scared," he said in little more than a whisper. "I'm scared I'm going to end up alone. Again."

"I'm not going to leave you, Howard." She heard the words and corrected herself. "I'm *never* going to leave you. But I'd be lying if I said I knew how to fix this." Her voice trailed off, along with any semblance of confidence.

Howard reached out his trembling hand and placed it on her arm. "We have to find a way."

"Alright," she said quietly. "But you have to understand—the miscarriages, they broke me. I'm not the same person I was when we met, when we moved here, when we got married."

"I know. I'm not either."

Amber stepped toward him and rested her forehead on his chest. They stood there in the humid autumn air holding each other as the darkness enveloped them. For a moment, brief yet eternal, it was just them, clinging to the fragile threads of their marriage, hoping that they were strong enough to survive the storm.

19

Wolf Valley, 2002

In which Howard is 48 years old

It isn't until the shelter pulls into view that the weight of the situation hits him. Before that point, all he could think about was this woman and who she was. And leaving Coby behind. And going back for Coby. And the chaos and destruction that has overwhelmed Wolf Valley. And his house—or what will be left of it. But now he is thinking about those two jackasses again.

It's not quite daybreak, but you certainly wouldn't need a flashlight to see the boat approaching. The reality of his situation: he is returning to the scene of a crime with the stolen boat. Or is it a *stolen* stolen boat? The differentiation should matter, but he knows it won't to the two men who previously used it.

Before they get too close, Howard turns to maneuver around a small building. He knows he should be able to remain fairly low-key and skirt around the area, pulling the boat up to the back of the shelter and sneaking inside—that is if no one has seen him yet. The greeter at the door the previous night was not standing there and Howard didn't see any other movement. Still, 'in the clear' is an expression that has lost most of its value to Howard in the last several years.

"Where are we headed?" asks Edna.

"Just coming in the back way to the community center." He contemplates if he should tell her, but decides that at this point, after all they have been through, there is little point to lying. "Borrowed this boat to go save Coby—and you too."

"I see."

"Dogs aren't exactly welcome in this shelter. At least not by the folks toting the guns."

"I should say that surprises me, but nothing shocks me these days. Should have known folks 'round here can't even lend a hand without going on some kind of power trip."

Howard nods. "That's about right. But we'll pull around back. I have a woman who will sneak us in the backdoor."

"That right?"

"That's right. Dog owners stick together, I suppose."

With a keen eye trained on the building, Howard lets the boat glide to a stop where the water ends. He looks for grass, but it is all pavement. The friction causes them all to grasp for balance. Howard hops off first, then he steadies the boat for Coby and Edna to follow. Maybe it is just his way of counteracting their fatigue or maybe he knows he has no choice, but as they both struggle even to walk he finds a new strength in his stride.

Once clear of the boat, he takes hold of the bow and drags it up from the water, careful not to cause any damage to the underside. The slope up to the shelter is steep, but fortunately, Howard spots a set of stairs they can take. Stairs, he realizes, are not much better. Even Coby, who would have bounded these in a few strides a few days ago, is taking them one at a time. His raggedness is alarming. Howard has an arm around Edna, who is still clutching the envelope in one hand, the railing with the other. He helps her until they reach the top. The entire way up, he watches closely, monitors the area to ensure they are not being outed. It occurs to him how unbelievably ridiculous this all is—rescuing a dog and an old woman and feeling like he's the one who is doing the wrong thing. Misplaced guilt.

The backdoor that the old lady inside showed him opens to an alley of sorts. The adjacent building, a warehouse of some kind, is close enough that this alley feels more like a concrete corridor. Whatever light has crested the horizon at this point in the morning doesn't reach them here. On the ground, broken bottles and trash are littered around, with weeds poking through uneven cracks in the cement. In a past life, Howard never would have allowed Coby back there for fear he would cut open his paw. He no longer has the privilege of those concerns.

The three of them reach the door. Howard gathers himself and focuses on the special knock that he and the old lady inside had rehearsed. He asks Edna to stand back and then he steps forward and knocks on the door. A moment passes. Then another. They give it several. He doesn't want to stir up too much commotion.

"You sure you did it right?" Edna whispers.

"Sure." He steps back up to the door and knocks again. Coby is standing by his side. This time, the door swings open almost immediately. But it's not the old lady. It's Jerry the jackass.

Howard knows this is the worst-case scenario. Scratch that—this is what leads to the worst-case scenario. Oblivious to the situation and without hesitation, Coby tries to dart inside the building for warmth.

Before either man can utter a word to the other, Jerry snatches the dog and throws him back through the door. Howard tries to catch him but misses, and Coby tumbles onto the pavement near Edna's feet, screeching and whimpering.

Howard jumps back to attend to Coby, who quickly regains his footing and stares at the man in the doorway. For the first time, Howard hears Coby growl. Then, when he knows his dog is okay, he stands back up to face Jerry.

"Don't you ever touch him again," Howard says. It's a threat. There is a fury inside him. It's been building for over a year, though mostly beneath the surface of grief and guilt, so he hasn't realized it. But it's here now.

"No dogs allowed," Jerry says arrogantly. "You should know that."

Pinky is standing over Jerry's shoulder. Howard can't see the old woman. That adds to his rage as he thinks about what these two men might have done to her if they discovered her hiding out backstage. He is breathing heavily now, trying to think of what to say.

"I see you're the fella who stole our boat," Jerry adds.

Coby growls again and takes a slow step forward. Howard crouches and puts his arm on the dog to keep him from attacking—if he's even capable of that.

Jerry takes notice of the situation and pulls his gun from his waistband. "That dog's not comin' in here. And you keep him at bay or I'll shoot him." The gun is trained on Coby when Howard stands again to face Jerry. The barrel follows Howard. "And I'll shoot you too if you try any funny business."

Howard can barely hear his own thoughts. Blood is pumping through his ears and his chest is heaving with each breath. At his sides, his fists are tightening. But before he can say a word or make any movement, his choice is made for him.

With quick and unexpected precision, the old lady's dog inside the shelter lunges for Jerry's leg and grips down with force. He begins flailing to free himself. Howard has one chance: he rushes forward and grabs for the gun. He pushes inside and now Coby is beside him barking. The two men stumble back onto the stage. It's a fight for their lives. Howard ends up on top. Both of his hands are on the gun now and he's banging the man's wrist into the floor, trying to break his grip. He's waiting for Pinky to rush in and pull him off, but he doesn't come. He stands idle, watching the scene play out until two other men rush past.

"What the hell's going on here!" one shouts as they each grab for arms and pull Howard and Jerry apart.

They stumble backward until they can regain their composure. Jerry still has the gun in his hand, but it's lowered now. Howard looks around to assess the scene. Most of the shelter is now looking their way. Behind him, Edna and the other old lady are standing by, observing with blank stares. Coby is sniffing at Howard's pant leg. The little dog is already back in its owner's arms.

"Just what the hell is going on here?" says one of the men who broke up the fight.

They are all breathing heavily, looking around, wondering how much blame to start assigning.

Finally, Jerry says, "This man stole our boat and is trying to bring a dog into this here shelter. Which ain't allowed, Sheriff."

Sheriff. That one catches Howard off-guard. The man isn't dressed like a sheriff, with boots and jeans and a sweaty t-shirt like the rest of the folks in here. "Sir—Sheriff," Howard says. "It's my friend Stu's boat. I borrowed it to go save my dog." He takes a step back toward Edna. "And while out there, I brought in this woman as well. Would have been left out there for who-knows-how-long." Then he nods back toward Jerry. "*This* man would rather have me shot than let me save these lives. And quite frankly, sir, that doesn't scare me anymore." Howard snaps his fingers and Coby is at his side. No one says a word, and the two of them walk past the group toward the steps. As he passes Jerry, he notices a twitch in the gun. He knows the man wants to point it at him again but refrains. He stops and looks him in the eye. "This time you'll have to shoot me," Howard says as he walks off stage with his dog at his side, waiting for a bullet to pierce his back that never comes. It's one of the first victories that he's had in over a year. And yet, nothing about it feels victorious.

The scene settles rather quickly. Edna and the other old lady—dog in hand—sit down backstage and strike up a conversation. Jerry summons Pinky and the two of them storm out the back door to go inspect the boat. Howard, with Coby by his side, walks across the large room over to a table where someone is handing out water bottles.

He takes one graciously, though without saying anything, and the gentleman giving them away—a short fella with a round belly and balding head—says, "Quite the stir back there."

Howard nods but still doesn't say anything.

The man looks around. "Between you and me, that guy's an asshole."

Howard appreciates the comment.

"Here," the man says, reaching under the table and pulling out a small bowl. "Here," he says again, and then cracks open a water bottle and pours it into the bowl. "For your pup."

Howard takes the bowl. "Thank you. Thanks a lot."

"I wish more of these folks coulda brought their dogs, if I'm tellin' the truth. Dumb rule. Makes no sense, if you're askin' me."

In another circumstance, Howard would have been happy for the support, perhaps even eager to continue the conversation, but he was running on fumes and was starting to come down from his adrenaline rush. So instead he nods and says, "I appreciate this, sir," and then walks away with Coby.

They maneuver through the gym or auditorium or whatever this space is, heads tracking their movement the entire time, until they find a spot against the far wall to sit and close their eyes. When he looks around, stares—endless stares—are meeting his. Surely, there are people in this room, like the water man, who support them— proud, even, that Howard did what he did. For some others, there is likely a feeling of jealousy bubbling up, or even guilt, for they made that regretful but necessary decision—in the moment—to leave their animals at home. Then, finally, there are probably some others who are indifferent but entertained or scared by the commotion. Howard doesn't care about any of them.

Before he drinks any water himself, he sets the bowl down for Coby and points at it. "Here, bud." The dog moves his mouth over the water and sniffs. Then he drinks, and drinks, and drinks—like he's never drank water before. As Howard tilts his bottle back, out of the corner of his eye he sees the sheriff walking his way. He scoffs and wants to get up and head in the opposite direction, but he doesn't have enough energy left.

The man who Jerry called a sheriff steps up to them. Coby lifts his head from the bowl and presses his body against Howard in solidarity. "Sir, I'm Sheriff Percy Connor with the Wolf County Police Department," he says. "I just wanted to apologize for all that back there."

Howard looks up at him but doesn't say a word.

The sheriff continues. "I understand you've been through hell the last twenty-four hours. I'm amazed. I respect the hell out of you for it." He pauses and thinks about how to say what he has to say. "Truth is, the 'no pets' policy was communicated by other emergency response units from past events like this and we followed suit. Think it's a crock of shit, myself. I'm dreading what we're gonna find out there once this water recedes."

"It won't be pretty."

"No, it won't." Sheriff Connor is standing with his hands on his hips. "But listen, thank you for doin' what you did." He gives a nod, bends over and extends his hand. Without standing, Howard reaches up and shakes hands, and then watches the sheriff turn and walk away. Coby huffs and presses his head under Howard's chin and the two rest like that on the floor, against the wall, as their eyelids fall.

What could be seconds or hours later—Howard has no gauge on time—they are suddenly awoken by another commotion. When he gets his bearings, Howard sees people rushing toward the stage.

Someone screams. Everyone is shifting and looking. Howard stands and walks cautiously toward the stage to see what's happening. Then he sees Edna. She's pacing back and forth, a look of worry washed over her.

Without hesitation, he heads straight for her—Coby in tow. He climbs on the stage.

"Edna, what's going on?" There are people gathered in a small crowd backstage.

"She just slumped over," she says through hurried breaths.

"Who?"

"The old woman. Her name is Patrice Vernon. Or,"

"Or...?"

"Or... was? God, I feel terrible just saying it."

The urgency of the situation hits him. "What the hell happened?"

"She just slumped over! We were talking about her dog. She said she had just rescued him from a place down the valley. Wolf Valley Farms, I think she called it. And then—and then it was the weirdest thing. She started to smile and then her head just dropped and her dog popped out of her arms and I didn't know what to do—I just called for help."

"Okay," Howard says, and he puts his arm around Edna, who is now crying. "Okay." He doesn't know what else to say.

A tear streams down Edna's cheek and lands on Howard's boot. And it dawns on him that for the first time in days, his boots are dry.

The tag hanging from Patrice's dog's collar says "Chester" so that's what they call him. The four of them—Howard, Coby, Edna and Chester—are gathered in a small group sitting along the wall. The dogs have water and someone comes by to give them all some granola bars and pretzels. It will do for now.

Edna has her eyes closed, but Howard's not convinced she's sleeping. The dogs, on the other hand, are snuggled up beside one another and look to be out cold.

A short while earlier, a couple of men with semi-official-looking uniforms wheeled Patrice away on a makeshift stretcher. They didn't seem like there was much urgency, which was bad, but they also didn't cover her with a sheet, which was good. For the second time since the storm hit, Howard bows his head and says a silent prayer. Then he looks around at the carnage: people from all over the valley displaced. Some are alone. Most are gathered in small groups, presumably family or close friends, but who knows—tragedy brings people together.

Edna's eyelashes flicker and then her eyes stumble awake. "How long was I out?"

"I'm not entirely sure," Howard says. "I dozed off myself."

And then in an instant, he sees the memory flood back over her, as if experiencing the trauma of Patrice collapsing all over again.

"Is she...gone?"

"I don't know," he admits. "But it didn't look good."

Tears well up in her eyes again. "She was so lovely."

"She saved my life. Or Chester did, anyway."

"You saved *my* life," Edna says. "There isn't a thing in the world I can do to thank you for that."

"Thank the dog. Coby saved your life. I was just there for the muscle."

"Well, thank you, Coby." She gives him a pat on the head and his tail starts wagging.

"So, there's something I have to ask. You came to my house after my wife died, right? Am I remembering you correctly?"

"Yes, I did."

"Oh, well...thank you. I was in the lowest of places back then."

"I know you were. Well, I could imagine, anyway. I wanted to share my condolences. And I hope the prayer card helped."

"It did," Howard lies as he recalls the memory of tossing it in the trash. The two sit there for a moment. Howard is thinking about

Amber again. What this entire chapter in *his* life would have been like had it been a chapter in *their* lives. "Did you know her?" he says finally.

"Only through her books."

"So you read them?"

She turns so that she can make direct eye contact with him. "When I tell you this, I want you to know how genuinely I mean it: your wife's books changed my life. They saved me."

He knows the feeling. "Thanks for saying so. She was a gifted writer. Even better person." Then he thinks for a second. "Do you mind if I ask another question? And you can tell me to go to hell."

She smirks. "Go ahead."

"Can I ask what's with that letter you're carrying with you? Must be pretty important if you had to grab it before leaving your house."

For a moment, it doesn't seem like she will answer—maybe she's not even listening. Then she takes a deep breath and says, "I don't think I am ready to share that." Then she says, "Can I ask *you* a question?"

"Shoot."

"Does anyone ever call you Howie?"

He can feel his heart rate pick up and his head tilts involuntarily. He looks at her, but she doesn't seem fazed by his sudden anxiety. "Only—" He catches himself. "No, not since I was a little kid, no." He's still staring right through her eyes. "Why did you ask me that?"

"Just curious. I had a son named Howie." And then she stands up and says she's going for a walk. Chester hops up and follows her and the two disappear into the crowd.

The entire time Edna is gone, Howard's head is spinning. He's waiting for her to return so he can press her more. *What's your story? Where are you from? Who is your son? ARE YOU MY MOTHER?*

But an interesting thing happens: she doesn't return. After a while, Howard stands and calls Coby to follow. He walks throughout the shelter, all around the gym, through the hallways, out to the lobby and even around the side of the building. Edna and Chester are nowhere to be found. As mysteriously as she shows up in his life, she vanishes.

While outside, Howard can see for the first time a sliver of blue cutting between the clouds. Maybe, he thinks, this can all be over now.

20

Wolf Valley, 2001

In which Howard was 47 years old

S ome things need not be spoken.

On Amber's fortieth birthday the year before, she and Howard sat in the quiet of their house and ate a home-cooked steak dinner with asparagus and potatoes. It was no different than any other night. They discussed the weather, the books they had read recently, the construction project going on in town, the water level of the river out back. An unease from stock market volatility and Y2K seeped into living rooms across the nation. They talked about that, too. What they didn't say: it's over. Not their marriage, but their quest for a family.

A year later, sex had become less frequent than ever before. Once per month, if that. Most of the time, Howard found himself withdrawing prematurely. He could tell it didn't bother her, either. Relationships like this simmer for years, to where hitting a boiling point can surprise both parties. That's what happened on a rainy evening that fall.

When Howard returned from a worksite, he knocked off his wet, muddy boots and went straight for the liquor cabinet to pour himself a drink. The rain kept him from the patio, and so he collapsed into a chair in the living room. He glanced toward Amber's office—but for the first time in his memory, she wasn't sitting there. He scoffed and rolled his eyes and kicked his feet up on the coffee table.

Not more than a few minutes later, he heard her car pulling onto the gravel of their driveway. He offered a glance through the rain-streaked glass but returned his gaze to the TV, which he had turned on and was watching reruns of old black-and-white westerns. The rain was coming down harder now. Once a soft day had turned into a full-blown storm.

From his vantage point in the living room, he couldn't see the back door, but he heard it fling open and he wondered why Amber—in such weather—would take the time to walk around to the back of the house instead of darting for the front porch.

A moment later, she crept around the corner and peeked into the living room. Without taking his eyes off the television, he said, "Yes?"

When he finally did look at her, she had a mischievous smile. "I have a surprise for you."

"Oh, good," he uttered sarcastically.

"Stop it." Then she disappeared for several more seconds before jumping back out to him. But she wasn't alone. In her arms, she was holding a brown and white, furry, slightly wet dog. She waited in anxious anticipation for Howard to react, but he just sat there staring at the animal.

Finally, he said, "Amber. What the fuck is that?"

"This," she said with eyes on the dog, "is our new furbaby. I adopted him from a shelter called Wolf Valley Farms."

Howard just went back to the TV.

"We need this," she pleaded.

"No, we don't."

"Yes, we do!"

He didn't even acknowledge her.

"Look at me," she said, stepping across the room.

Howard could smell the dog now—wet, stinky. It smelled like his past. It was regret. And sin. The last thing he needed in his life. "Get that thing away from me."

"Please," she said softly. "Can we talk about this at least?"

"What's there to talk about?" He could feel something building inside of him. Something out of his control. He'd never felt this before. "You went and got the dog without talking to me! Yesterday— *THAT* was the time to talk to me!"

She was crying now, tears streaking down her cheeks and landing on the matted back of the mutt. "Howard, please." Her voice cracked. "Please. Please. Please."

"Don't you get it?" He thrust himself up and staggered toward the kitchen for another drink. After filling his glass, he turned back to Amber, who was frozen in place. "I. Don't. Want. A. Fucking. Dog. I wanted a SON."

Dog still in her arms, she tore down the hall and went straight for their bedroom. The door slammed behind her. Howard, unperturbed by what had just played out, stood leaning against the kitchen counter and staring out at the rain penetrating the river's normally calm surface. He was certain that Amber would be shut into their room for hours, but only moments later she came shuffling recklessly across the house and out the front door. Howard shifted his position to the front window and watched her peel out of the driveway and speed off in the rain.

Some things, however much we feel them, need not be spoken.

The dog didn't blink. It sat there, in the center of the room, motionless, staring at Howard, who sat on the couch returning the glare. That's how they remained for quite some time. Only the occasional sip of his drink would break his stare.

She brings home a goddamn dog. A dog. Without talking to me. Why the hell would I want to take care of a dog? What the hell was she thinking?

A knock at the front door startled Howard. With the rain whipping outside, he hadn't even heard the SUV pull onto the gravel out front. He stood, beer in hand, and walked to the entryway and opened the door. There, standing on the porch, barely covered from the elements, was a police officer. He was holding his hat in his hand and his eyes looked like there was no life behind them.

"Mr. Lynch?" the officer asked in a deep voice.

Howard could feel the palpitations in his chest. "Mhmm."

"Mr. Lynch, I'm sorry to tell you this, but your wife has been in an accident."

"Is she okay?"

"I'm gonna need you to come with me, sir."

Without another thought, Howard set down his beer, slipped on his boots and jacket, and followed the officer into the storm.

21

Wolf Valley, 2003

In which Howard is 49 years old

Something Edna said in the shelter stuck with Howard. She said that Chester was rescued from Wolf Valley Farms. The name sounded so familiar. He couldn't quite put his finger on why. It took him a while, but he finally came to realize that it was the same place from where Amber had rescued Coby. It was one of the last things his wife ever said to him.

The importance of that connection doesn't strike him until several months later. The water has receded and the community has returned to a quiet buzz of respectful reconstruction. For all the evil that Howard witnessed during the flood, he now sees the opposite—the best humanity has to offer. People and dollars are flooding in from around the country. Many homes and businesses are either destroyed or have suffered such catastrophic damage that a full-scale renovation is required. Neighbors are helping neighbors. Strangers are helping strangers.

For his luck, Howard's home is salvageable—just salvageable. Compared to so many homes in the valley that needed to be demolished altogether, Howard is grateful his does not. He attributes that to its brick exterior—it just holds up better, he thinks. His neighbors directly next door, who had an old wooden farmhouse, had to knock their home down. The plan is to someday rebuild, hopefully soon, but time will tell. Driving down the streets, it's hard to recognize the sleepy valley as anything but a war zone—furniture and junk strewn about neighborhoods, homes in rubble, people looking as raggedy as the rest of it.

It's not until several days after the flood that Howard can step foot onto his property again. He has Coby by his side and they stand on the front lawn staring for quite some time. The house looks fairly normal on the outside, but as soon as he opens the front door the damage is immense. Virtually nothing can be saved. The walls are deteriorating. Furniture is destroyed. All of his belongings—clothes, electronics, decorations—must be trashed. Looking into Amber's study devastates him all over again. The shelves are almost bare, save for the few copies of books that tried valiantly to survive before succumbing to the flood. For a moment, Howard looks at the top shelf where he found Coby, and he wonders how on Earth the dog was able to find his way up there. Just as unbelievable, how was Howard able to then find the dog? Stepping out into the main part of the house, he eyes the route—down the ladder from the attic, through the kitchen and into the living room, and then finally into the study. He pictures it dark, filled with cold, black floodwaters. He is standing in a miracle.

In the attic, waiting undisturbed, is everything he had left behind. There is a box filled with Amber's books—the ones she'd given him, the ones with the personalized inscriptions. Survivors. *Thank the Lord*. Beside it, tucked partially under a blanket, is the pistol. Again, he thanks God that he'd left it behind. He knows that had he had it with him at the community center that day, he would have used it. Or wanted to, at least. And who knows how it all would have ended. Then he remembers what Edna had said that night about guardian angels. *That may be the only explanation left. Everything happens for a reason.*

As for Edna, Howard hasn't seen her since she stood up in the shelter and walked away with Chester. Though over the weeks and months, not a day has passed that he hasn't thought about her. On the drive back out of the valley to his temporary housing, Howard sees Edna's house and stops. Coby hops up to the window and pants happily, pawing at the glass. For all of its former beauty, the house is now in ruins. And it's the last time Howard sees it standing, for about a week later when he next returns to inspect his own home, Edna's place is demolished.

From the community center, Howard and Coby were taken to the nearest town outside the valley, where there was a strip of hotels along the main highway. That's where they settled indefinitely. Howard had to buy new everything—clothes, shoes, toiletries, books—at least temporarily. It's not quite home, but it'll do.

On warm evenings, Howard takes Coby for long walks through the woods that back up to the hotel. The top of the tree line is level with the first floor, so they descend and then follow the beaten paths that previous hikers have worn. Nothing is official in these woods, but everything is quiet. It's the only place Howard feels like he can think. Sometimes he brings a copy of one of Amber's books and they walk until they find a clearing, where Howard sits on a nearby fallen tree. There, he can read in peace while Coby walks around sniffing out the territory and claiming it for himself. It's amazing how removed from Wolf Valley he feels, particularly in the spring when the flowers begin to fill the field and a seasonal creek cuts beside one of their walking paths. It's a tiny creek, just a gentle flow of water that trickles over the rocks. Enough to remind him of home without all the bad stuff.

All this time living in the hotel feels a bit like a prison to Howard. He—and especially Coby—was not meant to live in a place like that. When he finally has the chance to begin gutting his home, he begins without hesitation. Volunteer groups from out of state, mostly from church organizations, fill the valley and offer to take up the work on his house. It's a relief for him, knowing how difficult it would be emotionally to tear that place apart, to see Amber's desk being thrown into a dumpster.

Not too long after the house is gutted, Howard secures enough insurance money and a construction crew to take on the renovation project. A couple times a week he stops in to check on the progress, but mostly he focuses his energy on his walks with Coby and the sanctuary of the book collection he is rebuilding. His instructions are to recreate the home as it looked before. Sure, updated tile and kitchen counters are fine, but he wants to walk in the front door one day and feel like he's home again—whatever that means at this point in his life.

Between Amber's death and the flood, Howard has a hard time discerning where his life stands. On one hand, he knows he is lucky to be alive. Yet there is still a nagging feeling in the back of his mind that he doesn't deserve to be alive, or doesn't want to be. He knows he should be grateful, and he tries to consciously will that on himself—gratitude. And yet despite—or perhaps because of—everything he has endured, there is still a massive hole in his life. For the last year, he has taken up prayer. He kneels on the bedroom floor and rests his elbows on the bed. Coby almost always joins him, sometimes even pawing at the mattress as if to fold his own hands. He prays for an answer. *Why did this all happen? What's the master plan?* And he prays the Serenity Prayer—over and over and over. What effect it will all have, he's unsure, nor is he particularly interested right now. The act of finding some semblance of faith is in itself helping to lift his spirits, albeit slowly.

The day he comes home again is almost exactly a year after the rain first started, a quicker timeline than he ever would have expected. Once again, fall has arrived in Wolf Valley. Howard's mind is trapped in a strange place. He is sitting in a new chair, in the same room, watching a new television, with the same dog at his feet. He feels the dichotomy of his life pulling him apart—it's been a million years, and yet Amber walked out of the house for the last time just yesterday.

On the counter, the construction crew left a box. He opens it and finds a few of the salvageable things from the flood—more survivors. Among them, Howard's attention is immediately drawn to the answering machine. *How in the hell did this damn thing survive? Wasn't it broken before the flood even started?* Of all the meaningless objects. Pulling it out, he sets it on the counter near where it was plugged in before, but then he walks away from it again. He knows it's full of memories from losing Amber and he's not sure, after all he's been through, if he has any strength left to face them. Or what good it would do.

His first afternoon back in his home should be a joyous occasion, but all he can think about are the scars. From Amber. From the flood. From those two jackasses. Over the last year, he has lost everything. Everything. Well, actually—he looks down at Coby. Not everything. This dog. The animal he never wanted. The one he refused to feed or even name for days. The animal he reluctantly kept, too fearful of the guilt that giving him away would bring. What Amber would think. It's what saved him, truly. For a moment, he tries to mentally torture himself again, picturing what his life would be like if all else remained the same, except for Coby's absence. But he cannot do it.

These are the thoughts streaming through his mind. He's not even paying attention to the television before him until something catches his ear.

"I'm here at Wolf Valley Farms," a reporter is saying as she slowly backpedals over to a kennel full of dogs. The dogs aren't what he expects to see. Rather than a pile of fluffy puppies tripping over one another to get to the reporter's outstretched hand, it's a pack of misfit mutts, sniffing calmly and curiously looking at the cameraman.

She continues: "What was once a busy shelter for animals in need, has now become overrun by strays in the aftermath of the flood. Countless pets have been captured roaming the streets and forests and farms in Wolf Valley. Countless more have been dropped off by folks unable to care for them after the devastation. For months, Wolf Valley Farms has taken these animals in, cared for them, and either tried reuniting them with their families or finding them new homes. Now, the kind folks at Wolf Valley Farms are asking for your help. They need people to foster and adopt these animals, and they are looking for volunteers to help keep the shelter running in the meantime. As one employee told me, it's all hands on deck. With Channel 5 News, I'm Grace Williams."

Howard stares intently as the screen flips back to the studio where two anchors make disingenuous comments and then begin pointless banter on another topic. But his mind is lost in thought about that news report. Wolf Valley Farms is the place where Patrice found Chester, and it's the place, he believes, where Amber found Coby. He looks down at his dog. The debt he owes to that animal shelter is significant.

When he pulls his truck into the gravel parking lot, he notices there are only a few others there. The scene is quiet. *So much for being 'overrun'*, he thinks. Still, he's wearing new boots and jeans and a t-shirt—out of character for him. Realizing the vast majority of his wardrobe had been destroyed in the flood, he decided to replace it all as close to the way it had been before. He isn't used to the new stuff, not yet broken in. Feels somehow restrictive.

Wolf Valley Farms welcomes visitors with a nice building that couldn't be more than a decade old. Despite its name, the farm sits on a hilltop that looks down into the valley, so it was spared from the worst of the storm and nearly all of the flooding. That doesn't mean it hasn't endured the wrath of the devastation—that all just came after the fact.

Behind the main building is a series of fenced areas with winding wood-chipped paths, all eventually leading to a separate barn-like structure on the rear of the property. Howard approaches the main building and heads inside. There is a round woman with thick glasses and short black hair sitting behind a desk. "I hear you need an extra hand around here," Howard says.

"We certainly do! Did you hear about us on the news?"

"Mhmm."

"Well, we sure appreciate your help."

She then sends him down a long hallway, out a set of double doors, and along one of those outdoor paths until he reaches the barn. Calling it a barn, he realizes once inside, is a bit misleading. While it may look the role from the outside—complete with red paint and white trim—that's not the scene inside. It's well-kept and looks nearly as new as the main building. The ceiling stretches to the high roof, but a series of rooms are sectioned off with walls that reach about halfway up. Two things immediately catch Howard's attention: the sound and the smell. There is no mistaking this building for anything other than what it is: a housing unit for dozens if not hundreds of dogs. Before he can see them, he can hear their barks and smell the unmistakable canine scent.

Without any semblance of a reception area, Howard stands inside the doorway looking around for a moment. He isn't sure if he should be exploring the rooms or waiting for someone to show up to give him instructions. So he gives it a couple of minutes. A short while later he hears voices approaching, so he steps aside and the doors behind him swing open. In come two teenagers, a boy and a girl. They see Howard looking somewhat aimless and show him mercy.

"Hi there," the girl says. "Are you a new volunteer?"

He nods. "Just want to help out however I can. My wife"—he pauses. Hearing that phrase come out of his mouth again momentarily paralyzes him. Then he tries again. "My wife adopted our dog from here a couple years ago."

The girl smiles. "We hear that all the time. Thanks so much for coming back and lending a hand. My name's Emmy. This here is Trent."

The boy nods but doesn't say anything.

"Have you met with our shift manager yet? She's usually the one who assigns work around here."

"Not yet. I was just told to come out to this building."

"No problem, I can help you track her down."

Emmy waves him along and the three of them—Trent is trailing behind—head down the corridor. Dogs are barking and scratching at kennel doors. Some are just sleeping in corners. Howard can see them all as he passes by each room. He tries to imagine Coby behind those bars—nameless, cold, lonely—and thanks Amber silently for saving him. At the end of the corridor, they make a right down another hallway and then turn into a large room full of supplies and dog food. There is a woman bent over rummaging through something across the room.

"Hiya, boss," Emmy says. "Got a fresh volunteer for ya."

Then Emmy pats Howard on the shoulder, says, "You're in good hands," and leaves with Trent.

Howard stands in the doorway for a moment before finding himself saying the same thing he did before. It'll be easier the second time, he thinks. "My wife adopted our dog here a couple years ago. Saw on the news you needed some help so figured I owed you a hand."

The woman stands, turns and smiles. Howard nearly falls over. It's Amber. She's much younger, back in her early twenties, but there she is. The same dark, wavy hair twisted in a braid over her shoulder. The same slender frame. The same blue eyes. Everything. It's her.

"Everything okay?" she asks.

"Uh, yeah, uh—yes. You just look like someone..." His voice trails off. He can't say it.

"I've gotten that before. I appreciate you coming to help us out." She extends a hand. "My name's Autumn."

"Howard."

"It's real nice to meet you, Howard." Looking into her eyes nearly breaks him. "Let me show you where to get started."

Nothing could distract him from that encounter. For the rest of the afternoon, he thinks about that girl, Autumn. And he thinks about Amber. And he racks his brain trying to put this puzzle together.

At one point, he is tasked with walking the dogs around the property along the various trails. On one of these walks, he crosses paths with Trent, who is also walking a couple of dogs.

"Hey," Howard calls.

"Hey," Trent says. "Forgive me."

Howard can tell he's looking for a name but can't remember. "Howard."

"Right, sorry. How's the dog walking coming? Everything you hoped and dreamed about coming to help at this place?"

He takes a breath. "To be honest, I'm not really sure what to think of this place."

"Hmm? How do you mean?"

"What's your boss, Autumn—what's her deal?"

Trent smirks. "Already tried that, sir. She's got a boyfriend. Pretty serious one, too."

"No, no, not like that. Just—is she from around here?"

"Everyone who lives in Wolf Valley is from around here. No one comes here otherwise."

"I'm not from around here. Not originally, anyway."

"Well, that would make you the first. Supposin' somethin' specific brought you here though, right?"

He thinks for a moment. "A girl," he says.

"Ain't it always."

Before he leaves, he makes it a point to stop by the supply room where he met Autumn that morning. He pokes his head in the doorway but it's empty. By the look of it, she's gone for the day.

Back in the main building, Howard offers a polite goodbye to the woman behind the desk and tells her he'd be happy to come back and help out again.

"I'm sure we could use you anytime."

The drive home is filled with winding roads that mostly descend until he's down at the river and eventually pulling into his driveway. Wolf Valley Farms is a couple of towns over and the drive is just long enough for his mind to sufficiently spiral. By the time he's arriving home, it's now racing a mile a minute.

On his way into the house, he checks the mailbox—a habit he hasn't needed for a year. Inside, he's surprised to find a single post-card from the Elmswood Post Office. He flips it to the backside.

Dear Mr. Howard Lynch,

Due to the destruction caused by the storm, a significant pileup of mail has accumulated in your name. Please come to the post office to collect it. As of today's date, regular mail delivery to your address will resume.

Sincerely,
Elmswood Post Office

The postcard catches him a bit off guard. It's a reminder that while he has wanted to forget about the world for the last couple of years, the world has not yet forgotten about him.

He takes the card inside and sets it on the counter directly beside the answering machine. Coby meanders up and presses himself into Howard's leg, and Howard tries to bend over and pet him without taking his eyes off the old machine. The thought of plug-ging it back in and listening to the messages—if they still exist—is tantalizing. He ultimately decides against it. But that doesn't mean the thought is expelled. For the rest of the evening, he glances over at the machine. He can picture the little red bulb blinking. It makes him want to both plug it in and throw it out the window.

The next morning, Howard heads back outside to drive to the post office. No point in putting it off. What he doesn't expect is that when he walks back out of the building, he's carrying a large box full of mail of all sizes. In his kitchen, he sits at the table and sorts through it all. Mostly junk. The occasional bill. Some deals he missed out on. And then his eyes cut across a name he hasn't heard or seen in two years. Kim Barnes. It's written on the return address of an oversized envelope that has some weight to it. He quickly breaks the seal and pulls out a stack of papers. The top page is a loose letter from Kim to Howard.

Dear Howard,

I haven't been able to get ahold of you since Amber's passing. I am so, so sorry for your loss. And I am sorry I was not there. I tried calling several times but I couldn't get through.

I am enclosing Amber's last manuscript. She sent this to me the day before the accident. I wanted you to see it. You deserve to see it.

Please call if there is anything I can do for you. Again, I am so sorry for your loss.

Yours,
Kim

Before he's even finished reading, a tear falls onto the page and he smudges the ink trying to wipe it away. He pulls the letter back and reads the title of the manuscript:

NEAR AND FAR BY THE RIVER

There is a feeling bubbling inside him. He doesn't know if it's anger, or fear, or guilt, or grief, or regret, or even joy. But it's strong. Without reading a word of the manuscript, he turns to the answering machine and plugs it in. He's not sure it'll even work, but a moment later, by the grace of God, the little red light flashes and he begins combing through the messages. He's listening for Kim's voice and disregarding everyone else. Finally: "Howard, it's Kim..." He listens until she leaves her phone number, which he writes down, and then unplugs the machine again.

Immediately, he dials. It rings. And rings. And rings. Then: "You've reached Kim Barnes with the Barnes Agency. Please leave your name and number after the beep and I'll call you back."

Howard contemplates just hanging up but hesitates. After a brief moment of deliberation, he says, "It's Howard Lynch," and then leaves his number.

For the rest of the day, he sits by the phone waiting. One can imagine the self-destructive, speculative, unproductive, painful, yet hopeful thoughts channeling through his mind. He picks up the manuscript and sits in his chair. *One final gift from Amber.* Page one. That's how he sits until hours have passed. His eyes are clouded over and burning from the tears and the swelling but he reads on anyway.

Sometime in the late evening, his phone rings. "Hello?"

"Howard, it's Kim."

"Kim. Thanks for calling me back."

"I've got to say, Howard, I'm not entirely sure you deserve this phone call."

He thinks about that for a minute.

"What, with you going silent on me the last couple years. I know Amber was your wife and I can't imagine the pain you felt losing her, but I was her friend and I cared deeply for her. Completely ignoring all of my attempts to contact you seemed selfish."

It's not the way he expects the conversation to begin, but he understands. "Kim, look—I'm sorry. I really am. I was in a bad place. A *really* bad place."

He can hear her sigh on the other end. "I understand Howard. What can I do for you?" She sounds reluctant to help.

"I just got the manuscript. The last one that you sent to me who-knows-when. The post office was holding it."

"You're just now getting that?"

"Yes. And Kim, I need to know—what is this? What is this story Amber wrote?"

Another sigh. "Hold on a minute." He hears her set the receiver down and then in the background can hear her rummaging through drawers and shuffling paper. After a few minutes, she returns. "Still there?"

"Yep."

"Good. I found the letter she sent me with the manuscript. It says, 'This story is about a passionate love affair that results in an unwanted pregnancy, but the girl gives the baby up for adoption instead of terminating it. Later in life, she's overcome with regret and tries to slowly, from a distance, reinsert herself into her daughter's life.' Does that help?"

Tears are streaming down Howard's face now. "Yes," he says, and then catches his breath. "Kim, thank you."

"You're welcome, Howard." Then, before hanging up, she says, "And, listen, I am truly, truly sorry."

"God works in mysterious ways."

Click.

Howard spends the rest of the night finishing the manuscript. He doesn't eat, or drink, or even use the bathroom. Coby is curled at his feet and occasionally falls into a fitful sleep before stirring awake.

By early morning, Howard turns over the final page. He takes a breath and looks around the room. His eyes are bloodshot and his brain is ready to melt.

Even through the shower he forces himself to take, the tears won't stop. And then, manuscript in hand, they continue through-out the entire drive. Coby is riding in the passenger seat, head poking out the window. At Wolf Valley Farms, Howard sits in his truck for a while until the tears stop and he can compose himself. Then he puts Coby on a leash and heads inside.

Cutting through the main building, he briskly makes his way to the barn and then down the corridor to the room where he first met Autumn, but again she's not there. So he waits for a short while before heading out to look for her. He checks in all the kennels, along the outdoor walking paths, and then back in the main building, but he can't find her anywhere.

Out in the parking lot, he's feeling dejected. He's leaning against his truck thinking about what to do next when a car pulls up in front of the building. A man is driving and he sees a woman in the front seat. She kisses him and then climbs out, and that's when Howard sees her hair and her skin and those eyes. The car quickly drives off, and just as Autumn begins toward the main building, Howard calls for her.

She turns and smiles, just like before. "Oh, hi there. Volunteer from the other day, right?"

"Howard."

"Howard, yes." She sees Coby and crouches to his level. "Hey, I remember this little guy. One of my favorites to come through this place." After giving the dog a pet, she returns to Howard. "So, back for more dirty work?"

"Actually," he says, and then pauses and looks down at the manuscript in his hand. His palms are sweating. "Do you like stories? Because if you have some time, I have one you won't believe."

Epilogue

What I didn't tell you at the start of this book is that the pretty bartender with the braided black hair who introduced me to Howard was his granddaughter, Avery. She facilitated this whole thing. I owe this book to her.

Shortly after that first meeting with Howard in the bar, I was invited to his home—a brick ranch that sat back off the road and whose back patio looked out across the lawn to the river. (But now you know all about that.) There I met Autumn for the first time. But, as I said at the beginning, this was Howard's story. So Autumn, Avery and I all sat together, sipping lemonade or iced tea and listening to the man recall those early days, those trying days, those hopeful days. Everything that you just read came directly from Howard, and in his honor, I tried my best to get it all right. I hope I did his story justice.

After he finally told me the whole thing, I had to ask him one last difficult question. "I'm sorry, Howard, but if I'm going to write this story I have to ask you this."

He looked at me like he knew exactly what I was going to say.

I hesitated because I wasn't sure exactly how I should ask it.

"You want to know if I had any anger toward Amber for keeping our child from me."

"Yes."

"There were certainly moments," he said. "Times when I questioned how she could do that. Pissed that I missed Autumn's childhood. Felt like our entire relationship was a lie."

I was watching him closely. I knew he wasn't done.

Just then a look of amusement came over his face and he glanced over at Autumn and Avery. "But our only hope for happiness in this life is through forgiveness. The way I look at it, Amber gave me one last gift. Something that can't ever be taken away."

"That's pretty profound."

"Yeah, well," he said with a smirk, taking a sip of his lemonade. "I'm a pretty profound guy."

Beneath a thick tree with low overhanging branches along the riverbank, Howard crafted a headstone for Coby, who had passed some years before. It was familiar soil to him, so it just felt right. I never had the honor of meeting that incredible dog. On that first visit to the home, before sitting down at the patio and before telling any more of the story, Howard escorted the group out there and gave him a moment of silence. Coby had become such a monumental piece of his life, and seldom a day went by when Howard didn't look up to the skies and thank God and Amber for bringing him into his life.

It's with a heavy heart I also report that in the year it took me to complete this book, Howard joined Amber in Heaven. He still felt too young to lose—a tragedy in its own right. Perhaps by fate, he seemed to know the day was coming. We had already wrapped up his story and I was working through the editing phase of the book. He must have felt some form of contentment. What I know for sure is that Amber was up there waiting for his arrival. *That's* the forever we mean when we talk about true love.

There are very few people in this life that we truly get to know deeply and understand the heart of their pains and joys. For me, Howard was one of those people. The girls had him cremated and on a crisp Sunday morning in the fall, they spread his ashes in the river and watched them float around the bend and disappear.

Several weeks before this book was set to publish and before I wrote this epilogue, I drove to Wolf Valley with my family to hand a copy of the final manuscript to Autumn. I wasn't sure exactly how it would go—if she would invite me in, if she'd be excited or nervous. It was a normal exchange. I stood on the porch and rang the doorbell, and when Autumn answered I gave her the book and we chatted for a short while. She asked me to stay for a glass of tea but I politely declined, as we were on our way to a vacation and still had hours of driving ahead of us.

My pregnant wife and young daughter were waiting patiently in the car, and just as I began to walk away, Autumn tapped my shoulder. When I turned she wrapped her arms around me tightly and, through glassy eyes, whispered, "Thank you."

"Thank *you*," I said back.

"My dad never told me the whole story before. I didn't know how badly I needed to hear it until you showed up."

I felt tears pushing at the backs of my eyes as I climbed into my car. My wife didn't say a word, only squeezed my hand to let me know it was okay to feel. On the remaining drive, I kept glancing in the rearview mirror at my daughter. As night fell over the highway, the darkness made it impossible for me to see anything in the backseat. But I kept looking anyway, because I knew what I couldn't see was still there.

Author's Note

Hey, it's Ed, the real author, not the fictional one.

This book took me well over five years to write. The idea first came to me many years ago, back when I was in college at the University of Michigan in Ann Arbor. I was walking through the Barnes & Noble on Washtenaw Avenue and inspiration struck. I remember jotting down the idea and then taking it home and thinking through it for quite some time. I wanted to write a novel about how mistreated pets have been historically in times of tragedy and how we humans are unworthy of their unconditional love. Obviously, the idea grew into much more.

What I know for sure is that between marriage, new jobs, homeownership, parenthood and a pandemic, the novel sat on the back burner for a while. Eventually, though, this turned into a passion project of mine. Along the way, new motivators appeared, often—far too often, sadly—in the form of tragedy. This book, for me, became a memorial to those we have loved and lost along the way.

I read somewhere, years ago, that everything in fiction is intentional. But that's just simply not true (and I am a fiction writer). Sometimes there is no deeper meaning; sometimes the curtains are just blue. That's certainly the case with much of what I wrote in this story. But then, *some things* are certainly intentional.

Take the title. I was originally going to call this book *Borne by the River.* I loved it. I thought I was clever. But then, in June 2020, we lost my 21-year-old cousin, Wolf. It's the smallest of deeds, but I pivoted the book at that point and set it in fictional Wolf Valley, in honor of my cousin.

For a year, I continued brainstorming and writing.

Then, in September 2021, our dear friends Kristen and Craig Knaffle lost their dog, a chocolate lab named Coby. At the time I'm writing this, my own dog is nine, and I dread the day that he's no longer with us. I know losing Coby was sudden and devastating for our friends, and once again I pivoted. I hadn't yet settled on a name for Howard's dog, but Coby felt perfect.

So I kept writing.

Finally, in the spring of 2022, my wife texted me with tragic news: her friend Jess's four-year-old daughter, Hannah, had been diagnosed with DIPG, an untreatable childhood brain tumor. The news floored me. I cried like a baby. This book, since I really gained momentum in early 2020, has been about celebrating the joy that daughters bring into this world. About how they save us. That's the joy I felt when my two daughters were born, and I know it's the same joy that Hannah brought all those who loved her each and every day.

So this book is for them. It's for Coby and all the good dogs who never wavered for a moment in their loyalty to us. And it's for Wolf and Hannah and all the beautiful souls God called home before we were ready to say goodbye.

In the famous Broadway musical *Hamilton,* Eliza asks her husband Alexander, "Why do you write like you're running out of time?"

The older I get, the more I understand.

Acknowledgements

There are some people I need to thank, without whom I never would have been able to publish this book.

First and foremost, I need to thank my beautiful wife, Cara, for her angelic patience and support throughout the entire process. You would not be holding this story in your hands right now if I didn't have her by my side.

I would also like to thank some friends: Greg Hummel, for badgering me for the better part of a decade to write a new novel, and for constantly believing in my storytelling ability; and Kevin Hall and Mackenzie Meter, for being the first eyes to read these words and for their kind, thoughtful feedback.

Truthfully, this book would not have made it into its final form without of all you.